My Name is Jared

My Name is Jared

A Novel

James Tauro Riley

For My Brothers,
Lost and Found

Prologue

Fourteen Years Ago

The Hurricane
Puerta de la Reina, Mexico

The women moved steadily through the chaparral, with no light other than the moon ahead and the sea of stars above to light their uneven path. Traveling on the roads was not an option; for the next few weeks, perhaps months, they would continue to live as they had for so long already, as if they only had each other, as if they were not really a part of the world. Eventually they would separate and return to whatever family remained that would take them in, but losing even one of them at this early point in their journey would jeopardize all those homecomings. And so, before the riot of gunfire, they had left town connected one to the other by long, colored pieces of fabric as they jogged over dry desert brush and hiked up the sides of mountains they had for years only viewed through grated windows.

Few bothered or cared enough to look backward as the fire spread behind them, as it leapt from roof to roof, from one street of structures to the next. From a distance, the gunfire sounded no more fearsome than the popping of fireworks, and still there was no distance great enough that they would feel safe from it. Those bursts traveled in the opposite direction tonight, and tapered until they could be heard only sporadically; the occasional flashes of light marking the sounds' origins moved away, telling the women that the soldiers were out of the town, and already headed to the plains in the south.

Lydia led the group into the hills pushing a hard pace. They all were surprised that she had remained with them, because she would have done better on her own, and they accepted her leadership without question. They knew that at some point on this road, at a time she had likely predetermined, she would disappear, probably never to be seen by any of them again, and the rest would have to rely on themselves.

Tonight, because she remained with them, they followed her silently.

At the end of the fifth hour, they paused on a mountain ridge to take what most present hoped would be the last view they would have of this place. The fires, whipped by the coastal breezes, had spread across the port; everything in that area was ablaze, the docks, the boats, the trees, the pier, and the stars over the township were blotted out by the black columns of smoke swirling up from the rising flames.

Julia sat on a rock between her mother, Marta, and her older sister Alma, wondering what had happened to all of the other children, what had happened to the rest of her friends.

"By the Goddess," Marta said.

"Let's move. You'll turn to salt," someone said.

"The town will be gone by morning," Sylvia said.

"They're all going to die," another woman said.

Someone else spat. Several voices wailed: "the children, the children! God will save the children."

"Amen," many of them said together.

"We saved ourselves; the rest of them could have done the same."

"Look there—those are storm clouds moving in, not just smoke."

Julia looked up at the sky hopefully.

A little rain might make it not so bad. A little rain might leave some small piece of the only home she had ever known.

"We didn't cause this," old Chaya said.

Lydia called out for them to move. She didn't like the looks of the clouds. On one side of her was a clear, moonlit night sky;

on the other, this storm was coming on too fast. They needed to move higher into the hills, and they would need shelter.

"This is the world when it is left to the men," Sylvia said as she stood and stretched. "These evil men."

Chaya said, "You never know. That fire might be our salvation. There's a chance no one will notice we're gone. And that no one will come looking for us."

————————

MEXICO CITY BUREAU NEWS FEED—Hurricane Manja, surely the most terrible offspring to date of an unexpectedly volatile El Niño season, was today officially declared defunct, despite reports of continuing abnormalities in weather systems reaching as far north as the Canadian provinces and as far south as Peru. From hailstones in the Caribbean to flurries of snow in Guam, the most powerful storm to ravage the Gulf of Mexico in recorded history continues to prove the experts' declarations of death premature.

For all the images of destruction left in Manja's wake, nothing matches that of the devastation visited upon the impoverished region of Mexico that bore the brunt of Manja's fury. For days now, survivors have been arriving in the capitol city. They come by car, by bus, by helicopter, by ambulance, and they come on foot, a few carrying armfuls of cherished possessions, most covered from head to foot in mud.

Of the coastal cities affected, two remote indigenous communities, Puerto Angel and Puerta de la Reina, seem to have been the hardest hit. In the latter city, flash flooding triggered massive mud slides on hillsides recently denuded by fire; whole neighborhoods were swept into a churning Pacific Ocean before the first warnings could go out. Today, lightning is still crisscrossing over an altered landscape grimly marked here and there by the bodies of some of the estimated 7,000 who have fallen victim to the deadly tide of mud and water.

"I thought it was the end of the world," one survivor said as she walked into the city of Acapulco, which fared better against the storm than its sister cities. "I was screaming and crying for my family, for my brothers, for my children, and I could not hear my own voice above the thunder. I climbed on the roof of one of the buildings that had not been destroyed in the fire, hoping I would be able to find them, to find anyone. But the lightning was so intense, so bright, and the rain so heavy, I could not see more than a foot in front of me. I could not see, but at times I could hear the cries of the dying. There was only water and mud rushing everywhere." She survived for three days on a section of the roof that broke free of the structure and carried her miles downstream to the south.

"When the storm was at its worst, I wanted to die; I felt as if it was alive, alive and angry, screaming at me to die, and I wanted to die because I wanted it to stop. After so much time I finally decided to end it, to jump into the current and let it take me.

"But when I finally jumped in, I found I could stand, with the water only as high up as my chest. And because I could stand, I walked and sometimes swam until I got to higher ground; and then, because there was nothing left behind me, I kept walking until I got here."

———————

It began with the coming of the storm.

It wasn't yet raining, though he knew it would soon come to that; as yet, the only accompaniment to the thunder playing overhead was a mist that made the skin damp to the touch and turned the dirt and dust to mud. A heavy, reddish-brown haze, backlit by the fires, muted the darkening sky overhead; the air was thick with silt and soot, clinging to damp clothes and flesh, making it hard even to look straight ahead. Ashes fell from the sky like a light snow.

There was the mercilessly steady breeze brushing leaves and loose topsoil into the brew, forming spinning witches that danced along the silent line of children in which he waited, taunting them with their spiraling grace and then tormenting them by filling open mouths and eyes with pieces that bit and stung.

It was only on a rare occasion that he bothered to wipe the mud from his closed eyes to mark his position. Never did he speak. That had always been the rule in this particular line. Slipping off the streets where chaos and bullets reigned, and into this back alley where the line of children waited in silence, had been a comfort. He contented himself with listening to the sounds of the wind dervishes whirling around him, imagining he could hear their pinched, wicked laughter calling out to him, calling him out to play.

He once held a piece of light hidden inside his hollow bones. It was but a memory now, the sound of a whispered voice; it was a piece of his lost self he had nurtured and fed upon, a thing to care for, a thing to light his way. He had once been able to hear the voice and see that light clearly. If not in his dreams at night, then that voice would come on the wind in the light of day and it would warm him from the inside as it spoke to him, assuring him that there was some constancy in this world.

But the words were lost now. His fists were curled at his sides as if they still held some part of the voice instead of the gravel the wind had deposited into them through the cracks between his fingers.

In front of him in the line was a girl in old tennis shoes wearing a thin cotton dress. Standing in front of the girl was a tall boy. When last he looked, he had barely been able to see the back of the tall boy's head; it had seemed to float there, faint and disembodied, disconnected, above and beyond the little girl's head. When last he looked he had not been able to see any further down the line beyond the tall boy, nor had he been able to tell how much longer he would be waiting.

He wiped the mud from his eyes to look again. To see if the line had moved forward at all. Not that it mattered, he knew. There were always lines, he thought to himself, there had always been lines. This was life. Lines for food, lines for water, lines for the bathroom, lines to get into the fairgrounds, lines to escape a burning town. There were lines to get into this world, and there were lines to get out.

The dirt in the air was beginning to cover things entirely; as the misting from the coming storm continued, as the winds grew stronger, the copper-colored air painted over things, casting them in a sparkling orange hue. Already much of the girl's cotton dress was covered. The jet-black hair of the disembodied head floating beyond and above the girl was caked by mud. When on occasion a flash of lightning broke through, the top of the tall boy's head sparkled.

Doubt flickered across his muddied countenance as he finally heard the first whisperings ahead, as unintelligible at this point as the sound of two rocks being rubbed together in the distance, a slight buzz and hum that came to him unevenly across the wind.

There had been a time when he knew better who and what he was. He wondered where that time went, who that person was, and why and how he'd been forgotten.

He wondered why he remembered (faintly) the feeling of fear?

He winced as flecks of sand caught in a flurry tried to sneak their ways into his squinting eyes.

The head of the tall boy bobbed forward into the haze, disappearing in the moments it took the girl in the cotton dress to step up and follow behind him. When finally it was his turn to move and he lifted his right leg, the movement was slowed by the mud that gripped his pants. It cracked and began to break. When he pulled his other leg forward with a shake and a stretch he knocked loose the copper armor that had formed over him. Patches of it fell with every ensuing step until he shook free of the rest of it, and immediately he began to be covered anew.

He stepped up onto a curb, where the choking haze was

too dense to see anything ahead. He heard only the scratching of their voices.

Gradually, the crosswinds built again, thinning the curtain of smog, pushing it aside enough that he could see the girl in front of him again, the tall boy in his entirety, and, outlined in the distance, he could even discern his destination.

He tried to shake the mud off his face as it ran into his eyes. Whether he could see it or not, he knew it was a wall he was moving toward. It stretched to the right and to the left to the edges of his blurred vision and beyond. That wall surrounded the town. And it was nearly impenetrable.

He could see the faintest signs of the angels who stood guard at intervals along its length—the flash of a weapon here or the glimpse of feathers in the distance. Although he could not yet see St. Peter, he heard the old one's voice rumbling, emanating from somewhere ahead.

If he stepped away from the line, walked over ten feet to the side, he would be able to see St. Peter. But then he would lose his place and have to go to the end of the line.

He'd learned that lesson once already.

The tall boy stepped forward to the sound of the angels applauding. The girl again moved behind him, brushing her filthy dress with her hands, as if somehow she could make it look better. Then it was his turn to move forward. His hands were clammy with anticipation. He was so very close.

The girl turned to him as if she sensed his anxiety. She knelt down in a fluid motion, and scratched a message for him in the mud, then stood and turned and resumed walking forward, as if she had never paused at all.

He could hardly read her writing when he came to it.

It said YOU CANNOT HIDE FROM HIM FOR LONG.

He watched the girl more carefully now, understanding that she too was pretending in some way, that she too had a plan to pass through the wall; she would not risk being caught by the angels doing anything she was not supposed to do. She tried to hide herself. She let her shoulders sag pitifully; she let her head fall forward a little as if in mourning. She folded her hands in front of her, and tried to look innocent.

When he stopped walking, he was close enough to see clearly the Gate in the middle of the wall. The tall boy now stood before St. Peter, who had to tilt his head downward to look at the tall boy's face.

St. Peter commanded the tall boy to CONFESS HIS SINS.

A hush ran down the line of angels, a hush that began with those guarding the Gate and then seemed to travel along the wall before disappearing off into the haze.

"I sold gum to tourists," the tall boy said, looking down at the ground, his hands behind his back in much the same posture as the girl, though appearing far less sincere.

"AND?"

"And," the tall boy said slowly, almost defiantly, "the ones who tried to chase me off, I threw rocks at them."

The whole chorus of angels immediately let forth with exaggerated statements of disgust and dismay; they called out insults from so far down the length of the wall that it seemed as if the smoggy air itself was castigating him. "THIEF!," they said. "BAD BOY! YOU SHOULD BE ASHAMED! BOOOOO!"

St. Peter turned dramatically amidst their heckling and walked to the wall, where he meets with an angel who stood guard with his horn in one hand and a sword in the other. St. Peter whispered in the angel's ear.

To them this was not a matter for entertainment. The angel Gabriel whispered something back to St. Peter moments later.

"FOR PENANCE," St. Peter said when he returned, "YOU MUST WALK ON THE GROUND LIKE A DOG. AND YOU MUST PAY ME EVERY CENT THAT YOU TOOK FROM THESE POOR, POOR, INNOCENT TOURISTS

BEFORE YOU CAN BE ADMITTED INTO HEAVEN."

The tall boy lost his beleaguered pose, became defensive. He said, neither meek nor pitiful, "Look at my pockets! It is gone." He pulled them out. Only gravel.

He didn't try to sound sorry.

"Let me in," the tall boy said, nearly begging.

There was silence for several moments.

The tall boy said, "I spent it, I spent it all. I'm sorry. Forgive me."

For another moment, all was silent between the tall boy and St. Peter. The winds slowed to nothing and immediately the air was thick again. He could barely see what was happening at the front of the line. It looked to him at first as if the tall boy's head was sinking down in the haze. Then the little girl put her head down in her hands and covered her eyes, giving him an unobstructed view as ever so gradually, with a terrible, aching slowness, the tall boy bent his knees until he was nearly in a crouching position. He sets his hands in the dirt and leaned forward onto them. And, just as slowly, the tall boy began to crawl across the ground.

The laughter of the angels that followed was harsh, their insults crueler than before, but the tall boy began to take it as encouragement nonetheless. He crawled around faster and faster, and then he barked and he sat up and lay down, and chased himself around in circles to appease them.

After several minutes, the jeering angels begin throwing pebbles at him, and when he didn't take the hint, small rocks, until, on all fours, bleeding from a small cut in his forehead, the tall boy darted away from the wall, away from the line, scurrying as if his tail were indeed between his legs, and he ran off into the haze.

He had to give the girl a little shove right then to get her to move forward.

"CONFESS YOUR SINS," St. Peter said to the girl, who was less than half his size.

She began to cry.

"That boy you chased away is my brother," she said, "he's my brother."

She stamped her foot in the mud in frustration.

"AND?" St. Peter was indifferent to this approach. She immediately tried another tactic.

"I haven't done anything." She shook her head side to side emphatically. "I've been good. I did my hail Marys and I gave the nickel my brother gave me from the tourists to my mother to buy food."

Standing ten feet behind her, he found he could not speak. He would not be able to speak when the time came. He had been waiting so long so quietly he had forgotten his tongue. He tried; he opened his mouth and tried to push out even the smallest of noises, and got only a mouthful of silt in return.

His voice, apparently, had been taken along with everything else. His sins must have been too many to count.

He looked around desperately; he strained to see through the Gate, to find the one who said she would be on the other side of the wall, waiting for him. Julia. But she is not there. The hole in the wall is all that is there, a yawning pit of black guarded by Gabriel on one side and Nuriel, the angel of fire, on the other. More desperately, he looked up and down the wall itself, as if there might be another way.

"WHAT IS YOUR NAME?" St. Peter asked the girl.

Behind her, he grimaced. He did not know his own name.

"WHO ARE YOUR PARENTS?"

He felt an icy grip on his heart. Who are his parents, should the question be asked of him?

While the girl named both her mother and father, and their mothers and fathers before them, St. Peter smiled approvingly, and patted her on the head. He stood aside as two angels descended from the brewing sky; they landed gracefully before St. Peter, and knelt. He could not see their faces clearly from even this close distance, or what the dark clothes were that they wore underneath their robes. He could only catch sight of the glimpse of laurel and the flashing of gold from the crowns each wore around his head. That, and the outlines of their magnificent wings, their beautiful wings.

Those wings would be freedom itself, he thought.

These escorts then stood at either side of the girl, each grasping one of her hands, and they carried her to the Gate, and lifted her.

Gabriel and Nuriel both made way for her to pass. They put her into the hole at the center of the wall, and she disappeared.

He swallowed a dry patch of air.

When St. Peter gestured to him, he stepped forward slowly, his eyes darting right and left and then back again.

I've been waiting for you, a voice in his head said.

Or was it only the wind?

The angels grumbled and mumbled with suspicion as he approached. They knew instantly he did not belong here among them. A pebble sailed out from the haze and landed at his feet. And then a rock. One of them spat in his direction

"WHAT ARE YOUR SINS?," St. Peter asked him when he stood ready.

He would lie now. He would say none or make something up about giving nickels to parents but his tongue had been stolen. St. Peter said, "COULD IT BE LUST?" As if he knew something. The angels gasped and tittered and snickered at him, as if the truth were written over his body.

He shook his head, no.

(*Let me find you,* the voice said in his head, *Let me see where you are*)

But St. Peter was louder. "DO NOT LIE TO ME!" His voice very much like the thunder above, he said, "I KNOW

WHERE YOU ARE FROM! I KNOW WHERE YOU HAVE
BEEN AND WHAT YOU HAVE SEEN!"

He didn't say anything in response. He could not.
He trembled.

He was too afraid to ask St. Peter where he was from,
though he would like to know.

St. Peter's voice distorted, deepened, sending a shock
through him.

He realized he had been staring at his feet all this time.

"YOU DO NOT BELONG HERE," St. Peter said.
"YOU ARE NOT WELCOME HERE. YOU SMELL OF SIN,
AND YOU WILL NOT PASS BY ME ON THIS DAY OR ANY
OTHER."

He said nothing.

He could only turn inside of himself for comfort,
searching for that keepsake, the memory that once had warmed
his bones. It was an unspeakable, inexplicable, overpowering
frustration he found in its stead, lying in wait in his heart. It was
anger, it was indeed a lust for the other side of the Gate; it was
greed he felt for all the things he had been denied; it was pride
in having survived this far, knowing he deserved far better than
this, coupled with a near-overwhelming hunger to be free of these
restraints, and, at the last, it was a deep, gnawing envy of all who
were already in the beyond. He would tear the wings from the
backs of the angels themselves to be free.

It was a voice that never stopped screaming inside for
what was lost, yet he, standing there covered with mud, so close to
release, said nothing.

The skies rumbled overhead.

The rain began in earnest.

He sprinted forward, but the angels were on him in a heartbeat.

He stared at that hole in the wall desperately as he fell to
the muddy ground under the weight of Gabriel. If only there was a

way to will himself through it with his mind.

The angels rolled him onto his back and pinned his arms before he could crawl away. Up close, staring up at them underneath the rolling sky, he saw they were not angels at all. They had only the wings. They were not fair, they were not gentle, and they stunk of alcohol and sweat; their faces were scarred and grimy, their skin rough and aged; in their eyes, he saw as they circled him, were the deaths of countless souls; their belts were lined with cold metal weapons and the stolen mementoes of their victims, their clothes were nothing more than fatigues; their hands were sullied with blood and dirt. What he had taken before to be laurel wreaths around their heads were only green bandannas marked with the brass insignia of the army.

It all went by so fast after that. He closed his eyes as they held him up and the first blow landed on his cheek. Another sunk into his stomach, and another after that, and by the time they all set in together, he was already numb to the pain. He found himself praying they would use only their fists, and not their stones.

He went for a moment to another place in his mind; in his imagination he went right to the heart of the storm overhead, and then above and through it, to a place where his cries of frustration were the very thunder itself. The lightning roared, throbbing electric blood through his veins, and his tears fell as heavily as the rain. He was aware of their fists pounding on him, he felt their nails cutting at his skin, their hot spit running off his face, and he wondered: Were they going to kill him today? He heard inside his head a million crackling voices as they roared in the wind screaming past his ears, and he was adrift, lost in that swarm of maddening, spinning, shrieking noise.

Were they going to kill him now?

His eyes opened again to a glimpse of the ascendant moon glancing through the moving clouds of the storm. Was it a crescent, horns on both ends pointed up into the heavens? He tried uselessly to pull away from them, and realized they had dragged him to a place where there was another hole before him. At first, in his delirium, he mistook it for the Gate, and he crawled gladly toward it. The angels cackling together herded him in that direction, and he, not thinking twice about it, scrambled happily forward to get away from them, grateful indeed for their mercy.

Grateful, that is, until he looked into the hole and realized that instead of being a passageway into the meadows beyond, it was a narrow chute that only went down into the ground, down as far, as deep as he could see before it twisted and turned out of sight. Once he was inside, it was apparent the space was much smaller than it appeared from above; his legs in a moment were too tightly pressed against each other to move one or the other comfortably, his back and his elbows were forced against the hard earth as he tried to find a grip for his hands. He began to panic. The men disguised as angels pushed at him with their hands, and then with their feet, and then when he was far beneath the ground, with tall sticks that they jabbed into the hole after him; they pushed until he was so far down the narrowing chute that he became wedged in. Until he could not move.

(The voice in his head said *Are you my son? Are you ready to make them pay?*)

It was after they started throwing the dirt on top of him that he finally found his voice and began to scream.

Break Me
Into a Thousand Pieces
I'll Always Find My Way
Home

Chapter 1

White Harbor University, Maine
March 14 (The Present)

Eric woke in a cold sweat. Same dream. He smelled beer and flowers. And his mouth was dry. The back of a hand was on his face, stinking of shitty perfume. At first, thinking it was his hand, he panicked when he tried to move it and it didn't move.

Someone knocked on the door. Traces of the dream washed away. Next to him under the sheets a girl moaned and shifted. He felt under his hand—his real hand—her breast moving slowly. One of her feet rubbed up and down his shin, and she moaned again sleepily when her nipple brushed against his fingertips.

Bianca the maid walked in.

Eric realized he must have ended up in his own bed, in his own dorm room. He moved the hand off of his face.

Bianca was wearing her horn-rimmed glasses, and in her hand she had a rag. Something metal she was carrying or wearing that he could not see jingled with her every step.

She wiped her rag along the heater, pretending to ignore him, but was obviously watching the bed out of the corner of her eye. Eric looked at the girl's face next to him and tried to remember her. Where did he meet her? Bianca moved over to the window, her spurs jangling. She turned her back to him and reached into her holster for her Windex.

When Eric pulled himself out of the bed, neither the maid nor the girl reacted. Bianca went right on spraying and cleaning. As if she didn't have a camera built into the handle of her feather duster snapping away pictures so she could let Eric's mother know where he'd been hiding out and what he'd been doing with all his time.

Eric moved to the window and stood there, letting her

snap away roll after roll of his backside until her cleaning was done and she exited the room.

Although he could not remember the content of his bad dreams, his first thought was that they must have something to do with whatever it was he did last night. The funny thing was, he couldn't quite remember anything that happened last night. Why did all the nights blend together? Why did it not seem to matter what happened last night?

Out through the window from his view of the Plaza, Eric could see Brother Matthew getting himself worked up while lecturing a group of freshman students. Brother Matt's evangelism took the form of him calling his listeners sinners and fornicators, and then shouting accusations of corruption and snippets of scriptures at those who inevitably took the bait and tried to debate him. Brother Matt's goal was to go after their identities, to see who wasn't firm in theirs.

Eric leaned his forehead against the glass.

The last time he was in his mom's house, Eric had ended up in the attic space, looking through the scrapbooks there. He'd been in that space before, and he'd seen the albums before, but this time had been different. This was because all of the other times he'd seen them, he'd always thought the pictures in the albums were of him. Pictures of him traveling with his mom and the dad he couldn't remember, pictures of him getting his first haircut, of him in his first little dress suit, pictures of him growing up. It never occurred to Eric until he looked at them this last time that he didn't remember doing any of those things. Not at all. Because he never did. Somewhere along the line, those pictures just about became his memories. He just thought that maybe back then he didn't look the way he did now. That maybe he wasn't a very good-looking kid when he was younger.

Eric had always known he was adopted. He just never really asked how long always was. Something about being in this new band, something about having these new friends, had made him wonder about it—maybe for the first time in his life. Why didn't he know so many things about his life?

But there it was, or part of it, in those albums. Year after year, for the first four years, there was a Christmas card with his mom and her husband holding each other and smiling. Then there was a kid with them on the following card. He started as a baby and grew bigger and bigger every year for 7 years. Eric had stared at the little boy in the photos, the one who wasn't Eric anymore. Then, for a stretch of 10 pages, there were no holiday card photos to be found, and no other photos of any kids. Until Christmas, fourteen years ago, for which there was a photo featuring Eric—the real Eric—his mom, and their dog Kennedy, standing together in front of one of the oaks behind the house, the one they used to decorate with lights.

So his mother, Eric had guessed, had once had another kid, and that kid was gone, and Eric had been his replacement. But where had he been before he was adopted? Why couldn't he remember anything before that?

Staring out across the campus, Eric spotted a familiar face in the Plaza. The gardener. Edge. Driving one of those snow machines, clearing the main walkway, leaning forward in his seat like he was trying to cut down on wind resistance, leering at a tall, melon-chested blonde on the walk ahead of him.

It reminded him that he had to get himself fixed up again.

He watched Edge until Edge passed by Brother Matt and his audience of listeners, and disappeared around a bend in the pathway. Eric needed to think about how and when he was going to hook up with him.

————

Office of the Dean

Victrine looked both ways up and down the reception hall before closing the door behind her, and listened for the latch to catch.

Lord, she thought, what and with all the activity going on around here I must be having a harder time than I realized.

This was something she would never be doing regularly, but she wouldn't be able to get anything done if she didn't take a moment to pull herself together and catch her breath, try to put some order back into her head.

She stepped out of her shoes in front of the couch, and when she was back in her chair and she'd had the chance to catch her breath, she pulled an egg sandwich out of her handbag.

It was an important thing, keeping the machine well fed.

"Glory," she said to herself when she saw how her hands were shaking.

Half the sandwich was on the way down when Victrine allowed herself to wonder what could be wrong with her? Could it only have been hunger? There she had been, crossing the great lawn outside of the dormitories in the drizzle, when this odd feeling came over her, as if someone had their eyes on her. True enough, it was not an uncommon sensation for a woman of her size—look around hard enough and there were all kinds of mannerless people staring with that shocked look. But this had been different. There she had been, strolling through the eucalyptus trees, and the next thing she knew the hackles were rising on the back on her neck.

There wasn't anything happening out of the ordinary anywhere around her, as far as she could tell. Students were here and there as they should be, walking about, hanging about, nothing that should have set her on edge.

Then she had looked up at the dormitory building she was passing underneath. She was responding to the kind of awareness a person developed after standing in front of a classroom for a few years, a talent for locating the source of trouble—whether he was in the back of the classroom or standing just outside the door.

And there Eric was—at least that was what she told herself—thinking about it now, it could have just about been anyone. But at the time she would have sworn that it was Eric Hartin she saw there, standing tall and full of life and naked as daylight in a window three floors up, two windows over from the left, in the Amethyst building, staring right down back at her. Looking the same as always, skin and bones, but without clothes. Like he'd been caught in amber.

Hunger was a likely assessment. But then again, she might be stopping off at the church on her way home anywho. Victrine would take it as a reminder to herself to keep the both of them, Mrs. Hartin and her son, in her good thoughts.

Maybe before that she would just have to try to run a check on whose dorm room that really was. For peace of mind. Too soon, she finished off the sandwich. She thought that maybe she would try adding a little ginger next time.

A voice close by startled Victrine nearly out of her skin.

"Ma'am, pardon me?"

"Now how did you get in here?" She said before she located the owner of the voice. "I just locked that door."

"Well, I . . . "

Big as a horse he was, and he had himself a thick head of dark hair, and he was dressed in a green campus maintenance jumpsuit, although his face looked not one bit familiar to her.

"Never mind that," Victrine snapped out crisply. Was he some kind of salesman? Selling what? "One thing at a time," she said. "What can be done for you, yourself now?"

He handed her a business card. She set it on top of the pile in the IN tray without looking at it.

"I'd like to speak with the Dean," he said.

Of course he would.

"Do you have an appointment?"

She knew already he did not. Ms. Hartin had booked herself up the rest of the week.

"Actually," he said slowly as he rubbed his hands together, a nervous tic for a nervous liar, "I spoke with Dean Hartin on her way out yesterday. She said I should drop by. Maybe she forgot . . . "

Victrine lifted off her glasses, narrowed her eyes at him. She made it clear she knew what kind of man she was dealing with.

"Traditionally, Dean Hartin doesn't handle things that way, at least not to my knowledge, and I've been here quite some time now. If I could have your name, and a phone number, I'll try to arrange an appointment at the earliest convenience to the both of you."

His name was Edge, she could see from his name tag. Edge was a little flinty-eyed for her tastes. The kind of man who thought he shouldn't have to deal with women like Victrine.

"Is she in now?" And there it was, plain as day. Ignoring her words.

"Edge . . . " She left the question of his last name up in the air.

"Wow," he fairly sneered at her, "you can read."

Well.

He turned his back to her. Marched away from the desk just as he did coming in, talking under his breath.

Victrine didn't allow herself the time to be irritated by him.

She waited a moment after he had left, grabbed her keys and followed after him, just to double-check the lock. In the going, she clipped the edge of the desk, knocking a few papers to the floor. She would have to widen the walkway a little, she guessed. That was twice she had spilled papers that way in as many days.

But she would have to worry about that later.

Strangest day already. The hospital had been calling again, and Victrine was near ready to tear her hair out waiting for Dean Hartin to finish her turn at the orientation so she could pass along the message. Victrine knew that Dean Hartin had been up at the hospital looking after the poor boy only last week, and all had been relatively well. It was never anything good when the hospital called.

Law Offices of Steven Shank
White Harbor, Maine

"Please come in, Rachel, isn't it? My name is Steven Shank. Have a seat."

Shank was a pug-faced man, and very well groomed. Stepping into his law office was like stepping into a cozy den in someone else's home, where Shank the dog was up on the leather chair again. "I have a one o'clock—so we're going to try to get through this as quickly as possible."

"Fine with me," Rachel said, already feeling intimidated, defensive.

"This is Betty McClean, from Halifax General Life and Health Insurance Systems." Betty was obviously the lower paid of the two, and that meant something here. Shank's confident manner Rachel interpreted in the same way she did the box of Cubans on the corner of his desk, as evidence of pedigree. "Betty is here to observe, because that is undeniably her legal right. Don't feel obliged to address her."

"Hi."

Betty nodded at her.

"This is Margaret. She'll be transcribing the session."

"Hi, Margaret."

"Hello."

"This is going to be like I'm testifying in court?"

Betty and Shank exchanged knowing, furtive glances.

"Yes, but informally so," Shank said. He cleared his throat. "Now, Rachel, let's begin. We have gathered here today to take a deposition from you in the hopes of clearing up questions relating to the insurer's obligations toward one Eric Hartin. If this case does go to court and the testimony given today is found to be relevant, then you will again be subpoenaed to testify."

"The fun never ends."

"Let's begin. Please state your full name."

"Rachel Cummings."

"Miss Cummings, how do you know Eric Hartin?"

"We're friends. Or at least we were starting to be before this happened. He might feel differently now. I might not have done him a favor."

"You were with Eric Hartin on the night of November 17th?"

"Yeah. I thought it was understood that was why I was here."

"Is that a yes or a no?"

"Yes."

"Will you please describe the events of the night of November 17th?"

"Sure. We were in Weatherton for a show. Eric Hartin came with us because my friend Marty, our regular guitarist, was too whacked out of it to make the trip. We knew Eric because he used to hang around a lot at the recording studio on campus when we were rehearsing. Other than that, I never saw him that much, because he wasn't a student. We hadn't been getting all that much band work at the time."

"This show was performed on the Weatherton campus, is that correct?"

"Yeah."

"Yes or no?"

"Yes."

"After the show in Weatherton, where did you go?"

"We rented a cabin near Weatherton, stayed there for the night."

"Hayward Cabins."

"Exactly. You don't even need me for this, do you Mr. Shank?"

"Is that a yes or a no?" Shank sounded slightly irritated.

"It is a yes. We'd all had a lot to drink and we thought it was going to snow again. We'd already run into a surprise squall on the way up. Plus, the show went well, so we were all kind of stoked and wanted to celebrate. "

"Was there anything you noticed about Eric that night?"

"He was in a strange mood, Yeah."

"When you say strange mood, are you saying he was depressed?"

"More withdrawn than anything."

"Depressed is not the right word?"

"No."

"Please continue."

"Well, much later, after we'd partied for a while . . . "

"Partied?"

"We drank beers."

"How many did you have?"

"Three."

"And Eric?"

"He must have had five or six before I fell asleep."

"Something woke me up early in the morning. Like snap!, suddenly I was clear and awake. It might have been the bed. I need to practically sleep on a board to be comfortable. My back is really messed up going back to when I was a kid. Or it might have been the beer. I never sleep too well after drinking. What happened was that I woke up just in time to see Eric slipping out, closing the cabin door behind him."

"So you left the cabin as well?"

"Just, you know, to see if I could help him out. Part of the band thing. I mean the truth is, Eric and I weren't that close to start with. I'm not talking about romantically, either, not at all, so don't think that. He was a very out-there guy, and I appreciated his perspective. He might have been a little annoyed by me, I think. Because I'm so direct. And I talk a lot. I like to get everything on the table—the better to figure it out. Eric was a real introvert. I thought maybe he might have been gay or something."

"Ms. Cummings, do you know if he was gay?" Betty had finally found her voice.

Shank glared at Betty.

"You don't have to answer that, Rachel."

"Why doesn't she, Steven? She opened it up."

"I'm closing it. Leave it for the courtroom, if that's how you want to behave. Have some class, for God's sake." Shank rolled his pug eyes at Betty, then turned back to Rachel.

"Rachel?"

Rachel would have felt bad for the older woman, simply due to the hostility Shank directed at her; but then, truth to tell, Betty didn't really seem to be a particularly nice person either.

"Uhm . . . what?"

"When you say you followed Eric, are you saying you were right behind him?"

"No. I was a ways back, and to his side. He had a head start on me. I actually wanted to see what he was up to before I interrupted him. He could have just been taking a leak in the privacy of the great outdoors for all I knew."

"Fine."

"Well, anyway, I reached the top of the climb, which was—I don't know exactly where it was because of the snow—but it seemed to me to be a small field that ended at an overlook. A few hundred feet above the cabins. It was a beautiful night. Nearly full moon, crystal clear sky. The storm we'd been worried about never showed."

"How long was the climb?"

"Twenty minutes, I guess. I had to catch my breath a couple times."

"Could you hear anything Eric might have been saying?"

"No. I didn't hear him say anything the whole time. He was just standing there when I finally found him again at the top. He had gone straight up through the middle. I came up around the side, so I could see what he was doing."

"And what was he doing?"

"He was crying. Just standing there, crying."

"Until," Rachel said, "well, until he started to move."

"Started to move where?" Shank watched her carefully.

"Towards the edge of the field. Walking at first, then jogging. I thought he was planning to run right off the edge."

"That's very speculative, Rachel." It was a schoolteacher's tone Shank used, pointing out that she might be mistaken, that she might want to do her math again.

Rachel cleared her throat nervously.

"It seemed clear to me, Steven."

"How could you be so sure?"

"I . . . guess I couldn't be? Sure, I guess I couldn't be." Rachel shifted uncomfortably in her chair.

Shank cleared his throat.

"Moving on, Rachel, what did you do when you allegedly saw Eric Hartin walking, then jogging, in the direction of the edge of the field?"

"I started running toward him. God, I think, even before I knew what I was doing. I didn't understand any of it. Just like I don't understand any of this. Except that you're both assholes, aren't you? "

"Would you like a Kleenex?"

"Fuck off. Shank."

"Miss Cummings?"

"Is that a yes or a no? I mean no. No, Steven, thank you. I don't want a Kleenex."

"Would you like a moment to compose yourself?"

"No. I want to get this over with."

"You ran after Eric . . . ?"

"Yes. Everything happened too fast after that. I mean, I know logically it was longer than I remember because I noticed that the snow was slowing us both down so much. But then, at the same time, it wasn't taking long enough either, because he was getting closer to the cliff. Eric's eyes were squeezed shut—I don't even think he knew I was there, I don't think he knew anything was there. I was coming from his side, and I could see his face clearly and no, I didn't even think of calling out to him . . . don't ask me why . . . " Rachel took a deep breath, "and the next thing I know . . . he's right there . . . ," she reached out in front of her with her hands to show how close he was, "right there in front of me jumping right into the air, no second thoughts about it . . . right there at the edge he jumped and pulled his legs up, and held his arms out like he was jumping into the air and he thought he was going to be able to stay up there, like he thought he was going to be able to fly or something . . . and then I decided to try to catch him . . . "

"You tried to catch him?"

"It wasn't as if I felt I had any choice in it. I didn't feel heroic or anything . . . I was so caught up in the motion, so terrorized by the idea of the cliff, so determined to not let him do this. Even though he didn't know it, we were locked together for a few seconds, tied together; when he jumped, I did, too—to stop him. I mean, in the back of my mind part of me was sure it was all over—life unlived flashing in front of my eyes and everything, the ground seeming like it was moving away from me too fast— and then suddenly I had him, I had Eric. And he had me. My arms went around his waist, and my hands closed together on the other side of him, and he grabbed onto me and then we were both falling together and I wasn't letting go. It was our combined weight that saved us, I'm convinced. I hit him at an angle and our weight together brought us down inches, not even feet from the edge."

"Do you think Eric Hartin wanted to die?"

She was quiet a moment. "I know I didn't want to die."

Betty snorted.

"I don't think many people truly want to die," Rachel said. Shank cut her off with a smile.

"What happened next, Rachel?"

"When I realized he was out . . . "

"Eric was unconscious?"

"Yeah."

"Yes or no."

"Yes, Steven, he was unconscious. He was breathing, although for a minute that fact didn't register on me and I totally freaked out. Even though he was in my arms, I somehow became convinced that I had missed him, missed him completely, that he had gotten away from me, gone straight over the edge. That was when I started yelling. At first I think I was calling for him, because I was thinking still that he wasn't there with me. Which is what everyone in the entire valley probably heard that night. Me screeching like a banshee in the hills. I think Nate heard me. One of my band mates. He was the one who called the cops. I just plain started screaming because I didn't know what to do to make it right."

As the two lawyers discussed things she didn't care to understand, behind Rachel's eyes danced fleeting glimpses of the memory of her rush from Eric's hospital earlier in the day, and her great desire to be out in the open air. Sprinting down the last hallway before the exit, watching out of the corner of her eye the legs of her shadow sliding gracefully back and forth on the white enamel wall alongside her, Rachel had recalled the exact way the moonlight had flashed and broken between Eric's running legs as he had raced with her across the snow . . .

Earlier in the day, Rachel, who had visited Eric at the hospital regularly since that night, had been in the middle of updating Eric on the whereabouts of the former band members when Eric's eyelids had fluttered open, so that he appeared, at least momentarily, to be staring blankly at the ceiling. Then his eyes had rolled upward into his head. And before she could even fully take in that this had happened or what it could possibly mean, his whole body had started to convulse. Rachel had called for a doctor while Eric lay there on his back with his hands up in front of him as if he were a dog begging, the whites of his eyes flickering out from behind his fluttering eyelids, his whole body shaking uncontrollably. She had called out into the hallway again for a doctor and what she had gotten instead were two muscled attendants who pinned Eric down far too forcefully, elevated his legs, and then placed a stick in his mouth, to keep him from biting his tongue or to keep him breathing or, she had thought, maybe both.

"He's starting another one," one of the attendants had said.

The other attendant had turned to Rachel to suggest that she might want to consider returning to visit him another day.

––––––––––

Office of the Dean

Victrine stepped gingerly as she crossed the threshold of the Amethyst dormitory. Here they were, she was thinking, on the brink of really being able to start off a year on the right foot, and there was never an end to the problems that arose. Today there were thirty protesters camped out in the administrative lobby, with none of them even being able to agree on what they were protesting. As if they had any legitimate complaints in the first place, the way the school catered to their needs. But tomorrow, when they were gone, it would be something else, and the day after something new yet again. And here Victrine was, a single mother raising two boys, always being asked to make that extra effort for the sake of the team, for the sake of the school, for the sake of the students. Where was all the extra effort she was making going to make a difference to her boys? When were they going to be getting back some of the time they were losing with their mother?

Lord, Victrine thought, she was nearly at a point where she was regretting tossing that worthless boyfriend of hers out of her house. He may not have done anything more than lie around watching television, he may not have had any kind of work ethic, he may not have done any housework, he may not have had any money or even cared for Victrine at all, but at the least, having him there had meant having someone home for the boys when they needed it, the poor little bairns.

It took all of 10 minutes to find the room she was looking for. That was where she had seen the naked young man. Three floors up and two windows over from the west of the building. It turned out to be number 319.

Victrine knocked on the door.

No one answered.

When she merely touched the knob, the door pushed open.

The least she could do, she had decided when she had left her office for the day, was answer this one question for herself.

Sure and there it was, she assured herself as the door swung slowly open to reveal a barren, unoccupied room, it could have been just about anyone she had seen the week before. It could have been any transient or bum who had pushed hard enough on the door to let himself in.

She stepped into the suite carefully, took a slow walk about the place. It was noticeably colder inside than it was out in the drizzle. Someone, she thought to herself, making a mental note, had been sitting down on the job to have let an empty apartment like this slip by, what when there were hundreds still who'd be happy to have that kind of roof over their heads. It was a fine apartment—a one-bedroom, one-bath apartment with clean carpets, newly painted walls, and a clear view of the Plaza and the eucalyptus grove. She closed the open windows, latched them.

Nothing much else here, she thought, glad now that she had come to investigate the room. Nothing wrong with it but the feel from it, the feeling that something was not right inside it, or something out of place. And that she could easily attribute to the fact that it was empty now, when it was intended to be lived in. When she closed the door behind her and locked it, her thoughts had already returned to her boys, who would still be at their school, waiting for her to pick them up. They were probably out on the street already, keeping an eye out for her car. They liked to do it that way—they were already at the age where they didn't want their mother to be making an appearance in front of their little friends. Maybe she would try to plan something fun for them for the weekend. Something non-athletic for once, something they would all be able to do together.

Eric had been her only clue, the only hope she had of understanding what had brought him to her, or so Evelyn Hartin had wanted to believe.

When she returned to her office to discover two messages from the hospital—the first indicating the occurrence of another seizure, the second informing her that the seizures had ended and Eric had settled down again—she had an epiphany: it occurred to her that perhaps there was something more she could do, one more avenue to venture down.

First things first, she thought, and she opened a drawer and pulled out a small notebook. She opened the notebook to the first page and wrote:

Fourteen years ago, as I was beginning to truly invest myself in my new career, I had the luxury of time to spend an entire month searching for a name for my soon-to-be-adopted child, the child I had found, the child who found me.

There was a name that would describe his slight build, his almost sickly thinness, and the startling light blue color of his runaway eyes. A name, after all, was not to be trifled with. The right one would best guide him through life, serving many times as an anchor, giving name to his tribe, reminding him where he has been, where he was from, and where he was going. Although he wasn't able to tell me who he was—either because he wasn't able to remember or because he didn't want to remember it—it was my belief he wore the name he had been given at birth, spelled out all over him, if a person were looking at the picture in the correct light.

Every day for a month I burrowed through books of names—names in English and in several other languages as well, although his dark skin later turned out to be only a deep tan. I dug through phone directories and old class rosters for a wider selection. At first, in the days when he was literally gulping down every bit and scrap of food, I would simply set myself down in front of him and read the names to see if he would respond. He and Kennedy were a perfectly matched set at dinner time, both anxious the other (or maybe someone else) was going to steal his food. They both ate voraciously, usually side by side, with Eric at the table and Kennedy right next to him.

During my first attempts at instruction, when I tried to teach him to eat his food slowly, I read from the same small, blue, lace-embroidered book I used to pick a name for Curt years before. For weeks I tried new names on him at every opportunity. When he climbed in the trees in back, when I called him for breakfast, lunch, and dinner, even when I was telling him to brush his teeth—I would be calling out one name after the other after the other.

The poor child. He must have thought I was mad. He must have been terribly confused. But it seemed to me to work, at least to an extent. I noticed there were several names he responded to, or at least that he responded to more than he responded to others. I soon had a list of names that I held as potential keepers. At the end of two more days of working down the list, I had a shorter list of choices.

It seems to me now that what occurred in the end, when I was comparing the names on the short list, looking for commonalities, I realized there was a name I hadn't been willing to try out on him, which was the name of my first child, Curt. Even now, I remember the deciding moment distinctly. Eric was seated at the top of the staircase and I called up to him without knowing he was so close by. I just about bellowed to let him know that lunch was ready. And I called him Curt when I called him.

The moment after that name, Curt, flew out of my mouth, I saw him sitting there watching me. I felt so ashamed, as if I had revealed to him the most painful secret of my life, and my heart's desire—that is, that he might somehow be Curt, brought back to me. And before this new child could respond, even as it came out of my mouth, I knew that I was wrong and that this was not and never would be the son I had given birth to and lost.

I named him Eric later that day.

Evelyn Hartin set down her pen, closed her new journal and dropped the small, bound book into her bag. She reached across her desk, and picked up the business card she had found lying on the carpet just outside her office door. She studied it silently, leaning back in her chair.

Brighter Day Services
Providing 24-hour Security
Edge Harwood, Investigator

She would dig through her storage when she got home, to find the journal she'd kept fourteen years ago, when she first met Eric. Maybe there were answers still to be found.

Chapter 2

White Harbor University
March 15

When Eric walked around the corner of the last in the row of dorm buildings, he saw the gardener standing in his usual spot, by the stairs to the basement laundry room.

Eric stuffed his hands deep down into his pockets as he walked up to the gardener. Eric asked if the gardener could set him up. The name tag on the gardener's Staff shirt read EDGE. In cursive.

Edge said, "Name it." He smelled like a pile of shit.

"I want a black one," Eric said.

Edge said, "Forty-five." Eric pulled a twenty out from the bottom of his right pocket. His only twenty.

Edge looked around. He said, "I don't have time for this shit." He snatched the twenty. He looked around again, shoved the bill into his jacket pocket, at the same time with the other hand removing a bottle. He shook out four red ones.

Eric sighed.

Movement behind Edge caught Eric's eye. He squinted against the night, and around Edge's arm Eric saw someone kneeling on a spot of pavement cleared of snow in the Sapphire building parking lot. It was a girl. She had a spray paint can in her hand.

She was writing LOVE IS GOD.

Edge saw as he was dropping the four pills into Eric's hand that Eric was looking at something. When he turned his head, he saw the girl and said in a low breath ONE OF THEM RIGHT FUCKING THERE.

Two of the four pills missed Eric's hand and fell . . .

Edge said WATCH YOUR NOSE, KID.

Both pills landed in a weed.

Eric didn't see where Edge went when he left. Eric was on his knees on the ground, squinting his eyes . . .

One red one was wet when he found it. It crumbled to pieces in his mouth as he swallowed.

Edge and the girl were both gone. His knees were cold and wet. Eric heard the sound of drums echoing faintly—either a band playing or someone practicing down at the Soundbox, the campus music center. When he stood up, he decided he might as well check that out. He didn't have any other plans . . .

Eric reminded himself that he needed to be in his own bed in the morning. Just to keep an eye on that maid.

———————

Office of the Dean

It wasn't as if Victrine minded being at work this early. No problem in dropping her boys off a bit before their classes, she thought. Her boys were at that age where they preferred that, she thought, because no one saw them with their Mommy.

Although the University may not have been her proper element, she did well on campus as Executive Assistant to the Dean. She always had. What and there was no wonder in that, she thought, everything being so big. The desks were higher, the doorways were wider, the ceilings taller, even the paintings in the hall stretched near as far as the eye could see. You were only as big as your mind allowed you to be, Victrine liked to say, and in a place like this, there was a need for a lot of space.

It was a close thing when Victrine almost left it all behind.

She knocked on the door twice, and gave Dean Hartin a moment. Although she knew the Dean wouldn't answer. She took a deep breath and pushed open the door before picking the breakfast tray up off the floor.

She did not like to be in the Dean's office on these mornings.

Victrine was also feeling self-conscious: she shouldn't have worn stripes.

Just in walking in, she felt uncomfortable immediately. The windows were open wide, the curtains were open, and as a result the heating system was going full bore, so that the books on the shelves were shaking a little. Sure enough, Dean Hartin was setting out on the window ledge, facing the rising sun, smoking, busy reading through what looked like an old journal, looking so peaceful. Almost angelic. Never mind that the horizon to the north was brimming with storm clouds, or that the air was crisper than usual.

The night before, when Victrine was locking up her desk—which everyone in the building found themselves having to do now—the Dean was pacing about, snapping down her cigarettes one after another. Almost as if she knew what kind of day today was going to be for her.

"There was a message from the hospital," Victrine said steadily. "They indicated you may want to clear your schedule later in the afternoon. But I'm thinking you might want to leave earlier than that, before the storm has gone the distance. I can juggle around your appointments easily enough . . . "

Victrine went on for a few minutes, talking about the boys mostly, as much for the Dean's benefit as for her own, warding off the silence. When she had set the tray at the Dean's desk and pushed and pulled the more pressing papers and messages into more prominent positions, she walked back to the door and slowly pulled it closed behind her. The Dean had her mind on a hundred things at once.

Victrine heard her say, simply and sincerely, "Thank you, Victrine."

That was enough for her, Victrine thought to herself.

White Harbor, Maine

Stumbling through the damp cold of the night, it was a much bleaker picture inside than it was outside. His ragged breath came and went in a cold blue manner, with a puff of steam. Although the rain had finally ended, the air was still thick with wind and moisture and the cold charge of electricity; water still ran steadily from the saturated earth beneath the rose gardens and the landscaped hillsides into the gutters; the cars parked alongside this endless road were all gleaming from their recent rinsing. Everything looked shiny and new.

Where all he could remember before this, and faintly at that, was a nightmare of smoke and fire.

The boy was alone here, more alone than he had ever been before. He didn't know where "here" was. He didn't know how it was he was here or why it was he felt he should be keeping an eye on the road behind him.

It was harder to walk on the second night after the storm. More painful than the first night. Hungry and numb, his cold legs were moved on by the bright burning light at the top of a hill that might as well have been in heaven it was so far away.

That light drew him, and the breeze coming down from it. A western wind that carried with it the smell of fresh, raw meat . . . Otherwise, he would still be sleeping half-buried in a snow bank down by the harbor.

From one of the parked cars as he approached there came a clicking noise. In the driver's seat the darkened silhouette of a head wearing a wide-rimmed hat turned to see who was coming; the man inside, seeing the boy in the side view mirror, gasped in surprise, and the car immediately began to move, rolling forward silently for a hundred feet.

The car stopped again and sat still at the curb. Where it seemed to be waiting for the next move to come.

The boy took twenty more cautious steps forward toward the light, close enough to be close to the car again; again, the car began to roll forward, going farther down the road this time before pausing for another moment. Maybe the driver was nervous, or afraid, or both.

The car then continued rolling forward, up around the corner, where its headlights came on and the engine came to life. And then it moved off.

Much later, standing beneath the porch light of a gingerbread house with candy cane columns, the boy faced a smaller door built into a larger door, a graham cracker flap that swung open and closed with the breeze rhythmically offering puffs and wisps of the flavor of the food nearby. All while the greater door around it remained closed.

Just inside the flap was a large metal bowl filled to the rim with pieces of animal flesh, the fat all removed, enough to make his dry mouth water . . . an offering for the gods, a meal fit for a king. Just as the boy was about to make his move, the witch who lived there strode into view.

———————

Evelyn's Old Journal
Entry Date: May 9

It is suddenly as if I am living with a stranger.

I can no longer deny that something has affected Kennedy, that somewhere in the process of moving to our new home and his graduating from the Academy he has become a living terror. Of course it has been a trying transition for the both of us, and the poor beast of a dog had already been on edge for weeks—an obvious result of the torrential weather (and who could blame him?). I had assumed by now that he would have come around.

My worst fears were confirmed earlier this evening when I returned to a plethora of messages on the answering machine from several of my concerned new neighbors. It seems my little boy concluded a whirlwind of destructive afternoon activity by herding three sobbing neighborhood children (who were on their way to school) into the Mitchelson's pool yard, where apparently he held them captive, taunting them with freedom for more than an hour. (When I went to pick him up, Mrs. Mitchelson told me that he would let them take two or three steps away from the cabana each time before chasing them screaming back inside.) One of the little girls involved soiled her dress, which puts today's grand total—adding in the cost of the roast dinner I'd been preparing for our annual Women's Night, which he consumed—at close to one hundred dollars.

There are times now when I see him that I am simply terrified of what he might do; it is a feeling I truly believe—for the sake of the child (even when the child is a dog)—a parent should never experience. It breaks my heart, especially when I feel this way, to see in his eyes only open love and affection. He must sense my fear, I am sure of it, but I do not think he understands at all that he is the cause of it. He merely attempts to drive the fear away.

Yet, at the same time, he has become more distant and aggressive. There seems to be a certain air of expectancy, of tension and violence to his presence, as if he is just waiting for something. At times, it's all I can do not to avert my eyes from his and back slowly away . . .

———————

Fourteen Years Ago

Evelyn Hartin knew she had seen an ancient-looking typewriter tucked away in a corner underneath someone's desk in the administrative secretarial pool, and of course it would turn out to belong to that strange woman Victrine. The engraved brass plate mounted just above the keyboard bore her name; it was obvious the machine was well cared for, although Evelyn had yet to see it in use and doubted she ever would again after tonight.

As she started typing, enjoying the action of the keys, Evelyn promised herself that she would make a more sincere effort to overcome her prejudice toward Victrine. Whatever form she wore, Victrine did appear to be a kindred spirit.

Evelyn typed:

Entry date: June 4
I tried to sleep, but my mind would not rest without arriving at an understanding of exactly what it was I experienced this evening. The memory was still so potent and viable as I tried to calm myself at home in my bedroom, as I tried to slow the beating of my heart, as I waited and waited for even the slightest hint of tiredness to creep into me. Women's Night only served to remind me after it was over that I was all alone in this new place. With Regina back on the road to Saugus, there isn't anyone here or nearby I can turn to.

In the end, tranquilizers or not, I felt it best to leave the house entirely. Every noise there signaled the breaking of some lock buried deep in my mind, a rattling at my nerves; every settling sound was to my ears the creaking of a long-closed door swinging open.

So it is I find myself back at the office.

In the midst of the traditional giddiness of our gatherings (and shortly after my well-received dinner) we retired, at Regina's urging, to the living room, where Candace, her younger sister Megan, Diane, Regina and I seated ourselves in a circle on the floor.

(I haven't seen Megan in years. She's rather high-strung—we had to lock Kennedy away upstairs because he made her so nervous.

The poor boy. I gave him a heaping plate of leftovers as an apology).

Regina labeled it an exercise in broadening perspective. It was vintage Regina, typical of the woman who had introduced us to Ouija boards and Tarot cards and any number of other so-called mystic experiences. What we were going to be doing tonight, she said to us as we sat there, was called projection.

At her urging, I remember closing my eyes. Regina instructed us to focus our minds on an image—an object, a person, a thing—until that image was all that was in our thoughts, until we felt we knew the object, the person, the thing, inside and out.

I played along only half-heartedly; I was actually thinking that Regina had gotten a little bit more outrageous, maybe too outrageous now, with each passing year. Diane has always been fairly convinced that Regina was out of her mind, but she is also always willing to humor her games.

So there we were, breathing properly, eyes closed and concentrating, and it seemed like it had been going on that way for quite some time. Without opening my eyes, I mentioned this to Regina, that nothing seemed to be happening. I asked if indeed something should be happening; and, at that exact instant, I was jolted. There was a terrific tugging, an unrecognizable sensation from above, that seemed to pull on me, seemed to send a vibration almost like a shock from my toes to my head. My first reaction was to assume that it was Regina pulling me, and that thought calmed me almost instantly. There was such strength in Regina's soft hand. (This gave me great comfort, too—her grip was so firm I knew I was safe.)

I opened my eyes to discover that although I was still holding Regina's kind hand with my left hand, I had somehow risen out of my body, off the carpeting, above the floor, to a height where I was looking down at myself as I sat on the floor with my eyes closed, holding the hands of my dearest friends. It was very disorienting at first, to say the least, and the sensation in retrospect seems to have had a certain dreamlike quality to it, almost like an extended hallucination. Candace, describing her experience afterward, said that in a similar state, she had looked me in the eyes, but I don't remember seeing her, or Megan, or Diane. Not at all. I can only distinctly recall the room being filled with light from this new perspective, and that Regina, risen above herself, was one of the sources of illumination. I couldn't keep myself from staring at what I can only describe as her spirit, so beautiful was the light that shone from within her.

It was at this point, I think, that I became aware of something else occurring in my vicinity. A quickening in the air. This new sensation was caused by something toward the back of the house, I was sure, and I turned to look at the back porch door (which from my vantage point I had a perfect view of through the kitchen and the laundry room).

Almost as I was turning to look, Regina somehow indicated that we had to be ending the exercise unexpectedly, as Megan seemed not to be feeling well enough to continue.

I agreed, but I continued looking at the door; more specifically, I remember looking out through the window at the top of the door. Although the sun had long since set, out that window I would swear it was as bright as day.

Something was out there. Regina sensed it too.

I felt her turning at my side to look in the same direction, toward that light.

In the pale yellow glow of a sun that wasn't really there at all, in the window at the top of the door, I saw rise the unkempt blond hair and face of a small boy who was likewise peering in at us, his features darkened and covered by hair that glowed golden yellow in the sunlight.

The next thing I knew I was opening my eyes on the living room floor, momentarily disoriented, hearing Candace and Megan breathe out sighs of relief in unison and noticing the sound of Kennedy baying upstairs at one thing or another. I looked again at the door, but it was still night outside, and of course there was no one there in the window . . .

I have been asking myself one question over and over since: Was that Curt I saw?

I can't get over the impression that, whatever it was, he was as shocked and startled to see us in that condition as we were to see him.

Entry Date: June 10

Back at home again finally, but I have to return to school, and I only have time for a short note. Candace called me at the office this afternoon, terribly depressed. Her sister Megan has checked herself into a hospital up north.

Apparently because she's had a nervous breakdown.

———————

Fourteen Years Ago

White Harbor, Maine

On Monterey Street in White Harbor there was an elementary school surrounded by a chain-link fence cold to the touch yet somehow reassuring to feel, to hold onto and to hang from. Inside, mostly white children in brightly colored new clothes played like a frenzied swarm across the asphalt playground, filling the air with a steady, healthy hum of noise that was punctuated here and there and there by childish shrieks or whistles blowing or bells ringing out.

Several children stood inside the fence, staring back at him, and yet seeming somehow to be looking right through him.

They were not frightened by him.

Ten blocks up Kearny Street, at the top of the hill in the yard of the witch's house, there was a large, orange spot that moved and shifted along the length of the yard. Gradually, it came into focus; likewise, the spot came to a halt and directly stared back at him. Judging by the rapt attention it displayed—the agitation in its suddenly animated movements as it started again and jogged and strutted back and forth along the length of the witch's yard—it had made a great discovery.

All the while with its gaze firmly fixed on the corner of Monterey and Kearny.

Where the boy stood in his grey clothes.

The orange spot with its curled tail then began jogging down the long road, its great form gaining speed with every loping step. It occurred to him only after it had closed half the distance between the witch's house and the school that it was actually coming down the hill not only toward him, but also to get him.

In a voice filled instantly with terror, a voice that shocked the boy with its force, he screamed "NO!," the sound going in both directions, up the street and across the schoolyard. Unexpectedly, the approaching monster stopped in its tracks, equally surprised, if only for a moment. The children inside the fence said nothing.

Across from the school, on Kearny, was a complex of town homes. To him, it was an escape, if indeed he was the one being chased. Racing across the street and up the sidewalk, he quickly lost himself in the walkways winding in and around the living units. It seemed to him he had lost the beast, as well, if it was really after him in the first place. This confidence lasted for all of a minute, until he heard the loud crashing of the shrubbery at one end of the central gardens at the very moment of his arrival at the other end.

The dog had done this before, he realized.

"Why, why, why," the boy said to himself. Everyone else acted as if he wasn't even there . . .

It took all of five seconds and no effort to be spotted.

With a bark and a salivating growl, it charged, sprinting around the circumference of the gated pool yard.

Repeatedly he screamed for it to stop, to leave him alone,

to no effect. He backpedaled, and then turned down another of the cement tributaries. This path, he knew, would lead him back out to the street. He jogged by a porch where a baby carriage was rattling clumsily out of an open front door. There was a blonde woman with a baby in her arms struggling behind it.

Once past her home, an alternative presented itself. There was a fence behind the home, separating a neighboring community of similar-looking town homes from this one. An easy out, with a trashcan conveniently on hand as a stepladder. Rather than heading back to the killing ground of the street, he hopped over the fence.

As he ran down yet another blind walkway, he heard what could only be the blonde woman screaming as the beast charged by her, "No, No, NOOOOOO . . ."

Followed by a terrific crashing sound.

Evelyn's Old Journal
Entry Date: June 20

My mother used to have a hand-sewn homily in the breakfast nook, hanging in between her four seaside lithographs of the coast at Martha's Vineyard. It read: "Sit Ye Down And Find Repose. With Chat And Cheer Good FriendShip Grows." Add food to the equation and it is the motto that has always underlined my relationship with Regina, one based almost exclusively in the sharing of our lives—as well as good food. The two of us would spend entire evenings seated on the kitchen counter under that frame, talking the hours away while one sweet thing or another heated up in the oven.

The reason for the nostalgia is that I have found some respite—Regina returned unexpectedly this afternoon. She is resistant to any particular interpretation of whatever (or whoever) it was we saw on the 4th of June, except to say that the occurrence merited greater investigation. Yes, she said, it could have been a visitation from Curt, or then again, it might not have been that. Yes, it could been that there was some message for me in the vision. Or not. Yes, she said, perhaps Kennedy's odd behavior of the last few months (just this afternoon he somehow managed to chain himself to the tree out front) might be explained by a visitation from the dead (an occurrence he might be more sensitive to than I), or his actions could simply be a reflection of my own mood. And, she said, there is always the possibility that something we had done that night might have inadvertently caused it to appear. That she returned at all indicates to me that she is more disturbed by what happened than she was trying to make it appear.

These days I find myself doing things I haven't done for twenty years. Remembering and seeing things I'd hoped I'd long forgotten. The feeling of helplessness is what is so confusing to me—this feeling of being pushed back toward a place I do not wish to be in again.

———————

Fourteen Years Ago

The scene played repeatedly in the boy's mind as once again he stood outside the schoolyard fence, this time leaning against it, watching as a group of children played a rope-jumping game inside.

The girl jumping in the middle of the two swinging ropes sang a song as two others turned them. While they all seemed to have taken notice of the boy's presence, they ignored him.

Something was different about him. Something had happened to him when he returned to the witch's house, he was convinced. That was when they had cast some spell upon him—a spell that continued to bewilder him, to play tricks on his mind.

On this second visit to the house, the dog had been for some reason locked away inside. The boy had arrived to find, unguarded and enticingly close to the door, in a metal bowl with the letters K E N N E D Y on the side, a bowl filled to the rim with scraps from a meal.

Should have known it was a trap, he thought now.

He couldn't touch the food, did not dare because the witches had been seated with too clear a view of the door behind which he sat that night.

He waited until he was queasy from the hunger, until his stomach hurt and his head began to ache. As he sat on the edge of the porch, holding his stomach, he had closed his watering eyes, and tried to ignore the spinning blur of images rushing behind his eyelids. Nauseous almost instantly, he had opened his eyes moments later to end it.

Opening his eyes, he found himself standing in the air high above the ground. High above his own body. What was worse at that moment than the sickness in his stomach, worse than being right exactly where he was, was the feeling of being flushed out of hiding, the feeling that this had been a trap all along, that someone had done this to him purposefully; he looked around, panicked at the thought, as if there might be someone right beside him, and, finding no one there, he realized that as long as he was outside his body he could do nothing to alter this predicament.

The room where the witches were gathered was filled with light—and they were in the same state as him, clumsily towering above their bodies. They had done this to him, he thought as he gazed in through the window at the top of the door, and so, logically, they were the only ones who could undo it. The same force which pulled at them obviously had affected him as well.

And as he gazed inside, the witch who lived in the house turned unexpectedly, terribly, as if at the very sound of his thoughts. She met his stare with piercing eyes that opened wide in shock as they settled on his face.

Then, a voice—hers he had been sure, although it had been a lower and far more menacing voice than he would have attached to her—whispered into his ear.

(*Are you my son?*)

The shock in recoiling instantly tore him free of their spell; he snapped instantly back into in his body, and once he'd affirmed that was so, he was off, running into the night while the dog began howling upstairs in the house . . .

The boy closed his fingers around a link in the fence and squeezed. Just to make sure he really was standing there on Monterey.

He had found himself inexplicably drawn to the house on the hill since then. The food always did taste better than the food he found in other houses in the neighborhood. Further, he had come to view the challenge presented by the house's main defender well worth the risk—because in truth the dog wasn't very bright.

At the same time, somewhere in the back of his mind, he was sure that one day if he continued to take that risk, the witch would catch him and he would be the sweet-smelling flesh that drew other lost souls to her doorway.

———————

Evelyn's Old Journal
Entry Date: July 17

I've spent too many hours these last weeks thinking endlessly about Curt.

His life was so short, I cannot even see it as a life lived. Only as several lives lost.

It has been well on twenty years since that time in my life came to such a complete end.

There are other habits I've not managed well. Long after Jonathan Hartin's passing influence on my life, I still prefer to find a dark corner of the house to hide away in at times of duress.

After the accident with Curt, it was the attic space to

which I most frequently fled, that unlit cubbyhole where Jonathan would leave me alone for days at a time at my request, where I would spend hour after hour looking through old photo albums, old journals, trying to recapture what exactly it was that had been taken from me.

At the same time, unnoticed by me in this shroud of mourning, day by day Jonathan would remove from the house below, piece by piece, first any and then all allusion to the child we'd raised and lost together, setting it just inside the attic door beside me before closing the door behind him and heading back down the stairs.

For a half a year, I was content with this situation, with rearranging the furniture and the boxes in the attic, making the space a memorial to my young son. The more distant, the more hostile Jonathan became, the happier I was to have the things I most wanted to be around with me while I was staying away from him . . .

The simple truth in the present is that for all the calm and confidence Regina brought to me with her visit (and her vow to return), I feel haunted, if not by the spirit we saw then by the memories it has invoked. I feel already as if I am more lost than before Regina arrived. I find myself ill at ease in the house, although the slight improvements in Kennedy, I must admit, have provided some solace. (As an experiment, I began feeding him in the evening when I return, in addition to the meal he gets in the morning from the maid. If nothing else, he is somewhat calmer; I believe I am beginning to see emerging signs of the wonderful pup he once was.)

———————

Fourteen Years Ago

When the boy woke, it was with a start both because he did not know where he was or how he arrived here in this bed in this dark room and because he did not know what exactly it was that woke him. Only that it was a certain coldness that touched him as he slept in this feathered bed. Perhaps even a threat to him.

All of this was somehow familiar, he thought, his mind beginning to clear.

It was the soothing sound of the rain outdoors that brought it together, that reminded him that the small house he'd found at the back of the vacant lot, a child's playhouse up in a tree, the house in which he had been living these last weeks, began to leak late in the afternoon. Too late in the afternoon to take shelter in one of the neighborhood houses that were his daily source of provisions, where mothers and fathers and children alike were all returning for the evening.

He had turned again to the one available option. Where else was he to go?

The witch who lived on the hill always returned late in the night. It hadn't turned out to be too difficult a trick locking the beast that lived with her in the cellar. Nor had slipping inside.

The boy walked over to the window, hoping to tell by the position of the stars how late he had slept. Surely by now the witch had come home, just as surely as the beast was no doubt free and lying in wait patiently outside the bedroom door.

The night was clouded over, with no stars in sight.

After a minute of looking, though, he saw something else; something out on the street, something happening three houses down from the witch's house, something that looked as if it was floating in the air outside an upstairs bedroom window.

As he watched this thing, which was blacker than the night, it moved from the one house to the next, where it stopped at another window and seemed to look inside as well. Then it moved on. This procession continued until, as he watched, nearly choking on a combination of fear and curiosity, it floated over to the house the boy was in, and it stopped outside the window he was staring out. A blood-colored, jelly-like thing, with a roundish body that shimmered darkly and hypnotically as it moved; it came to a stop right in front of the window, right in front of him.

He stepped away from the glass, five steps, backing to the bedroom door almost, where instantly he could hear the beast in the hallway, sniffing along the bottom of the door. The boy saw that the thing in the window had a face, a human face inset at the top of its beanbag body. Like a jack-o lantern had a face, misshapen and twisted by the odd form it wore.

As the boy watched, the face stretched forward from the body, pressed up against the glass, and then into the glass, and then through it. Once inside, the face looked left and right around the room until its eyes rested on the boy.

Its voice a low hissing vacuum, it said, "Are you my son?"

The boy shook his head emphatically NO—although there was no way he could be sure. He prayed not.

It eyed the boy for a moment.

It believed him.

Pulled back its face instantly, and without a look back, moved on.

In the middle of the night, Evelyn Hartin woke to the sound of a high-pitched whimper from Kennedy, who was apparently out in the hallway.

Tired from yet another long day, and groggy on top of that, Evelyn pulled herself out of bed and peeked out her bedroom door. It took a moment to follow the restless whine to the place where Kennedy was lying at the far end of the hall, outside the door to one of the guest bedrooms. Lying there low on the carpet in the shadow cast by the tree outside, with his chin resting on his paws, his nose pushed to the door.

The wind rattled the window behind him. Kennedy lifted his head at the noise, but turned to her when he realized she was there. He wagged his tail, folded his ears back. Spending the day in the cellar had taken its toll, Evelyn thought, although she couldn't imagine how Kennedy had managed the trick of locking himself in there. Earlier in the evening, he'd been acting as if he thought he'd be punished for it.

All she really wanted to know was how and why he managed to do these things to himself.

As she approached him, she said his name once and again, in a careful, calming voice.

"What's the matter?" She didn't bother to switch on the light—the moon behind the veil of clouds had lent the night a pale glow.

Kennedy let out a low growl . . .

Evelyn started to assure him that the storm would pass, when the door handle began to move . . .

. . . began to turn . . .

Then it was clear to her that what Kennedy had been doing all along was waiting. As if to confirm this, Kennedy thumped his tail once, twice . . .

Then the house came alive around her.

A burst of wind hit the west-facing side of the house, knocking the windows there, upstairs and downstairs, open with a mad banging—that was all it took to send Evelyn screaming and scrambling toward her bedroom. The wind that rushed in around her was strong enough to shake the chandelier over the stairwell, strong enough to send papers on her desk fluttering into the air around her as she ran.

She remembered there was Kennedy to be concerned about. She turned in time to see the door to the guest bedroom swing open, and to watch as Kennedy leapt inside.

"KENNEDY!," she screamed after him.

And out of the door not a heartbeat later, with a bloodcurdling scream that lifted and rose and held clear above the reigning disorder, it came running, nearly flying down the hallway toward her: the blond-haired, dark-skinned boy who was definitely not Curt, who was wearing the greyest of clothes, a boy with a look of terror and torment on his face.

"WHAT DO YOU WANT WITH ME? WHAT DO YOU WANT HERE?" Evelyn screamed, jumping backward clumsily as he approached her. She tripped, but somehow managed to slam the bedroom door behind her as she fell. Then, screaming Kennedy's name, she pulled herself up and braced herself, waiting.

She ended up listening as the screaming child moved down the stairs and then into the living room. She held her shaking hands together in her lap as it went through the kitchen directly below her and then out to the dining room.

All the while with the outraged bark and growl of Kennedy close behind.

Evelyn dropped to her knees. Started to rock herself from side to side. The voice was now outside of the house. And, after a rolling crash punctuated by the rumble of Kennedy's growl and the rattle of the doggy door, Kennedy was outside too, still in hot pursuit.

And the house was quiet again.

Kennedy returned some ten minutes later, timidly approaching Evelyn where she sat at the top of the stairs, her face in her folded arms. She was still crying from the shock of it all.

Kennedy's sniffing at her ear startled her. When she realized who it was, she put her arms around him and sobbed even harder, glad that at the least he was all right, that that thing hadn't hurt him. Only after a few minutes of holding him did she notice the odd smell coming from Kennedy. She pulled back for a careful look. That was when she understood that there must be a more logical explanation to all of this.

For in Kennedy's mouth as he sat holding his head morosely, was a tiny piece of dirty, mildewed cloth. A piece of fabric from someone's grey pants.

———————

Fourteen Years Ago
July 23

The dog, the boy thought as he licked his lips, was in fine form this morning. Full of energy, full of fire. He turned the handle of the outdoor faucet as the beast barked itself into a frenzy just a few yards away, locked away once again in the cellar.

That'll teach you, the boy thought, proud of himself.

After drinking and then washing his face and his hands, he tucked in his shirt and seated himself on the edge of the porch with his back to the door, watching the horizon.

His timing today had been close to perfect.

He reached inside the door silently as he heard the cleaning lady begin with the dishes.

Sometime after the witch drove off in the morning, the maid made her pass through the back of the house. That was when she put out the food for the dog, although generally she waited to call in the beast until she was done with both the dishes and the laundry that sat by the door; the maid, like everyone else but the witch, was terrified of the animal, and would put off seeing him as long as she could.

Once the bowl was in his lap, the boy began chewing down the wet chunks inside, savoring the pungent flavor of the meat. He was always so hungry.

———————

This was where it finally ended, Evelyn Hartin thought. This was it, little friend.

She stepped away from the sink as soon as she saw the small hand pulling the metal dish out through the doggy door. She left the water running and moved stealthily to the porch. Each yelp she heard from the cellar hardened her heart against this intruder a little more. Once she'd known what she'd been looking for, that is, a filthy, dog-tormenting child, it hadn't been a hard thing spotting the little monster. The housekeeper had been only too happy to take Evelyn's car down to the market, while Evelyn had put her hair up in a bun and, for the morning, played the part of maid.

Kennedy made the perfect alarm system, once Evelyn knew what had been setting him off. It made her furious to think that this little boy had been putting her pet through such torment. That he had nearly managed to turn Evelyn herself against Kennedy. And then the nerve of returning even after being discovered, as if this were a game . . .

Urchin, orphan, runaway, or plain old neighborhood troublemaker, Evelyn thought as she crouched just inside the back porch door, he was going to be sorry his path had ever crossed hers.

As quietly as she could push first her hand, then her arm through the doggy door, she was even quieter, breathlessly reaching, reaching, reaching, until she was up to her shoulder, until the side of her face was pressed flat against the door.

Her hand closed on air once, twice. Then her outstretched fingers found and closed on a shirt collar.

She smiled at the sound of his gasp, at the feel of his surprise, relished the sensation of connection, of yanking him toward her with all her strength. She relished the unbelievably powerful rush of satisfaction, of regret, of release, of vindication, of righteous anger. The mixture of emotions coalesced into a perverse joy that almost made the last few months of pain and confusion worthwhile.

Almost.

Now, she thought, she was going to see who had the last laugh. Then she pulled the boy kicking and screaming into her home.

———————

Evelyn's Old Journal
Entry Date: March 15 (The Present)

With this final page of what remains of this old journal, I am completing a circle of sorts, albeit unintentionally. I returned home last evening to a feeling of familiar regret and moved directly—almost unconsciously—to the attic space, where I was greeted by the sight of the cedar chest opened and in disarray, the contents and the memories they invoke scattered across the floor. I've been up half the night now, working to get the mess back into some kind of order.

I started feeling a little claustrophobic in that closed space, and discovered it was much nicer down in the living room (surprise, surprise). Though I guess when you're sitting in the dark nursing an old wound the environment doesn't matter all that much.

It's 5 am now, and the sun is beginning to light the day. The storm has already moved on. I've been reliving my afternoon at the hospital, feeling fresh the helplessness that overcomes me as the seizures weaken and Eric's body relaxes and shuts down again, and he slips back into the motionless state in which he's been held hostage for the last fifteen months. The new doctor does not understand what is triggering the seizures, but has somehow drawn the conclusion that drugs are the only effective way to control them.

Eric is fighting, of that I am sure. Each time, when he stops struggling, it is obvious that he gives up on his own, that it has nothing to do with sedation. I've memorized by now the stages in this fight, and I know well the sight of surrender when it comes to those needle-scarred arms.

Afterward, the doctor was wondering if it might be best to hold Eric restrained overnight. I could forgive him, because he's new to the job. But my son is not going to be kept like an animal.

The older attendants and I knew there would be no more seizures this evening, not for another month or two, if past history is indicative. All there is to do now is wait.

Chapter 3

White Harbor University
March 16

Eric woke with a jolt. Although he remembered crying in his sleep, awake instants later it was only a hoarse rasping noise coming out of his dry throat.

He waited, lying still for a moment—trying to get a grip on the mix of panic and relief he felt at being able to open his eyes, nearly hyperventilating as he gasped for each new breath of air. His heart was pounding in his chest, his head throbbing with the pressure. It almost felt like he wasn't going to wake up this time. It was such a heavy dream. Something or someone was after him. His eyes darted around, a little nervous, making sure no one had followed him out of his sleep.

Whoever it was chasing him through his dreams . . .

Eric moved his arms and legs a little to make sure there wasn't anyone else there still holding him down.

The dream was too heavy. It felt like he was drowning.

He looked around to see where he was and where the cigarettes were in relation. What he found, to his surprise, was that he was on the carpeted floor in the hallway right outside his dorm room door. At the least, it wasn't far from home.

He wondered, Where the fuck was I last night?

He stood up, brushed himself off. But when he tried to turn the doorknob to get into his room and it didn't turn, didn't budge, it took a minute to register that someone had gone and locked the door. Locked him out of his own room. He rattled it, as if he could shake it open, hoping it was only jammed or something like that, but nothing inside gave way. One of the maids locked it, or some fucking helpful Samaritan, maybe one of Eric's stupid, helpful neighbors, someone who didn't know him well enough to know he liked to keep it open for weary travelers like himself.

And him without the key.

He'd had enough of this shit, all this shit, all the time.

He sat down cross-legged in the middle of the hall, facing the door.

Damn it. Damn it. Every day there was something more forcing him against his will farther and farther away from himself. Locked out of his own room—that was only the least and the last of it. The worst was that part of him was starting to feel the person he was losing wasn't much worth keeping anymore, wasn't worth holding onto. When did he become such a waste case? What, Eric wondered, and who was he before he turned into this?

———————

Evelyn Hartin watched silently as the doors to her office suite closed behind the exiting form of Mr. Edge Harwood. Her shaking hands were clasped tightly in her lap. Outside her window could be heard the sounds of protesters singing songs and chanting slogans from the ground below as they took advantage of what promised to be a lovely day, free of rain or other elemental intrusion. Arriving on campus in the morning, she had negotiated a path through no less than twelve separate, fairly organized groups soliciting membership and calling for action on a variety of issues.

They were students and non-students alike, with concerns she classified as both legitimate and otherwise. They hadn't antagonized her on the way in, perhaps not recognizing her in the early morning hours; during the course of the interview with the investigator, however, they had interrupted her several times. Twice by dialing up her private line and shouting insults for a few seconds before hanging up, and several times after that, as the campus shifted into its more active period of the day, by the sheer volume of the combined voices chanting in protest.

Evelyn had already felt harried by her conversation with Mr. Harwood. There had been a need, she felt, to be circumspect with him, to avoid certain details, such as those entailing the exact route she had taken through the adoption process. And yet the very act of discussing her son's case with this heretofore unknown person had the strange effect of unburdening her. She had wanted to tell him everything. She had stopped herself several times to keep from crying while describing Eric's current condition, and the method by which he had arrived at that condition. At times during the conversation, she had felt herself balanced on a precipice of her own, very close indeed to giving in to the anguish and uncertainty of the previous sixteen months.

She was not sure, afterward, if she had revealed more about Eric, more about herself, more about their family than had been necessary. Mr. Harwood was a seasoned listener, and, oddly enough, she'd found herself fairly at ease with him by the end of her explanations. He'd wanted more, it was clear, but of the type of information she could not provide. She simply didn't know any of the details of Eric's life before his arrival in White Harbor. In her heart, she held little hope of Mr. Harwood getting any further with this than she had on her own.

Mr. Harwood had said not two words by the time she had finished. At which point, after a particularly pointed look at her that suggested he suspected her of withholding relevant information, he had cleared his throat and tilted his hat and risen from his seat then said, "Ma'am, I'll get right on it. See what I can do. I won't promise you anything."

Foolish woman, she thought now as she finally unclasped her hands and reached across the desk for a cigarette. As if this man would be able to do anything more than she or anyone else had done, other than string her along until the hope he inspired became too tired for her to carry.

———————

It was late in the day when Eric found himself standing in a foul mood outside Rachel's room on the far side of campus. He'd given up on locating the gardener at all the right spots around campus. That joker, he thought, was nowhere to be found.

What kind of business did that guy think he was running, anyway?

Eric might just up and decide to take his business elsewhere. If he could find an elsewhere.

The door here was locked as well. But Rachel had told him before that she kept a spare key under the mat for emergencies. Even though this was the first time he had taken her up on it, she'd told all the band members many times over she didn't mind if they crashed, as long as they left her a note.

Once he was inside, although he was sure it was not what she intended when she gave him clearance, the first thing he did was head for the medicine chest in the bathroom. Because he knew she wasn't going to have any booze lying anywhere around in the kitchen, because Rachel was a good girl.

Rachel was not much of a drinker. Not much of an anything-er, total corn seed, although she was somehow still fun to be around.

Crap was what he found in the bathroom, no hidden stash or anything resembling it. Midol, deodorant, shaving cream, girl's stuff, buffered codeine-free aspirin, basic toiletries. And what did he come up with after digging through everything, praying for some reason his goodie-goodie friend from a conservative Midwest home was going to have a vial of coke stashed in her bathroom for emergencies?

A bottle of cold medicine with about a capful left of it.
He downed it in a gulp.
Shit.
A better buzz than no buzz at all. He needed something to settle his nerves.

Or else, he was thinking as he wheeled around from his image in the bathroom mirror, he could be losing his mind. That could happen.

Next, he tore through her kitchen cabinets, looking for that cooking sherry.

When he came up empty-handed, and he caught his breath, he tried to think of where to look next. He was about to move into the bedroom, ready to tear the place apart, when something clicked in his head, and he looked around and realized what a mess he'd already made of his friend's place.

What a fucking mess he'd made here.

It took him a minute to think more clearly, but the best thing, Eric eventually decided, was to get out before he ended up trashing the whole place. It hadn't been smart coming here like this, he knew.

On his way to the door, he stopped at Rachel's desk, looking for a piece of paper to leave her a note. That was the rule. Then he thought better of it, because the only thing he could think to write would be SORRY FOR THE MESS.

Seven Years Ago

Evelyn's Old Journal
Entry Date: February 7

Regina spiked my tea this evening with some sweet herb, leaving me wide awake while she and Eric sleep soundly ten feet away. I have been beguiled for a good hour now by the campfire and by my own reflections.

I've decided that there have been times in months past when I've lost touch with the fundamentals of my relationship with Eric. It is one thing to find a child in need, and out of impulse and

perhaps more than some instinct to decide to care for him. That
was the easy part, particularly with someone so desperately in need
as Eric, and particularly for someone with as imposing a void to
fill as I. It is quite another thing to come against the constraints
presented by both our pasts. My frustration with his performance
in school, coupled with my workload—specifically the cursed book
tour—had us both alienated. Trouble with tutors, then trouble with
his school, followed by more trouble with different tutors, trouble
with different schools, and so much unresolved tension at the end
of it, most admittedly generated and suffered by myself. I was
unwilling to admit that he has already been shaped by this world,
and that at this point the prerogative for change in his life must
come from him.

All I wanted, from the beginning, was to give him a home.

The morning after our arrival in Saugus, we attended a
sunrise service at the House of the World, a natural grouping of
rocks that resembles an outdoor amphitheater, and which has been
used, Regina has said, for performances and sermons and meetings
and rituals for locals in the area for more than a thousand years.
Eric was more than convinced that I was dragging him to a coven
of witches—nothing could have better confirmed his suspicions
than my leading him up the path behind Regina's house, into the
trees and then into what he said looked like "part of Stonehenge."

There is a singular beauty to that place. It is still very much
the same as I always remember it being. There are thirty-two steps
above the theater that lead a person above the tops of the pine
trees, to a hilltop view of seemingly endless miles of unsettled
mountains and prairies. There remain the white rocks littered about
on the rust-colored carpet of pine needles, rocks that I once used
to spell out my name on the ground. There remains an air of the
primeval, where all around the dark grey stone, ancient trees reach
in a silent tangle upward.

What I will carry in my mind from this trip until my
days' end is the look that came over Eric's face when the choir,

eighteen strong and not a male among them, opened the service. We could hear their voices before we could see the line of them approaching through the trees. Many of them were women from the community we had already met. Their voices vibrated off the stone benches and the walls of the amphitheater, filling the clearing as they entered with a beautiful sound. Eric was instantly enchanted. By the time Regina finished speaking half an hour later, I think we were all similarly mesmerized. Whether she is sermonizing or leading a discussion or politicking on a topic relevant to one or all of the communities she represents, Regina shows such strength and wit one can't help but be inspired by her perspective. To see her in that place is always to see her at her most formidable—although, again, this has probably done nothing but strengthen Eric's conviction that she is a witch. That was fixed from the first moment he saw her.

This was the final evening of our camping expedition. How very different it is to vacation with a son again. It is the way I remembered it, and imagined, and hoped it would be. He's enamored of Regina's recollections of deer and bears and wolves and what have you. He is equally fond of simply wandering away without notice to investigate this or that, much the same as he is at home. Regina says I shouldn't worry about that, as long as I can be sure about him knowing the way home.

I guess I am.

I ended the day watching as Eric joined Regina in an impromptu rain dance—a civic effort of sorts, intended to bring an end to the current dry spell. One of the congregants had suggested to Regina that while she was in the mountains, she might take the time to appeal to the skies for some relief.

The moment did provide the second image I will carry with me from this trip: Regina, stiffer now than ever, beseeching the skies with arms open wide, looking very much like the trees reaching to the sky above her, words of appeal falling from her lips like an incantation, while Eric whoops and hollers and dances a slow circle around her, his shadow cast by the fire against the darkness of the night, grasping pine needles and throwing them in the air as he goes, kicking up his legs and calling to the clouds.

Entry Date: February 25
An epilogue to my last entry: Regina called today to let me know that after two and a half weeks, the torrential rain has finally ended. There have been requests from several congregants that in the future she leave the weather to the heavens. She sounded fairly pleased with herself.

Cassette Tape #1: Dated March 17

(Lonnie, Lonnie, look)

    (Say what?)

    (Sayonara. Hasta la vista. This is the finale)

    "Hello? Hello, Hello? Is this on?"

    (When I'm walking around here I think I'm going to die)

    "Okay, right. We're recording now. My brother and I used to pretend we were celebrities and interview each other with this cassette player when we were kids. It was my dad's—he used it to keep track of ideas for sermons.

    "Thank god I had it put away in the bedroom."

    (This is the real dying uh the uhm the dead)

    "I wish those guys would shut up."

    (the dead guy or something like that. This is it)

    "Well, anyway—hi, Eric, this is Rachel."

    (this is today's dying, this is today's dying, look)

    "WILL YOU SHUT THE HELL UP YOU INFANTS!?!"

    (pound pound pound pound)

    "That's the sound of my fist on the wall. My neighbors are complete losers. They sit around saying stupid pointless things all day and laughing at themselves."

(pound pound pound pound)

"ARE YOU GOING TO SHUT UP NOW? ARE YOU?"

(. . . . .)

"Good. That's more like it. If my voice sounds like I'm talking from inside some kind of drain, don't worry, it's this tape recorder. My cords are intact, I'm happy to say."

(. . . . .)

"Okay, good. They really did shut up. Let's get started. It is, let's see, nine-thirty in the morning on St. Patrick's Day. I am two days late in getting to you. As if it makes a difference.

"Have I been out of it lately or what? On the way to the White Harbor police station this morning—for reasons I will share with you later—I realized that it wasn't raining at all. It was snowing. I had been so convinced it was raining that I didn't even notice it wasn't. I'd had my umbrella out for the entire two-mile walk there and most of the way back without noticing. It must have been snowing the whole morning judging from how deep it was in some places. Isn't that strange? That I wouldn't even have noticed snow on the ground? That I would have been so convinced otherwise I didn't even register the reality? The rain was the reason I waited until morning to go to the police station, because no one I know has a car and I didn't want to be tramping out in the rain in the dark. Snow you can get through without getting drenched.

"You should have seen the way the cops treated me, by the way. The officer I talked to at the station was entirely patronizing. He complained about the paperwork he was going to have to do and the forms he was going to have to file for a crime that in the end really wasn't all that big of a deal; basically, he wanted me to walk out of there and forget the whole thing.

"Now that I'm home I'm feeling a little better. My cramps have kind of been bothering me, actually. Hopefully they'll find the person who did this to my place. I can't even be comfortable sitting in the living room. It feels to me almost as if my apartment has been possessed.

"What I've decided might be best would be to step out into the fresh air and take you on a tour of the campus you've been away from for so long. I found the 1980s tape recorder my dad sent me with to school, like I said. This is going to be a hellish day, not least of all because I didn't sleep much last night."

Harbor View Hospital, White Harbor
9:45 am

The undercurrent of disquiet inside the hospital was not immediately apparent to Evelyn Hartin as she crossed the lobby; she was herself gripped by a dread-filled anticipation of what this day had in store for her. From the moment she'd opened her eyes, lying curled in bed, she'd felt the weight of the dawn hanging like a stroke about to fall, and known it could mean there was nothing good ahead.

It was not that the hospital was inordinately quiet. To the contrary, there was a great amount of activity going on, particularly in contrast to the brooding vacancy of the streets outside, where to all it seemed a storm was soon to break. Evelyn moved past electricians, construction workers, and staff alike, hardly aware of their presence. One would have to look deeper than Evelyn was of a mind to in order to see the unease in some of their eyes as they tried to hurry through their shifts.

Out the windows on either side of the corridor as she moved toward the west wing, kindly referred to as the convalescent wing, there was only an oppressive gloom. Storm clouds to every horizon, lying seemingly inert upon the land, withholding for now. It always seemed to be overcast when she was at the Harbor View facility; she had wondered on more than one occasion if Eric's seizures might be influenced by the drop in barometric pressure.

There were voices ahead.

"You walked away from me just now," a woman's voice said. "We were in the middle of a conversation. Do you remember that?"

"Yes," an older voice responded. Much older.

"Was there something I said that upset you?"

"Yes, dear."

"What did I say that upset you?"

There was no immediate answer.

"Was it too cold outside for you?"

"Oh, yes it was."

"Or did you just forget we were having a conversation?"

"Yes, yes. Please forgive me. I'm not myself. I forget things all the time."

"You said something about a man."

"Oh, yes, there was a man here, in the lobby right here. That's my room right over there," the older woman said.

"The attendant. We discussed him already. Let me say again that he's very sorry for ignoring you."

"There was another man, too."

"Another man?"

"Yes, that's it. He scared the dickens out of me."

Evelyn emerged from the hall, then moved past the nurse's station. Sitting side by side on a couch in the waiting area were two women, one a young doctor, the other an elderly patient. They both looked up and watched Evelyn for a few moments as she crossed the room, and the older woman spoke again, loud enough for Evelyn to hear.

"He was walking down the way just like that lovely woman there, heading right where she's heading, I'd bet."

"What exactly did this man look like?"

"Oh, he was thin. And sharp, with edges everywhere. Parts of him looked so thin they might as well have been butterfly wings. Parts of him, they would just disappear when he moved them. The legs and arms almost flickered. It was because the lights went out that I saw him. I could see exactly where he was, coming down the hall . . . ”

Evelyn stepped into the adjoining hallway, and shortly thereafter, still in the range of the voices, she came to a stop.

“Please sit down, don’t walk off again. I want to help you. Why did this man upset you so?”

“He was here looking for someone . . .”

The door to Eric’s room was blocked off with yellow tape. There was a steel plate grafted onto the door, sealing the entrance.

“ . . . I thought it might be me.”

An odd feeling of disorientation, of confusion, took hold of Evelyn as she stared at the door, at the yellow tape. At the solitary flowers and the bouquet lying on the floor.

Evelyn’s plan had been so simple. She had brought along a letter from Regina to read to Eric, and a collection of short stories written by White Harbor students as well.

“Why would this man be looking for you?”

“Why would he be looking for anyone? I knew who he was. There’s only the one reason.”

By the time the incompetent at the front desk had redirected her, Evelyn had worked her way through a surprising array of recriminations, ranging from the fact she had left the beeper in the car overnight (thus she hadn’t received any of the messages from the hospital until the morning), to the anger she had with herself for failing at parenting, to her choice of Harbor View for Eric’s care.

Her eyes found Eric as she pushed into room 108B. That was her first relief of the day.

The gentleman in the room with Eric, she assumed, was the shift doctor.

He looked quickly at his clipboard lying on the counter. “Ms. Hartin?”

“Yes.” There was something she noticed immediately . . . a

faint scratching noise.

"My name is Jonas Peterman. I've taken your son's case."

"How nice of you to inform me. I was quite satisfied with the care Dr. Samms provided." She looked around the room as she spoke, away from him, trying to isolate the source of the scratching sound.

To affirm, in her addled state, that there indeed was a sound.

"Dr. Samms has left Harbor View for a public healthcare position. It's a positive career step for her and we're all very happy about it."

"Spare me."

She pulled up the sheet and blanket covering Eric's feet.

He was pedaling them as he slept. His toenails had been scratching against the sheets.

I'll have to trim those.

"Why is he here? Why was he moved? Why does the door to his last room look like a memorial? Why haven't I been informed?"

"As I understand it," Dr. Peterman said, actually taking a step back from her, "there was a problem with some of the equipment in," he had to look at the clipboard for the name, "Eric's room last night. Two of our staff, who were with Eric at the time, were injured in an electrical accident in that room. He was apparently administered a mild sedative by the night physician in response to a particularly strong seizure, and the seizure unexpectedly intensified. We were neither able to reach you nor did we have the staff on hand to properly restrain him while we were dealing with the situation in his room, so at about 2:00 am I authorized a heavier sedative. He leveled off approximately forty-five minutes later. We've had staff with him the entire morning, and there have been no further incidents."

Evelyn thought for a moment that she might finally start to cry. Either from relief or because of the continuing frustration, she wouldn't have been able to say. She didn't want to lose him, and he was drifting away. That was what was happening. He was fighting harder because he was running out of time.

The doctor slid his pen into the pocket of his smock. As he turned his back to hang the clipboard at the base of the bed, he pulled an artificial smile seemingly out of the air, a smile that he turned with, a smile that he held frozen on his face as he looked directly at her and extended his hand.

"I'm sorry to be off so soon, but I have several other patients to check on. Give me a call if you have any questions. Nice to have met you."

Cassette Tape #1:

"I have a great story for you, Eric.

"Right now, I'm walking down the pathway between the apartments and the Price Center. I'm working in the Grotto today. Lunch shift. Just another fine, living example of our school helping to make our educational dreams come true. It buys me part time status and meets the rent, so I guess I should be grateful. God knows what I'm going to do when I finally graduate and they force me out into the unemployment line. But that should be a worry five years or so in the future at the rate I'm going.

"About two weeks ago—hard to believe because it seems like so much longer—I answered an ad in the White Harbor Register for a singer. It was this band—old guys—all string players, old-timers—who were looking for someone to sing on two or three songs a show. It isn't much, but at least it's something. Four people responded, and I was the only one who was interested in doing it after I heard all the details. i.e., no pay, little exposure, required to look interested and interesting between bits. I'm sure my new status as a brunette had something to do with it, also. I really like the music they're doing, very bluesy, very classy, even if their age is slowing down their swing a little. I'm not even sure I'm good enough to be doing it, but I figure, you know, it's obvious to me that they aren't the hottest either, so maybe it's a good match. There's a show tonight at a boat club down by the Harbor.

"Okay, I'm about to cross over into the Plaza. I'm taking the short cut past the labs, where I have to be at four. There's a lot of noise up ahead. Can you hear it? The Greeks must be having a having a rally . . .

"Oh, my goodness.

"Wow, Eric. I wish you could see this! There are so many people out there. I had no idea . . .

"I can't believe it. I cannot believe it. They're flippin' everywhere. It's like a carnival. And they're not all frat people. No, No, there's Gerald. He hates the Greeks—oh!—okay, he's wearing his Kill the Greeks shirt right now.

"I didn't know any of this was going on. That's what happens when you live in the dorms. They isolate us like they're worried we're going to riot."

(Rachel)

"This is what it looks like: The frats all have booths together on the side of the Plaza where the Grotto is. My luck, they're all going to be wanting to eat. Lunch shift really bites these days. There are clubs and teams and I guess you'd call them special interest groups with kiosks all over the rest of the place. I can't tell what is for what or who is for who because there are hundreds of people who just seem like browsers, spectators, people from campus, people from town, hanging out; I can see some graduate students and a few of the professors. It looks like most of them are having fun. Shoot, this is probably half the reason they look forward to college. All the regular stuff is still going on, people studying, vendors out selling trinkets, guys playing hackey sack in the shade. There are six boxes, huge cardboard boxes, all sitting back to back by the fountain, and it looks like there are people in them. I don't know what that's about."

(Rachel, Rachel, over here)

"What's that?"

(Rachel!)

"Someone is calling my name? Oh, look! Pam! And Bob! Hi you guys!"

"Hi, Rachel."

"Hi, Ray."

"Hi, Bob. Say hello to Eric, too. I'm making an audio letter to him."

"Hi Eric, it's Pam."

"Get better soon, buddy."

"So Pam, what are you guys doing out here today?"

"Oh, that. You know, we really felt like we were missing out—because we've been studying so much lately, gotta make the grades, you know? So we decided to take the day off, see if there was anything we could participate in. And, well, you know, I'm pretty much a vegetarian, so we decided to gather signatures for the Vegans. At least until we see something we like better."

"You really are a civil activist at heart, aren't you, Pam?"

"Huh? Oh yeah, well, kind of. Do you see that guy over there? The Rastafarian?"

"The guy with the sign?"

"That's him. He's in one of my Poli Sci classes. I think we're going to switch movements soon, actually. I think he's from one of those amnesty groups. He stopped by before, seemed interesting, even though right now I can't even remember what he was saying about that guy, the one in prison. You know. I don't know anything about that, in case you were thinking of asking me."

"So what's going on with you, Ray?"

"Oh, the same, the same, Bob. I still hate it when you call me that. My name is Rachel. My place was broken into last night."

"What? Are you kidding? Were you there?

"What happened? Are you all right?"

"No, I wasn't there. My cabinets were gone through. Things pulled apart. It wasn't as bad as it looked. I guess."

"Oh my gosh, I'm so sorry."

(You're kidding)

"Yeah, it's the big hassle at this point. I reported it to the White Harbor Police, but it looks like my chances of catching the person are bleak."

"I'm so sorry."

"I know. Me, too. Ah, well, story of my life. Listen, I have to get to work now. But tonight, if you guys are interested, I'm doing a St. Patrick's Day show down at the Bay Club at about 9:30. Not a whole show, just a few numbers—but the guys said I could invite a few friends."

"The guys?"

"I'll tell you about it if you show. I have to go now. Bye."

"Sure. Bye, Ray. Take care."

(Bye, Rachel)

"Bye, Bob. Bye, Pam. Aren't they lame? Sometimes they embarrass me."

———————

The only relief through a night of the withdrawal shakes was a joint Eric shared on a dorm balcony with a couple of frat boys. He had actually ended up in their room by following the scent of bud in the air.

He had to listen for too long a time to their stories about all the great pussy they'd been getting. They meowed at each other once in a while, while they were telling tales—like pussies, Eric guessed was the point of that.

But then, they finally agreed to party him out. They were impressed that he had actually risked getting his ass kicked for asking them to share. They thought that was cool.

Cassette Tape #1:

(where's your green, where's your green?)

(pinch me you fag and I'll)

("What a marvelous day. Can you feel it in the air? That quickening in the air as the Good Lord contemplates opening the gates to yet another storm, the energy in every breath you draw? I should tell you that is not the sole source of the invigoration I feel on this day, although it does remind me it is good to be alive. No, I draw my comfort from a vision visited upon me last night as I wavered on the edge of sleep.")

"Eric, Can you hear this? It's your buddy, Brother Matt. He has a crowd around him."

("That's what I said! I had a visitor in my room last night as I knelt by my bed praying.")

(probably had an erection and didn't know what it was.)

("I WAS NOT ALONE! I felt a presence, a pair of eyes upon me.")

"The frat crowd is eating it up. The rank and file. The rank and vile."

("After a moment, I asked, 'is there someone beside me?'")

(In my freshman year, he was only here a couple months of the year)

(Don't pinch me)

(He's been barred from the Universal Chapel because he lets the transients in)

"Hold on a minute Eric, There's too many people talking around me."

(Pardon me for living.)

(It just seems like he's always around here now.)

("There was no answer in the silence of my room, no word from my companion, although I could certainly, undeniably

75

feel his presence. After a moment, I asked again, is someone there beside me?")

"If you can hold on a second until I clear the crowd, Eric."

(watch it, stupid bitch)

"Oh, hey, take it easy, I'm going, I'm going. It's not like he's saying anything different than anyone's ever said before."

(fuck off)

"You fuck off.

"Everybody is staring at me now. There's nothing going on here. Thanks, yeah. Move along, now. Everyone's probably wondering what I'm doing with this tape recorder. There's been this ongoing debate in the newspaper about government recruiting—you know, for the CIA and FBI. Your mom denies that anything is going on like that, but you know how it is—a lot of people won't believe an authority figure no matter what she says. This is one of those times I'm glad I colored my hair. I really do feel like I'm in disguise like this. Even if Pam and Bob recognized me right off the bat. For some reason it make me less concerned with what anyone else might think of me."

("When my visitor remained silent, I think I began to understand. This was a warning to me. It was a message, a sign. But a sign of what? There was to be no answer from my companion, although I could certainly still feel his presence. Perhaps, I thought, it has to do with the direction this ungodly university's ungodly administration seems to be moving. Perhaps it has to do with their Millennium Fundraising drive, the latest thrust by these institutionalized, government-approved moneychangers to tax others that they might continue their tradition of inculcating the spirit of lawlessness rather than feeding the homeless and the hungry souls who wander beyond the narrow confines of the campus.")

(My opinion of Jesus Christ—and mind you I'm a fan of the Jesus Seminar—)

"There. I'm in a much better position in the crowd. 2:00

in the afternoon now. I've just finished lunch shift, which was basically madness. I thought things would die down after a while, especially since the sky looks like it's going to pour later on, but that hasn't happened. If anything, there are more people here than before. No news cameras, though. Not yet.

(If you look past the myth, if you see him as a person like the rest of us.)

(Only cooler.)

(Uh, yeah, I mean, a rebel.)

"Excuse me? Could you keep it down? I'm recording. "

("The scent of danger is in the air, I fear, dear children. Look about you now, and you will see if your vision is clear that the race to judgment has begun in earnest. This dissension you see playing out before you is only the smallest step further down the slope the angels themselves have fearfully watched us slide. We are turned away from God, sinking into a war of attrition with our own souls, of degradation against our spirit and the bond shared by that spirit with the Almighty. We have sunk finally into a state of constant and bitter infighting with our own selves, and in that division we trust not our own instincts, not the instinct of our forbears, not our own innate connection with the essence of the Lord of Heaven above . . . ")

(Why does it have to be so melodramatic? Do we really need all the smoke and mirrors to understand that the world would be a lot better place if we could all just be good to each other? You can stop me if I've told you about this already, but I've been reading about the Gnostic bible . . .)

"Actually, sudden change of plan, I don't think I'll be able to hang here after all. I'm sorry. I know you like hearing people getting themselves all stirred up, but I really am sick of the whole church thing. It just turns me off. The words are all the same; the epithets for Christ are really all that seems to change from preacher to preacher. I had enough of that growing up. I just can't live my life anymore afraid that the God of Love and Forgiveness is going to turn me into a pillar of salt for advocating individual choice. "I always think I'm going to be able to be tolerant, but I never really can be. I don't have time for conflict like that. I want the most informed, provable answer. And I don't have time to find prospective comrades in any movement, so I don't think I'm going to take you through the rest of the crowd, like I'd planned to earlier. I'm just going to do my best to avoid them all."

———————

By noon, Eric had wandered back toward the dorms, and his hands were shaking pretty badly again.

He rounded the corner of a building, and then he heard Rachel's voice incoming. She was talking to someone, words coming out in a steady flow; this was forewarning enough to duck into the shadow of a stairwell before she passed by.

He had torn her place apart. What had he been thinking?

———————

Office of the Dean
4:30 pm

"I don't mean to be interrupting when I know you've got a mile of catching up to do, and forgive me for making an already sorry day that much the worse, but there's something you should see," Victrine said over the intercom. "Have a look out your window."

How nice to hear from Regina, Evelyn thought, as she refolded Regina's latest letter, and slid it inside the cover of the book the letter arrived with, titled *Viewed From A Distance: Puerta de la Reina.*

Evelyn swiveled her chair and gazed out the window. Across the sky the clouds hung dark and ominous, still and burdensome. On the ground beneath the grey horizon, Evelyn thought as she scanned the Plaza, there were now quite a few more participants than there had been earlier.

"I've had a handful of calls from friends of mine at the neighbor campuses," Victrine said slowly, "They're just now realizing that some of their wayward charges are headed in our direction, presumably to join the party in our front yard."

There were school buses in the northeast student parking lot behind the library. Seven of them, and two more were just now arriving at the front gate. Both of the arriving vehicles had banners on their sides, and when Evelyn had found her glasses, she confirmed by the seemingly arbitrarily arranged letters of the Greek alphabet that these were indeed reinforcements. Students in orange vests were directing the buses across the parking lot and into designated parking spaces, where other arrivals nearby were being armed with placards as they disembarked.

"The good news I have," Victrine's voice continued, "well, judge it for yourself. Mayor Rutner apparently gave you a roasting at a fundraiser the other night. Might mean the little bugger is considering a run for higher office, God help us all. The media outlets have been harassing the girls in the University office pool all morning for any reaction from you. The girls have been faxed a dozen or so copies of a flyer with conservative-themed Dean Hartin jokes on it. And you know the girls; they're all having fits and chuckles over it downstairs, so I guess it isn't a total loss. I'll have a copy in your inbox as soon as I can pry it out of their hands."

Evelyn continued watching out the window silently. She reached behind the planter on the windowsill, pulled out a pack of cigarettes.

"The reason I describe that as good news by-the-by is that none of the reporters who have called have caught scent of what's afoot here. I'd be surprised if we have the period of grace for much longer, though. Would you like me to put a call in to the White Harbor police?"

"No. No yet," Evelyn said.

Those on the fringes of the crowd below were only beginning to realize, as the steady stream of new arrivals flowed into the Plaza main fare, the import of what was happening. It was growing. They were growing. The cheering intensified in volume as more were swept along by the moment. For a while now, it would be pandemonium.

"Caught us with our pants down this time, they did," Victrine said with a sigh.

Cassette Tape #1:

"Hi, Eric. Back home again. I have about half an hour before I'm off to my Chem lab, so I'm going to be getting ready while I'm talking to you. It's a special section today dealing with viruses. E. Coli, the plague, all the really ghoulie ones.

"I just want to scream when I look around my apartment. Last night, I got home about 11:30, after my dress rehearsal with the band, after my 3-hour Chemistry class, to find my front door swinging wide open. I turned on the lights when I finally had the nerve to go inside alone—of course, my neighbors were pretending they weren't home and wouldn't come out. Thank God I wasn't being attacked or I'd be dead before those losers would lift a hand to help.

"So there I was, middle of the night, trying to make a little noise, hoping nobody's inside, and all of a sudden, for a few minutes, I was almost convinced that what had happened to me was that I had mistakenly walked into someone else's apartment. I mean, the place was all messed up.

"I'm looking at it right now. Thank God they didn't touch anything in my bedroom, because then I would have to move. Really, for all the mess, the only thing I could see that they took was the last of my cough syrup—I brought the bottle and plastic serving cup to the cops for fingerprinting. It looked worse than it was . . .

"So that's why I was up so early today. And why I was up so late last night. I kept thinking I could feel this other person's presence in my place. The Campus Residents Office referred me to Campus Security, who referred me to the police and so forth and so on. I called my mom for the first time since Christmas and that just left me depressed.

"I placed an ad in the school newspaper this morning, in case anybody saw anything. I guess I have to start questioning my neighbors, just in case anyone saw or heard anything unusual."

Rachel left the tape recorder running on the table and stepped out onto the balcony. Clouds everywhere, the sounds of megaphones and microphones and the voices of hordes of people echoing off the gray buildings. One of her neighbors was walking up the pathway to the building. She watched him a moment without really paying attention to what she was seeing.

A strange thing happened then, as she looked down at the ground. First, she thought she heard the sound of rain. Then she remembered, a very sharp, clear remembering of the way Eric had looked that first night they had met, when she and Eric and Bobby had gone out stomping in the rain. Eric had been soaking wet, dancing through the puddles, celebrating the storm. He was not a very impressive person at a first glance, just looked like some kind of recently strung-out dropout.

But he had made such a strong impression on her over time. And now he isn't here, Rachel thought to herself. She stepped back into her apartment, locked the sliding glass door behind her.

"Well, I guess this is the end of my little tape to you. For now. I'm going to be totally busy the rest of the day. I'll come to the hospital in a couple days to see you, unless of course you wake up before that. I'll let you know how the show turns out tonight. Wish me luck!

"Bye Eric."

Chapter 4

My Dearest Evelyn,

Here again am I, my minimum of daily necessities in a carry-on bag underneath my seat, headed for parts dubious and unknown. Knowing the Mexican mail system, by the time you read this I may very well be back in Saugus, reflecting on these latest experiences. I thought perhaps if I composed this on the flight and dropped it off at the airport in Mexico City it might have a chance of reaching you sooner than that—it is a rather long time to be away without notice, and I didn't want you to be worried about me.

The flight will mercifully be followed immediately by a two-day drive by school bus to a town called Villacuerda, found somewhere along the southernmost coastal edge of the Sierra Madre. Mercifully I say because of the quality of the air in Mexico City. It's bad enough to choke on. Really, the last trip through, I was ready for intensive care after only a week of walking around breathing that filth. How can anyone truly enjoy life without fresh air?

But I digress. I still find myself getting excitable on airplanes, especially when I've had a drink. I've just now been observing that all the stewardesses seem to have rather persistent coughs.

A handful of my friends have been to Villacuerda in the last few years. It is a town apparently on the verge of becoming the latest of the New Age meccas. You know I'm hesitant when all the various ingredients in the movement commingle—witness what happened in Sedona—so I've decided to visit now, before the spirits of commerce and capitalism merge once again over sacred ground. What convinced me months ago that it would be worth two days' bone-jostling travel through the countryside was a book I purchased by a young photographer—one of Georgia's friends—a young woman who visited the area for her doctoral thesis. I am sending you my copy of that very book with this letter; perhaps it will give you an idea of where I am walking on this earth and what I am seeing even as you read this.

Chelsea (Gretchen's daughter—one of the group I am traveling with) has informed me it is still 'cool' to travel to Villacuerda. Still too hip to be trendy, were her exact words.

From what I understand of it, Villacuerda offers a panoramic overview of a plain that ends in a natural bay off the Gulf of Fonseca. It appears quite scenic, though you'll notice if you look closely at the first photo in the book that the entire plain beneath the township is barren. Among the Travelers this area is known as the Burnt Spot. Fifteen years ago, it was an impoverished harbor town surrounded by small, cooperative farms. It was razed first by a horrendous fire, and the remains literally scoured clean years and years ago by Hurricane Manja, which came right on the heels—days, even hours—of the fire. Do you remember that storm? They called it a 500-year storm. I've never witnessed anything like it. It was a terrible experience for us at home, and we were 1500 miles from its center!

In the book, there are photographs of Puerta de la Reina before and after the storm—you can judge for yourself definitively how easy the rest of us really had it. From the conversations I've had, the destruction has already taken on the trappings of myth among the locals in the region. The official estimates are that 7,000 died there, either drowned in the torrents of mud and water that poured down from scorched hills, or else simply dragged into the ocean—that is, if they'd somehow managed to escape the fires. Everyone I've conferred with has told me the estimates are low, because the government didn't pay very close attention to the locals before or after the damage was done. They were too poor, apparently, to merit the consideration.

When Gretchen returned from the site last month, she described it as a place with a burdensome air about it. She believes the psychic and emotional energy resulting from the violence of the inhabitants' deaths tore a hole in the psychic ether that is still on the mend. I couldn't even tell you the meaning or the significance of that, nor how exactly she came to that conclusion; but honestly, I have to say I was enough intrigued by her reaction to want to understand what she had experienced there.

I'll be sure to let you know how it goes.

All my Love,
Regina

White Harbor University
March 17

Things were getting sketchier for Eric. He couldn't understand it.

He had drug sources everywhere, for just this sort of eventuality. There was always someone on campus or someone just off campus. He knew people further from campus, in his mom's neighborhood, and he knew people between campus and town. The idea was and had always been that the flow didn't end. It was important to always have stuff. He was well-connected and had always intended to stay that way.

The farther away his sources were, the more complicated the logistics of getting there, and although Eric was already mentally prepared to begin any journey necessary, his body was not so ready. And look at me now, he thought. I'm all dried out.

Every dealer on campus was gone? People had moved, people had married, people had graduated or dropped out or transferred somewhere else? When did those things happen? Just like that?

It couldn't be, he thought. And he just couldn't understand it if it was. How long had it been? It couldn't have been that long.

Too long. He was getting itchy. It had been too long. His skin was starting to crawl. Like little spiders.

His hands were clammy.

One more circuit around his spots around campus, he decided. One last time.

Maybe he would see someone.

He'd spent so much time on the hunt, he hadn't even tried to get his stuff out of his locked room yet.

When he started feeling light-headed again, he took a breather under a tree outside the computer labs.

Poor Rachel, he thought. She didn't sound like she was very happy. Obviously, she hadn't been taking enough time out to party.

Eric's luck was no better at the graduate housing units.

His buddy's roommate in B-9 told him he might find his buddy in the crowd at the rally in the Plaza.

Eric was halfway there—walking the service path that ran behind the music hall to the Communications building—when he realized he was not going to make it the whole way.

His legs felt wobbly.

His stomach was aching. He was suddenly sweating like crazy.

His shortcut dropped him off on the main walk. The few people who were trying to live their normal school lives sans rally, they didn't pay any attention to Eric.

People today don't even bother to look up long enough to notice when someone right in front of them might be dying, he thought. Suits me fine.

There was a faint buzzing in his head.

Farther off, he could hear the crowd cheering. The buzzing

in his head was louder.

He crossed the main walk. Nearly slid down the two sets of stairs behind the main gymnasium. From there it was a short lurch to an alcove where there were two benches.

It was empty.

His was the first set of footprints through the new snow.

He fell on one of the benches, rolled over on it until he was lying on his back.

Everything was spinning when he looked up. Eric closed his eyes, tempted at the thought of trying to sleep it off, but his heart started pounding as soon as he closed his eyes—he was scared because he couldn't see anything.

He was still feeling a little uncomfortable when it came to sleeping.

Still scared about not waking up, he knew was the problem.

So he just stayed there, panting. Trying not to scratch.

———————

Harbor View Hospital

Nurse Lewis was not concentrating on her work.

She had problems of her own. Once again, she was the only one scheduled for this shift; she decided if that was the way the management was going to handle things, she was going take her time doing her job.

Besides, it was hard for her to find quiet time like this.

She was always careful never to take too long, because she needed her job if she was going to get through this mess with her soon-to-be ex. His constant phone calls, his two most recent scenes at the hospital, one for each of the two weeks he'd no longer been welcome under her roof . . .

It had been a difficult time.

Today, Nurse Lewis asked Leonora at the front desk to

intercept the calls. Marcia, her supervisor, took her aside yesterday to tell her the interruptions were getting to be "distracting."

She needed to hold on to her job, that was the bottom line.

That man was supposed to have been her hero, she thought as she pushed open the door to room 108C.

The patient inside, a young man new to her ward, was convulsing slightly. His feet were pedaling, his legs and arms spasming slightly, his head jerking methodically.

A soldier in need, she thought as she put a tongue depressor between his teeth and sideways across his mouth to keep him from chewing down on his tongue or his lip. Those were the ones who always stole her heart.

That was who she'd been looking for. That was who she'd thought she'd found.

She scanned the patient's chart.

Brrrr. Gosh, it's cold in here, she thought.

She turned only slightly away from the patient to prepare a sedative.

Nurse Lewis' shift had ended in the early evening the day before; everything had been normal when she'd clocked out. Today she walked in to find the atmosphere among the staff far more subdued than usual. Everybody was a little off, she could sense that immediately.

Eventually, she'd found out two people died doing exactly the type of thing she was doing now . . .

Of course, it had been an electrical accident. Lightning had hit a circuit box. It had had nothing to do with the patient they were attending to.

A strong sedative, nonetheless.

She gave him the same dosage he received early that morning.

Stick with what works, she thought.

That way he'd sleep right into the next shift.

Leave it to someone of a better mind to handle it.

———————

Eric closed his eyes again briefly when he'd managed to sit up.

Licked the sweat that had formed just above his dry lips, and then planned to ride out the chills and shakes that were soon to follow.

Sitting up was better for him.

He opened his eyes again when he felt something cold and wet on his arm.

He looked over to his right.

There was a skinny woman with stringy, bleached blonde hair sitting right there next to him on the bench. Wearing an old-fashioned Red Cross uniform, with a skirt and a cape and a big hood.

She was rubbing a piece of damp cotton over a spot in the middle of his arm, looking for a vein to mine. He could smell the alcohol vapors. He liked that smell.

She looked up at him, smiled when she saw him watching.

She smacked the inside of his arm with the flat of her palm a few times.

"You've used up most of the good ones in there, haven't you?"

Before he could answer, her smile tightened into a grim line.

She'd found one.

Eric swallowed. He didn't know if she was really there or not. He hoped she was.

He tried to pull himself away from her, but there was no strength left in him.

He tried to move his arm, but it refused. Not a finger wiggled. It might as well have belonged to someone else.

"I haven't done that for a long time," he said to her. "I stopped doing that when I was a kid."

The words sounded strange to him. Logically, he knew

he'd once had a problem because the evidence had always been up and down his arm. But the details of any of it were gone. He had obviously been hooked on needles at some point. He must have quit it somehow.

It is the truth, he thought,

(and the truth if you want it)

"Now, now," the nurse said. Her voice was like creamy pink syrup. "You've got more important things to worry about. Your daddy is coming to see you. You want to be all fixed up for him, don't you?"

Eric shook his head no.

When she sank the needle into his arm . . .

(my father)

. . . that sharp pain was almost as much of an electric rush as the sight of his thick, dark blood rising in the syringe.

"I don't do this anymore," Eric said.

She slid it back down, slowly pushing that heart-pounding and delicious panic into his chest, feeding that nausea in his stomach

For a moment, it was as if he was standing on a cliff looking down. The moment before he fell.

"Now, now," she said, a little irritated, "that's how you ended up here in the first place."

Nurse Lewis looked at the patient's face as she pulled the needle out of the IV.

Maybe she was searching for some sign of that lost little soldier in him.

She didn't expect his eyes to be open.

She gasped.

He was looking at her.

How long had he been watching her?

She was so startled she couldn't control herself. She shrieked, and thought, He's awake! He's awake!

He stared at her. He curled his lip at her.

"Hello, mother," he snarled as she stared back at him.

"You fucking bitch," he said. "I'll rip you apart."

Something was wrong with him.

She shivered again as she pressed the Call button beside the bed, and then looked away from him momentarily, to the door, wondering if she shouldn't just wait there.

When she turned back to him his eyes were closed again, and in fact, he looked like that had never changed.

The IV caught her eye as she backed to the door.

Her stomach knotted as it registered on her what she was seeing. The liquid inside the bag, which moments before had been clear, was now a dark, deep, blood-red hue.

She looked at his hand, where the IV was connected, to see if the setting had slipped loose.

It hadn't.

But further up his arm, much to her horror, she saw a fresh puncture wound amid all the other, more aged scars. There was blood leaking out of that fresh wound.

I administered the shot through the IV, she thought. I know I did.

She didn't even like giving shots. She always tried to leave that to someone else.

She looked at the used syringe in her hand.

Inside, there was blood.

———

Eric heard a sound overhead.

There was a flash of light. Lightning. And another flash immediately after.

He breathed in deeply.

The thunder clapped and roared as he felt his own heart racing and choking on the poison, breaking it down and spreading it back rushing through to his arms and his hands, to his legs and his feet. The sky above him was filled with lines of fire, lit by jagged bolts that cut across the grey sky as they rained down onto the ground.

He heard something coming.

Gathering whispers as the thunder rumbled on, a growing murmur.

Another flash. The breeze picked up.

The sound of voices approaching grew louder.

It was familiar, the coming of this rush; the feeling he was meeting again an old, once dear friend. Never meant to leave him behind, right? Eric looked down at the ground, at the single set of footprints through the snow leading to the place where he sat.

His little nurse friend was gone; only the puncture mark she left in his arm remained, a single point of reference to a life he didn't remember; his temples were throbbing while he stared at that wound in the arm he could no longer lift on his own. In his mind's eye, he drew a line from the puncture mark of the life he knew to the scars of the life he didn't quite remember, and somewhere inside a veil momentarily lifted. For an instant only long enough for him to understand clearly that nothing he knew about himself was right, everything was in fact so far off that he would never even have figured out the right questions to ask, much less which answers to seek.

In that flash in his memory, he saw an image of a girl, a beautiful, dark-skinned little girl. He heard her voice in the air of the alcove, as if it has been carried to him by the rising wind itself. She said to him, "You need a name to get through the gate; you need a name if you ever want to play on the other side."

There was a picture in the sand at our feet.

A diagram, a tree.

A family tree.

She pointed to the one that was you.

Then to the one above your head.

She asked, "What is her name?"

The winds would not allow him that answer. They carried the words away.

And this one, she said, pointing to the other. Who is your father?

He thought: My father?

"If you don't know," she said, "then we'll have to make something up. Don't worry," she said sincerely, "lots of us do it. Do you know who your father is?"

The thought of a father, of his father, filled him with a strange warmth and a surprising dread, followed by a surge of panic that just about made him want to run and hide. At the mere idea of him Eric felt like he had been exposed to him, uncovered and revealed, thrust into the middle of a spotlight because someone had said something too loud . . .

. . .when all it had ever taken was a thought . . .

It was a bolt of lightning that snapped him out of the memory, that dropped the veil and closed the door, freeing him from his panic. A flash of light so bright that for a moment Eric couldn't see—he could only hear the explosion of the lightning bolt that followed, a charge that fell so close by him that he felt the heat and the charge in the air as it exploded. His heart thrilled.

He was blazing now.

Office of the Dean

The first arc of white fire had been followed by another, and several after that, lightning strikes that for several minutes raked at the campus.

Victrine strode into the office and up to the window as the light show climaxed in a bolt that burned a trail through the sky and down to a tree just off the main walk by the main gymnasium.

"Goodness!," Victrine said, rubbing her eyes, and even Evelyn felt somewhat taken aback; they watched silently as a reddish-orange blossom flowered in the upper branches of the tree, a glow that could only be embers lighting.

Oblivious to concerns of safety, or else they were simply too mad at the moment, too caught up in their own carrying-on, the students congregating on the Plaza seemed to take this show of nature as encouragement rather than intimidation. The noise level swelled momentarily, as if they were cheering a fireworks show, as if the storm were staged for their benefit; they quieted just as suddenly when a rogue wind rose and surged across the Plaza, catching most unawares. Banners tore in that surprising burst of wind, signs were pulled from the hands that gripped them; as Evelyn and Victrine stood side by side watching, flyers were swept along with hats and umbrellas and various other articles of clothing, as well as much of the accumulated trash.

Evelyn ignored the pleased grin that crept onto Victrine's face.

Neither woman said a thing.

The thunder continued overhead for some time after the electrical storm had moved on.

When the sound had stopped, the wind just as suddenly died again.

"I'll go and put a call into the Fire Station, then," Victrine said.

———————

When Eric came back to himself, he was standing on the main walk again, well past the gym. He couldn't remember moving at all. The thunder had died down, the wind had fallen off again. There was all kinds of trash piled up along the edge of the Plaza.

He thought he might still be hearing voices. Or something like that. There was a weird static in his head. Nothing so specific as the little girl's voice. But it was similar to that. Nothing so cohesive or connected or in fact seeming to relate to him at all.

He closed his eyes, covered his ears, and listened.

Most of it was not even intelligible, like a bunch of static coming in on different frequencies inside his head. Someone who seemed far off was yelling out some kind of warning to someone else, but he couldn't make out the exact sounds of her words. A man's voice he did not recognize said something like "take the chain off the radiator!" and a kid's voice quietly whispered "I didn't, I didn't." That those voices were there was undeniable; for a few minutes, as he stood on the main walk listening to them, through his head ran a rambling stream of words and phrases that seemed not to belong to him at all.

It started to scare him, so he stopped it. He opened his eyes.

He tried to think of a song he could hum. Even then, there was a woman's voice he could still hear who kept calling out random names.

A few moments later, he felt his heart skip a beat when he thought to himself, "Am I still hearing the voices?"

It startled him because he knew he had wondered that same thing before.

But when?

It was a very strange place to fry, in the middle of a crowd.

Alone in that crowd. Knowing that his mother was up above him someplace, watching over the whole show, made it even weirder.

She must be coughing up a hairball, he thought, over all these people lingering about on her campus.

Someone with a megaphone said something about the Alpha Gamma Nu chapter from Vermont. Eric didn't hear what it was about them, but when people started cheering all around him, that was when he realized that these were frat people all around him.

On another megaphone cue, several people around him started singing a song that turned out to be the Alpha Gamma Nu theme song.

There were just too damn many of them.

Eric climbed up on a bench to see what was going on.

What it turned out to be was a large group of girls in white monogrammed sweatshirts coming down the walk at the south end of the Plaza. These were obviously the Alpha Gamma Nu chapter from Vermont, as they were not only singing their theme song but also walking in distinctive lines and performing an elaborate marching drill while they did so.

By the time the last line had marched into the crowd, every frat person within earshot was singing along, as if it was part of their rulebook or something that they knew and recognized the tunes of each other's hives; when the song was finished, the Plaza filled with the sounds of applause and cheering and chanting.

The vendors had taken up their positions around the fountain, and the area around their booths was the only place where there was any kind of open space to move around because people seemed to be building various structures out of cardboard boxes. Were they making tiny houses? Was it a visual arts project? Some sort of eco demonstration? Eric cruised into that zone, no longer really looking for his buddy from B-9, just kind of checking out all the action, wondering if there was anything he could get into himself.

He saw one of the beefy frat guys who had partied Eric out the previous night. He was tending a barbecue. His apron said HOT 4 SOCCER MOMS. In one hand he had a spatula. In the other was a joint. The guy wasn't even trying to be discreet. He waved Eric over with the hand holding the spatula.

"Dude! Hammered yet?"

"Toasty," Eric said. He passed Eric the joint. Eric took a drag, then handed it back.

"I'm pretty wasted too," he said.

Eric was sure he was the more fried.

The guy handed him a beer. There were hot dogs and patties on the grille.

He moved close to Eric, put an arm around his shoulder, patted and squeezed Eric a little too energetically. "Man," the guy said, "you want to know about the action? The action's gonna be out of control out here tonight. There's going to be four or five bodies in every bed tonight, dude. Killer bud, killer brew, you know what's going to be happening. Pussy, pussy, pussy. You should drop by."

Eric couldn't think of anything to say to that. Or to the fact that he was still massaging Eric's shoulder.

So Eric said, "Meow."

The guy liked that. He laughed.

"Check you later, man," Eric said when he turned to check the grill.

"Dude, see that you do."

It was like a school carnival that had spun out of control

Mom used to love having me here with her at work, Eric thought as he walked on. Who are we kidding? She would go through all the motions every day of letting me know how much of an imposition it was having to monitor my educational development so closely, having to practically keep me on a leash. But all of that attitude was gone by lunchtime everyday, when she would meet me after whatever remedial class I was in at the time. She was always happy to spend the time with me

I didn't mind classes on campus that much, he thought. Better than high school.

Nobody really tried to fuck with me here, he thought.

Everyone just goes his or her own way.

When he'd been on campus before high school, those were the days when he'd felt nothing but envy for all the students here.

They had always seemed to him to be so free.

Brother Matt was standing on a stool talking about redemption when Eric's tour of the crowd brought him to the edge of the preacher's small audience.

"It is not enough simply to say that you believe in one thing or another. It is not enough simply to ask for forgiveness. There is no entrance granted to the kingdom of God to those who are not truly repentant, who do not believe with conviction . . . "

Brother Matt was enjoying the attention. He always did.

"When, you may ask yourselves, when is it too late for me to guarantee safe passage for my soul into the next life? Is it enough to beg forgiveness at the end of a lawless, licentious life? Could a man knowingly sow war and hate, pain and dissension through all the days of his life, and still secure a place in Heaven by the mere utterance of an apology to the Lord above as he hovers near death's door? Though poets might lead you to believe otherwise, I say to you no. One can only earn redemption through love and dedication to love. The man who crawls to the altar only out of fear and self-preservation, out of boredom or out of political correctness, rather than out of awe and love and fear, he will not be saved.

"I say to all of you here today, put yourself on the road to forgiveness now, before the time comes that it will be too late, a time when all of you will wish that you had acted earlier to become a part of the Good, a part of the majesty of the Lord.

"Ask yourselves," he said, "ask yourself, what sins have I committed against my fellow man, what pains have I inflicted either knowingly or unwittingly, what acts of evil have I participated in, and what might I do as penance for these actions? Ask yourself this today. Tomorrow may be too late."

"And each of you," he said as he turned slowly, his eyes scanning the crowd, "remember that the day of judgment is all but upon us, the day when the dead shall rise and walk the earth, the day when all those who have lived lives both blessed and ungodly shall stand and be sorted. And know this, mark my words, that this day of judgment fast approaches, this day may well be upon us . . . "

Brother Matt turned toward the section of the crowd Eric was standing in.

When his eyes settled on Eric, he stopped speaking.

Eric wondered: Was he that obvious a trip case?

The preacher stared, and he did not know what to say.

People finally started to turn toward Eric to see what the preacher was looking at.

Eric ducked right down, and then practically crawled away on his hands and knees.

There were three girls playing jacks on the edge of the fountain.

Eric sat down on the edge of their game.

He couldn't keep from smiling, just smiling a big wide smile while he was sitting there, because this day was turning out to be okay after all. All he'd needed was to change his perspective a little.

He watched them play and they ignored him, this guy with the big grin on his face sitting next to them.

When he finally asked them if he could play, they widened their circle to include him, even though one of them seemed a little frightened.

They were not very good. Not much of a challenge. But that was fine for him. Their turns were short.

By the time he reached double-bounce tensies, he was more interested in spinning his favorite little jack—it was a black one—on the ground.

And when he discovered he could get two of them going at once, that was what he ended up doing for the next 20 minutes—trying to see how long he could keep them standing up and spinning.

He spun one. He spun two. At the same time.

Over and over and over, he didn't know how long it went on, but he liked watching them until they fell over. For a while, the three little girls copied him, and the four of them were spinning jacks and laughing, and giggling when a jack went shooting out of their hands, clapping when another jack managed to stay up an unusually long time. That was when Eric reached his peak on the high, when they are all laughing and he was feeling really heated and good. The Sigma Omega men of Virginia were making their entrance, all these jocks were yelling out the freakin' Sigma Omega mating call or something just like it, and he was feeling great making the jacks spin.

The good things never last, he thought.

Eventually, the girls got bored, and they wanted to play jacks again. He tried to convince them to leave him the black one. It wasn't like they needed all of them. They weren't that good.

An hour or so later, when he had come down a little, he covered his ears again.

The voices in his head were gone.

It was probably just a side effect, he thought.

He wondered what that nice nurse gave him.

He also wondered if he could find her again, and if she could score any more.

On his way out of the Plaza later in the day, he saw another group of sorority girls; this pack was walking along the south walk, from the Plaza to the parking lot. The girls were marching in two long lines, and they were singing quietly as they went.

What Eric didn't see at first because of the shrubs was that Brother Matt was waiting for them.

"Ask yourself, children, what force of fate it is that draws you to this place at this appointed hour."

Eric jogged forward far enough that he could see around the hedge.

Brother Matt was standing in the middle of the path on an old crate.

He was holding his Bible in his hands, standing so still he almost looked like a statue.

"Ask yourself, children, if there might not be greater powers at work here than your minds can comprehend. Ask yourself carefully if you are truly capable of assessing your roles in the greater schemes of the Lord."

The sorority columns split apart as they came to his position; one passed him on the right, one passed him on the left, like birds in the water floating around an obstacle. On the other side of him, they went back into a closed formation.

Although the sisters continued singing, they turned down the volume and they bowed their heads as they passed by the evangelical, so they didn't have to meet his eyes. It all looked very respectful.

"Ask yourself, children, if ever in your life do you truly have control over your destiny, do you truly have individual choices, or is it only a matter of the workings of fate?"

Once the girls were past him, they sighed in relief or giggled or else they looked back at him like they were looking back at an accident that could have been them.

Eric ducked into the library. A minute later, he was exiting the building on the other side.

He returned later to the spot where he'd seen the nurse, still aimlessly wandering, smoking the last bits of a cigarette stub he'd found on the ground, enjoying the last vestiges of his buzz, and thinking about heading back over to the Plaza to see if anything was really cooking for tonight. Maybe, he thought, he hadn't approached the goings-on with the right attitude.

It was still relatively early. But it was dark. Campus life was always more interesting after dark. Kick back for a while, he figured, enjoy the afterglow.

One last drag on his cigarette and he flicked it away.

It was a good shot. The ember traveled in a wide orange arc right into a bush.

The butt hung on a leaf, but didn't fall into the snow.

Eric walked over to put it out properly.

That was when he saw the heels of two feet sticking out from under the bush.

Little feet. Toes in the snow.

Surrounded by what looked like ashes.

It was the same filth that covered the little feet. Ashes the color of clay.

Eric pushed the branches of the bush aside.

The ring went all the way around a body lying face down in the snow, in a deep impression, as if the body fell there from the sky.

Eric dropped to his knees, rolled the body over. Still warm.

It was a kid.

Chapter 5

One Year Ago

Evelyn's Old Journal
Entry Date: January 17

I did not realize the day you arrived on my doorstep that I could not have been less prepared. That and every day since.

It is a sense of inadequacy inherent to child rearing, I believe. Not knowing where you make your mistakes until much later. Giving birth made me feel a part of a very select group; losing my own child put me into limbo. It was the realization of the worst of any of my fears.

I felt burdened by that experience from the moment I looked into your eyes

You would challenge my vulnerabilities time and again, in ways that would let me know I was not wanting. You gave me more than I had. In a way, I saw you as my chance to get it right. I should have known better.

I hired a sitter for you for the first few days you were with me. It seemed superfluous initially (and absurd afterwards), since you were obviously already self-sufficient; it made me feel better to imagine there was someone keeping an eye on you when I was away. I hadn't yet figured out what I was going to do with you. Every day for a week, as I would leave for school, I would say a silent prayer that everything would be fine, that you would be safe, that you would not run away, that you would not disappear as suddenly as you had come.

Disappear is exactly what you did from the start. Six-thirty in the evening would find me cursing the sitter, both of us sobbing while we searched this house and yard I was hardly familiar with to find you. A most exhausting and painful exercise that generally ended only when I had all but given up and gone inside to heat up a cold dinner . . .

You would appear at the back door of the house as the last rays of daylight were fading. Rather like a cat, you would never come when you were called, and you acted as if that were your right. You responded instead to the sound of the lid being lifted off a steaming pot, or the sound of dinner plates being set on the table.

My lost, silent boy. Always ready to eat.

I'm convinced it was there we established the enduring pattern of our relationship. My options that first night ranged from throttling you, to punishment, to simply yelling at you, to turning you over to the proper authorities, to simply dropping to my knees to praise the higher powers for returning you to me.

My course of action?

In silence—I dared not speak I was so overcome—I fed you.

You lived a secret life out of my sight, with friends I rarely met, doing whatever it was you did in your free time. I could monitor (and enforce) your schooling, give you chores, send you to camps and lessons, build the routines of a life around you, but I could never change the fact that as soon as you were done with whatever was scheduled, you would be gone and over the fence at the back of the yard.

That is how it happens now that I can sit here and feel so overwhelmed by the myriad stories of the life you appear to have lived here in White Harbor. My greatest concerns relating to you months ago would have been that I had never met any of the girls you dated and that you seemed—judging by the sporadic and meandering nature of your class selections—to have very few career ambitions. Today, if only a small fraction of the rumors I have heard are true, I would have to say, sadly enough, this is obviously the direction you've been set on since long before we met, and that I never really had a clue.

I've decided not to dwell on what are only rumors at this time. They will be addressed when you are past this.

I choose instead this night to recall the sight of you at the dinner table those first nights: perched on your chair in front of your plate, eyes popping out of your head in anticipation. You would never eat or touch any of it until I was done with mine. You would sit like that, wriggling in your seat, watching me eat, your face gleaming and delighted. I would ramble on and on, insisting the whole time that you eat, and you would seem to be listening, but you would never take a bite. Not until I had actually finished my entire meal and stood away from the table. Then there was no stopping you.

———————

White Harbor University
March 17 (The Present)

Before Eric did anything about the kid, he looked at what he thought might be movement along the edges of the shadows of trees for someone else who could help instead of him.

"Hey! Is someone there? Hello?"

No answer.

Someone who might now be standing there in the shadows, just watching? He wondered. It was the same feeling he'd been having this whole damn trip.

(he's watching he's waiting)

It was too dark to be entirely sure it could be written off as paranoia.

Eric put his ear down to the kid's mouth, listened for a breath.

Thinking all the while he should just keep yelling for help.

While his head was tilted sideways, he noticed it had

started to snow a light snow.

Nothing. No breath. There wasn't time to yell.

Eric felt around the kid's neck for a pulse.

Would anyone hear me yelling over all that crap going on at the Plaza?

Maybe there was a heartbeat. Underneath the layer of dirt covering his thin shirt, underneath that cold skin, a small heartbeat. Eric's heart was beating so hard so fast it was hard to be sure.

Eric tilted the boy's head back by resting his palm on his forehead. That got the boy's chin to drop open.

In the darkness, it looked to Eric like the mouth was filled with pennies.

But when he felt it with his fingers, it was only dirt. And clay.

And rocks and pebbles, some that glittered.

Eric tilted the boy to the side, cleared out as much of the dirt as he could with his fingers, then rolled him back.

Eric pinched the boy's nose. He gave him two short breaths.

Gently.

Eric put his hands on his chest.

Definitely a pulse there.

Remember, Eric reminded himself, he's a kid. And Eric felt pretty toasted.

Do it gently.

Little kid lungs.

The kid started twitching on the third set of breaths and compressions.

He coughed, he choked, he gasped and gagged on all the crud that was still caking his mouth and lodged in his throat, and probably in his lungs, and the best Eric could do was wince as the kid struggled to get it out. Eric pushed him back over on his side to make it easier, and then just sat there, watching while he puked mud and gravel. It sounded like he was choking up bones. In the night, against the snow, it looked like a pile of shit when he was done.

The kid drew in a rough, phlegm-filled breath and gagged and choked again before going through the same motions.

Eventually another pile came out of him, much smaller, beside the first.

A good sign.

He went on like that for a while before he seemed like he was doing any better. Eric sat him up, then pushed his head down between his knees while he panted for more air.

His body twitched, convulsed underneath Eric's fingertips.

He's still way fucked up, Eric thought. Glassy eyes and all.

Eric made a little snowball for the kid to suck on.

He shuddered and even jumped a little when Eric held the ice in front of his face. He closed his eyes. His eyes flickered open again, then closed.

The spasms started coming at longer intervals.

He opened his eyes and looked straight at Eric. Slowly, slowly, his blistered lips moved.

He said, "Paul?

"No. My name is Eric."

The Soundbox turned out to be an ideal location to deal with the kid—close by, but off a ways from the main walk, and Eric knew how to get in when it was locked.

Better, when they got there, no one was around. It was dark inside, quiet, and the heat must have just turned off, because it was still warm.

Eric took the boy straight to the cot in the room behind the booth, set him down there, straightened him out. The copper mud was now all over Eric's hands, too.

All Eric could find to cover him was a small towel that was

only a little bit longer than his legs. While he was looking for water, Eric wondered what he was going to do with the kid. Bring him to his Mom? Or should he call the cops?

What the fuck happened to him, anyway? Went out and got himself buried?

On his way back with water from the fountain outside the building, Eric found two jackets stuffed in a box in a corner.

They'll cover him up good, Eric thought. He's not a big kid.

The kid's eyes were glazed when Eric returned; still, Eric thought that something was stirring in there behind them.

I think he's on his way back, Eric thought.

He sat the kid up and put the cup of water in his hand, which closed around it.

The kid sipped it, choked on it, coughed a little. He spat a couple more rocks on the floor. Then he emptied the cup.

Eric went to the outdoor fountain, filled the glass again, and when he returned this time the boy was using the towel to try to clean the mud off his face. There was so much of it that it didn't make a difference. It couldn't possibly. He just smeared it around, got the towel all dirty in the process.

This time he emptied the glass in one breath.

He's the one who's going to decide what we do, Eric thought. I need to try to talk to him first. It could be simple. Could be he just needs a helping hand.

The kid looked around cautiously, slowly, more aware now. Checking out the surroundings, checking out Eric. Deciding whether or not he should bolt, Eric decided.

"Welcome back," Eric said.

The kid held his filthy left hand in front of his face. Clenched and unclenched it, and then wiggled his muddy fingers.

Eric tried again. "Can you hear me? How are you doing?"

He was almost surprised when the kid responded.

At least Eric thought that was what was happening when he started to speak. It took a bit of concentration to admit, when the words started coming from his mouth, started rushing out, that Eric had no idea what the kid was saying.

Maybe Eric's synapses were too fried out—he would admit to needing to consider that possibility, too. At first he told himself he understood what might be a couple words—scary angels, something about a fire—and his guess was that the boy was describing to him what he'd seen while he thought he was dying. It turned out Eric was not really getting any of it; he was so busy trying to catch up with the kid, so busy thinking that somehow listening harder would help him understand the kid, that it didn't register for a few minutes that it was another language that the kid was speaking. Dumb Shit, Eric thought.

Spanish.

"Slow down, slow down," Eric said. Like that would help.

How do I say slow in Spanish?

The kid said Something ayudame Something Something.

It was a question.

Eric shrugged. What did he know?

The kid paused, waiting for something more from Eric. When it didn't come, his brow creased.

The kid said something about Eric's ears. Eric thought it was actually kind of insolent sounding

But, more importantly, Eric could almost understand him. That was the oddest part of it all. The language was familiar.

Or better, the sound was familiar, the arrangement, from somewhere.

All Eric had to do was concentrate, he told himself. It was there.

Eric realized the kid was asking if Eric was deaf or stupid.

Eric thought, Do I know Spanish? Did I study Spanish?

The kids asked again, Where am I?

Eric understood him perfectly.

"You're in the States, the U.S."

The kid didn't follow.

He asked if Eric understood what he was saying.

Eric said, "Yes, yes, I do." For some reason, he couldn't say it in Spanish, although he felt sure that somehow he should be able to . . .

The kid said, "I don't think I believe you. You're just some crazy freak."

Eric said, "Are you giving me attitude?" The feelings that surged through him as he said it . . . because that or the equivalent came out of his mouth in Spanish . . . it was a rush of the familiar, at last, at last, at last!—a feeling of pleasure, almost of accomplishment; at the same time, it was like reliving an old, funny story, recalling something hilarious, something so absurd that it made him laugh out loud all over again. That was exactly what Eric did. He started laughing.

"I understand. I understand every word you're saying," Eric said. He heard it in his mind in English, but it was Spanish he spoke. "So watch what you say." Eric paused, thinking that maybe he did look a little crazy, cackling and talking tough. The eyes that looked back at him were clearly a little scared.

That made Eric laugh even harder.

Once Eric got settled down again, the kid settled down, too—underneath the jackets, at the opposite corner of the room.

Gonna keep his eyes on me, Eric thought.

Eric told him he should sleep. Not to worry.

He looked weirded out still, Eric decided. And why shouldn't he be? That's what the real bogeymen tell a person at the beginning, isn't it—don't be afraid?

Eric decided not to bug him anymore.

He could be a runaway, Eric thought. He could be homeless. He could have been kidnapped and then escaped.

Did someone really try to bury him?

He would have to wait it out until morning to hear it, Eric was thinking . . . when the sound of the front doors to the Soundbox closing let Eric know that the two of them were no longer the only ones there.

The lights went on in the recording area.

It was someone with a key.

They listened as whoever it was crossed the floor below.

Eric was thinking all this might go down better if they weren't hiding.

That kind of thing tended to put people on edge when they found you.

Whoever it was, they fiddled with the boom box. When the music came on, and Eric recognized it immediately as one of the tracks Bobby and he put down one of the days when they were fucking around trying to be songwriters, then Eric knew who it was out there. "It's Cold Outside," was the working title. It was a shitty recording they made on an ancient deck. It was just enough to give everybody an idea where the song was going.

It was Rachel.

Eric reached up to the control board and turned up the volume in the booth.

He closed his eyes when she started singing along with the tape. It sounded like she was doing other things while she was singing—walking around, moving a stool, strumming something unrelated on the crappy acoustic, rifling papers. She wasn't doing the song the way they'd played it as a band; instead, she was singing it exactly at the tempo of the demo tape. At the time, the band had all agreed it was too slow, because they all wanted it to rock.

It sounded beautiful this way, though. It made Eric wonder if the only reason it sounded good the other way was simply because of her singing. Because Rachel had magic in her voice . . .

Eric jerked back awake when he realized he was actually drifting off to that place where every good trip ended. He had taken a vow against sleep.

But with Rachel practically singing a lullaby, with the dirty little mouth-breather snoring not ten feet away from him, Eric started to feel like he was so tired he was ready to risk it again. Risk not waking up.

He closed his eyes, trying to get as comfortable as a person could get sitting up.

Here's hoping I wake up again, Eric thought.

Taking bets the kid sleeps right through it all, he thought, and has some pretty nice dreams because of it.

Chapter 6

White Harbor University
March 17

9:30 pm

I haven't figured out yet where I belong in this world, Rachel
thought to herself. I haven't seen much of it, just cornfields, a few
clubs, and this campus. Most days I go around barely managing to
keep track of what I'm supposed to be doing next. Is it wrong that
I'm actually sort of happy?

I work a lot. I study a lot. I worry a lot that I'm not very
normal. Which apparently I'm not. And that somehow I'm missing
out because of it. Which is normal, right?

It's not all that bad a life. I could have worse problems.

Rachel chose White Harbor University because it was the
farthest, smallest quality institution she could afford to get to from
her humble Midwestern starting point, and because she wanted to
break away from everything she knew, somehow show that she was
better than all of that, and see for herself how well she could survive.

Three years later, standing here shivering, watching the
snow drifting lazily down from a dark sky that had been hiding the
stars for so long now . . . she knew this wasn't the place she would
eventually end up either.

She missed the sun too much.

In the meanwhile, until she moved on, she kept telling
herself she was learning more every day that she remained.

Her original intent tonight had been to spend time at
the sound studio when she got back to campus, to work on the
song variation she'd been carrying in her head for what seemed
like forever. She wanted to stop spending so much time torturing

herself for not getting on it. But the truth she'd been avoiding was that it wasn't satisfying doing it the same old way anymore, being in the Soundbox alone. Until Eric woke up again, there were times, tonight in particular, it just seemed downright creepy.

That was part of the problem, too. She was wasting too much time dealing with this phony conjured sense of Eric.

Lately, it had been worse. At the strangest times, thoughts of him occurred to her, and she ended up wondering uselessly along some tangent, searching mentally through the remnants Eric had left behind, always finding nothing. Why couldn't they have just talked about it when there was still time?

She had to stop listening to old tapes, first of all. Stop dwelling on old memories, stop relying on old habits and the way we used to do things together. Put them away. For a while, if not for good.

She needed someone to play with. Someone awake and alive.

It was with a feeling of déjà vu that Rachel stopped and stared at the Plaza, standing pretty much in the same place she was this morning, when she first saw how the crowds had grown. Only this time, there was too much for her to take in at once.

The recruiting event slash rally had grown in all directions. The cardboard box structure had swelled in size—in six hours it had become a cardboard shantytown. In some places, there were tarps and plastic sheets serving as rooftops; in other places, it was open to the night and the snow. Surrounding the main, large structure were smaller, satellite campsites with tents and canopies and lean-tos scattered to the far corners of the Plaza.

People were having snow fights and building snow people, and sitting in clusters around portable heaters and propane lanterns, smoking, drinking, and laughing. Others were waiting in line with plastic cups in hand at the booth that must have had the kegs inside. There was music and dancing going on, and lots of laughter.

Coming from the inside of the cardboard structure, there was all kinds of noise, all kinds of pandemonium. Saws and hammers and drills, guys and girls yelling to and at each other or else singing stupid fraternity songs, music from a hundred competing stereo systems. So much noise. It was as if they had packed the entire dorm population in there. Whose great idea was that?

Even though Rachel could see no one familiar around, she decided to make her way out there.

That was where she would like to hang out, she thought. If she could find someone she could hang out in there with, then it wouldn't be awkward. This was the right atmosphere for her. Maybe she could even find a boy to kiss.

That was what she was hoping when someone bumped into her from behind. She turned, startled, as the girl who bumped her screamed her name.

"Rachel!!!"

The girl pulled Rachel into a hug. It was Pam. Before Rachel could react to the surprise of seeing Pam, Pam squeezed her, rocking her side to side, and planted a big wet kiss on Rachel's cheek.

"Pam?"

She'd been drinking. Rachel tried to break off the hug.

"Rachel, Rachel, Rachel! I'm so happy to see you!"

She renewed her hugging.

"Are you coming to play with us? Please say yes."

"Uh . . . "

"This is so perfect! I was just going back to our apartment. I wanted to get some fresh air and some more wine—and I was hoping I was going to be able to round someone up to join us." Seeing her now, surprisingly, Rachel felt fond of Pam. Almost comforted by the way she was always annoying in that same way. Maybe she'd been too harsh.

"One catch," Pam pulled her by the arm along with her. Towards the dome. "Just so you've had your advance warning.

Bobby's been giving me his bedroom eyes all night."

Rachel tried to pull free of her grip. Pam twisted her arm a little.

"Stop that. If we go back together, and we can get through a half hour of bad attitude while his erection subsides and the blood returns to his brain and heart, he'll come around and we can have some fun."

She stopped, turned to Rachel with a bewildered look on her face.

"I mean, really, what's this fixation on having sex with a thousand people partying two feet away? Does that make me a prude? I find it very hard to relax."

She said this very earnestly, but then apparently realizing that Rachel was not the right audience, decided to drop it. "Anyway, we could do something else with a protest theme, you know. Like we'll sing songs."

"That sounds great." It was a lame attempt to woo her, and Rachel was sure at that point that Pam would have said anything to draw Rachel along, but it turned out Rachel was actually glad for the invitation. Tonight she wouldn't let it bug her that Pam was only interested in the band because she was interested in Bobby.

Bobby had already had too much wine. In a crate from an industrial parts plant that he believed was larger than his first year dorm room, he was getting comfortably lost in his fantasies of himself and Pam in one of the myriad of imaginable positions in which they never had sex, daydreaming again what it would be like if she would let him do the things to her she would never do to him.

Pam had been on her booze run so long he was wondering why not just take the situation into his own hands and enjoy his time alone?

That way, if she wasn't in the mood again, it wouldn't matter that much . . .

. . . subtract the time it took to sink in 50 seconds later:

Yes, he thought, that was Pam yelling from somewhere nearby, "Bobby, you'll never guess who I ran into," and that left him about 15 seconds to panic.

He should have known.

There was going to be no lovin' in this hutch tonight. Lately it seemed she would do anything to avoid it. He pulled his jeans on. Freezing my blue balls anyway, he thought, waiting around here like this.

Fuck!

A quick look around the room for the most incriminating evidence revealed wineglasses on the table, they were fine; Billie Holiday on the player, fine; incense burning and the massage oil heating over the candle, fine . . .

. . . out on the floor beside the bed was the new pink nail-polish-colored lipstick-sized vibrator he bought for Pam. It had a bow around it . . .

. . . and the black nylon blindfold. Her string of pearls. All of that went into the backpack.

His back was turned, shirt was on, fourth button on his fly closed when the flap covering the front door opened.

"Bobby!"

It was Rachel.

Fuck, man. She's gonna be here all night long.

"Oh, this looks nice in here," she said. "You guys got a little love den."

He turned and tried to look her in the eyes when he said hi. Couldn't quite manage it. He felt rushed, and flushed and embarrassed . . .

"I don't want to interrupt you two . . . "

"There would have to be something to interrupt for that to happen," he said slowly, not looking at Pam. Then he smiled and said, "Actually, we were planning on fucking right around now. Right around here."

"Great! Do you mind if I stay and watch? I have no idea

what that's all about."

"The more the merrier."

"Oh, Bob," Pam said, "Can't we all just go out later and watch someone else? There's got to be other people with no sense of shame behind one of these cardboard walls. Or maybe we could just watch you, and everybody else can just listen in."

He tried to keep a good humor about it, hoping they didn't know how close to being right she was. But it was difficult for him to shrug off the central dilemma: Pam rarely wanted to have sex anymore.

"Make yourself comfortable, Ray."

"Thanks, Bobby."

"Who wants wine?"

"I'll have a glass. Thanks, Pam."

Bobby sighed. "Another for me, too."

"I love Billie Holiday," Rachel said as she seated herself cross-legged on the floor.

"You sure look happy," he said. Just making small talk.

"You sure don't." Ray looked him straight in the eyes. He looked away. She didn't understand, he thought, because she's a dork nerd virgin.

"I'll get over it. Where are you coming from?"

"From another great experience in my college life."

He had to think about it a moment, because she acted as if he should know what she was talking about.

"The show was great," she said. She took off her gloves, unzipping her jacket.

She had on a WHU sweatshirt underneath.

Pam asked, "The show at the Harbor Club?"

There it was. Pam knew what Rachel was talking about.

"It was so great, you guys." Underneath the WHU sweater was a turtleneck. Rachel got that off with some struggling. Underneath the turtleneck was a t-shirt. "Is it hot in here? You know, it's the first public thing I've done since we were in

Weatherton, and I was really nervous beforehand. It was just singing standards in a stuffy old country club atmosphere really, but fun, it was really fun . . . " She smiled at him. "And I was just at the Soundbox, trying to work on a song, but it wasn't working for me there. I got myself really spooked. I kept thinking I was hearing things, and then I didn't want to go looking around, because, you know, I mean, what if it is something, and I'm there all alone?"

He sipped his wine. Underneath the t-shirt was a thermal shirt, and under that was the tight, black, low-cut, nearly off-the-shoulders shirt that she must have worn at the show.

"The show wasn't at all like it was with us. First off, I had only five numbers in about three hours of music and most of the rest of the time all I did was sit around listening to them play songs I've heard too many times already . . . " He was waiting for her to start peeling off the layers of clothes on her lower body when she noticed that he was paying maybe too close attention. Then he'd swear her eyes wandered briefly to his lower body.

Rachel blushed a little, giggled her awkward way. "You don't mind if I take off most of my clothes, do you, Bobby? It must be 30 degrees warmer in here than it is outside.

"The truth is," she continued, "the only good thing I can find in the cold weather is that it has given me an added sense of security. Even in my apartment at night, I know anyone who tries to attack me is going to have to get through a lot of layers of clothing to get at me, including stuff that's hard for me to get off even under ideal conditions. "

She started unlacing her snow boots. He decided to sit back, relax.

May as well do that, and just enjoy the show, Bobby thought.

"Anyway, as I was saying, I decided tonight that from now on, I'm going to take whatever singing jobs I can get, wherever they come from. It's just too good for my soul to not be looking for chances to do it . . . "

As Pam sat there listening to and watching and laughing along with Rachel, all she could think to herself was this: Rachel Cummings, what planet are you from?

Pam could tell by the look alone on Bobby's face even while he was chuckling along with almost everything she said that he found her unbelievable.

But come on, it's Rachel we're talking about here, she thought.

And not just the Rachel they knew and loved. The one who long ago would wince when someone cursed, or when Pam burped out loud during a meal. One glass of wine turned Rachel bright red and babbling stupid. Any mention of sex and the blush would deepen to purple before she excused herself and left the room. Rachel was the one who would have been embarrassed to be seen wearing something like what she was wearing, much less performing a show in it.

Pam wondered: Did she actually wear that tonight? In front of other people?

We're definitely talking the new Rachel Cummings here, Pam thought. Whoever that is.

Pam emptied the last of the first bottle of wine into her own glass. It wasn't long before Bobby's attitude had mellowed—at least toward Rachel—while to her, he couldn't manage a word, even a glance. But the two of them, Bobby and "Ray," they just love to talk and joke and laugh, she thought, even though they have hardly seen each other since Eric took his dive.

Next thing, Pam thought, they're going to start poking each other and I'm going to have to scream.

I'm sorry, but no matter how much I love her new image—I think the new haircut is a flattering look for her most of the time, two hundred percent an improvement over what she used to go around looking like when she was a blonde—and looking at her now I constantly have to remind myself what she used to look like because the change has been so dramatic—but we've got to get ourselves together to face the facts: her taste in clothes has never been that great, and since her transformation, it's only gone from bad to tacky. She's still sort of a nerd and a dork, Pam thought.

"Rachel, how much weight have you lost, exactly? And how?"

"Honestly? I haven't been near a scale in two years."

"It's got to be about twenty pounds. Maybe twenty-five."

Rachel laughed. "Because I was really much fatter before, Pam?"

Sure, she hasn't been near a scale.

"It's really just poverty dieting," Rachel said, letting Pam off the hook, "Your body eventually uses up all the fatty deposits." Rachel pinched at her own belly, could barely grab an inch. "I eat lots of rice."

It's this trashy white urban thing she's going through, Pam thought, wanting more wine. I'm surprised she doesn't have a ring through her belly button or some odd part of her face, like everybody else.

Bobby poked at her exposed stomach with his finger, and Rachel squealed a little, and then punched him in the arm; for a moment, it looked like it might turn into some kind of wrestling thing. But before it could go that far, Rachel was up and on him, twisting his arm around behind him.

It wasn't that Pam had ever felt threatened by Rachel, or by the idea that she and Bob would ever get together—Bobby wasn't secure enough to be with someone who wasn't attractive; still, Pam felt a twinge of jealousy at the sight of them interlocked, even if they were hurting each other.

She definitely did not like it.

"Stupid boys," Rachel said, joking, and twisted his arm a little farther.

Bobby winced. Good.

"This is what happens," he said, "when you put a guy in a

small room with two women and a stock of wine. Next thing you know they're pinning him down and climbing on top."

He wishes. Mr. Raging Penis over there. Mr. Can't Keep It Zipped Up.

The sexual inference, though, was enough for Rachel to let him go. Pam felt grateful for Rachel's presence again.

"You're full of it tonight," Pam said as she pulled the cork out of bottle number two.

He smiled back at her. Leaned in, lips puckered, tipsy too, for a kiss. She leaned in, too. "I wish you were full of me," he whispered loud enough for the neighbors to hear.

Pam pulled away, poured herself a drink.

"Keep wishing."

Rachel was having a really good time.

"You know, I'm having a really good time."

"You're always welcome, Ray."

Pammy and Bob are so great.

"I'm going to hold you to it," Rachel said.

They were all quiet a moment. Rachel thought, I wish we could all be . . .

"You know," she said slowly, not quite sure if it was the right time to get into it. "I miss being friends with you guys. And I feel like . . . well, I feel like I need to talk about things before we can be . . . " Rachel paused, for no apparent reason . . . friends again."

"We are friends," Pam said.

"Things . . . " Bobby repeated.

"The one thing, actually, that is keeping me from having a really great time here tonight."

"Well," Pam said, "that's what it's all about, isn't it? We want you to have a great time, don't we?" Besides getting kind of catty when she drank, Pam also didn't handle confrontation very well, Rachel had observed before.

"Let me get some more vino, Ray. It sounds like I'm going to need it."

Bobby got up and turned his back. Rachel was supposed to wait, she knew. But she was ready to start. She didn't want to wait any more, even for him to sit down.

"I think I understand the reasons we all drifted apart from each other. Sad as it is to say, what it comes down to is that none of us wanted to talk about what happened, at least not honestly. None of us wanted to deal with it. And, after a while, because we took that attitude, none of us wanted to be reminded of it.

"And as long as we can't talk about it, we can't be around each other. That's how I see it."

Bobby said, "I don't know if that's one hundred percent true . . . "

"Well, I think it is. Even though it seemed like Eric was friends with everybody who liked to party, we were the ones he was spending most of his time with at the end. I think we were his closest friends. Maybe his only friends that he wasn't getting drugs from. I thought we were all on our way to becoming really good friends . . . and then after his accident you guys just cut out on me."

"Rachel, that is not true," Pam said emphatically.

"For a while I think I took it too personally. I'm like that. I really just felt like you guys had never really cared much about me, or about what we were supposed to be doing together. That I was just some big dorky nerd whose entertainment value had worn off."

What Rachel didn't say was that it had been clear from early on that Pam was more interested in Bobby than she was about being in a band. Probably went against her pedigree. And Bobby was into it, but then, without Eric around (and with Pam therefore in sole control of his brain) it suddenly wasn't worth it to him anymore, either. Rachel didn't say any of that.

"And I guess I translated that into meaning I wasn't worth your time."

"We're not guilty of anything you're not guilty of, too; it isn't any big conspiracy. It's just the way people react in these kinds of situations," Pam said, totally missing the point—that to Rachel, they weren't just "people" to each other. Rachel thought they were true friends.

"It isn't about blame . . . "

"You've focused your attention someplace else to get by," Pam pushed on, "just like us. We did the same thing. We all needed distance from it."

That was when Rachel started crying.

Pam looked mildly horrified.

"You see," Rachel said, "I need to talk about Eric. And I need to talk about Eric with people who know who I'm talking about. And I need to talk about him as if he's real. Like he was real, to us. Like our group friendship was real. Because I'm having a hard time figuring out where to put it, what to do with it, and I don't understand why it seems like it's getting worse and worse every day."

Quiet again. Pam moved next to Rachel, put an arm around her shoulder.

"I don't know how to talk about it," Bobby said. "I still don't like to. It takes me places I don't like to be. I miss having him around when I do that. It's easier not to."

This was why Bobby never wanted to hang out with Rachel, Pam thought. She always had to evoke Eric's presence whenever they were together, regardless of how uncomfortable it made him, regardless of the fact that Bobby always avoided the subject.

Before Eric started hanging out with all of us, there were other things we had in common; we were all friends before. Now it was always about him whenever the three of them were together. The most irritating part was that Rachel and Eric were never really very close.

Not as close as she seemed to like to think they were.

Bobby didn't know how to talk about it, either. He'd never been able to admit how much it hurt him. He wasn't willing to admit it was any more complicated than anything else in his life. Because he was a man, after all, and it wouldn't be manly to admit he needed help with it. So he kept the whole issue of Eric close to the vest, and Rachel wore it on her sleeve, and the end result was that neither of them left him there in his hospital bed, where he put himself without regard for any of the rest of them or anyone else who cared. A little bomb in all our lives, frozen part way through detonation.

Pam saw herself as the one in the middle who always had to pick out all of the emotional shrapnel.

"Did Eric ever tell you about the dark man?" Bobby was sitting back, propped up on his elbows, his hands playing with a little piece of black fabric he'd pulled from the backpack.

Rachel shook her head no.

He asked, "Did you think Eric was haunted?"

"Not before all this," she said. "In hindsight, it would obviously be an appropriate description."

"I always thought Eric was haunted," Bobby said. "When I first met him—it was my first year as a freshman and his fourth—I kind of had a superiority complex."

"Snotty attitude," Rachel said fearlessly. "You still do, a little."

"He's just more comfortable with it now," Pam said.

Rachel and Pam laughed.

He continued as if he hadn't heard a word.

"I thought Eric was the biggest scumbag when I first met him. It was at one of those lame dorm get-togethers. He got there late, showed up completely stewed. People told a lot of shitty stories about him. They said he dated junior high school girls, that he was a walking STD, that he'd been seen freebasing in the basement of the dorms or fucking some guy in the laundry room . . . "

Bobby's eyes were only half open, and he was slurring a

little. For some inexplicable reason, it made him look cute.

Or that might be the wine too, Pam thought.

When she thought he was not paying attention, she tried to snatch the fabric out of his hands. But he was more aware than she gave him credit for, and pulled it away before she could quite touch it.

"I didn't actually meet him, hang out with him, until the end of the first year, when I kept running into him at parties. Eric did know everybody, man. I mean, everybody. There wasn't a place we could go where we wouldn't run into someone he knew. You have to understand it was impressive to me, because I thought I got out there; I thought I was connected, but Eric knew the right people, and he knew the right places, he knew all the connections, if you know what I mean."

"Because he grew up here," Pam snorted.

"We'd all started practicing together maybe a month before he and I started hanging out regularly," Bobby said. "You two got to know him about the same time I did, which is when he started coming over to the rehearsals with me."

"It was just bad timing that we ended up with psycho Marty as drummer instead of him," Rachel said.

"It's not like he ever spent of lot of time talking about himself. Shit, I didn't even know he was the Dean's son until I got called into her office after we got back from Weatherton. At least we know how he managed to get into school here," Bobby said.

"That's just it," Rachel said, "I never felt like I knew him . . . at least, not as well as I should have. And yet, and maybe I'm just reading too much into it, I felt like we mattered to him. Like he cared about us. I guess I also felt kind of bad for him, kind of in that way you feel bad for a lost dog . . . "

"Eric was more like a stray," Pam said. "A stray by choice."

"But he touched me," Rachel said. "And now I feel bad that I didn't make more of an effort to discover why."

"He had high walls." Bobby said. "He had ways of making

you back off."

"Like always telling those freaky stories," Pam said.

Rachel rolled her eyes. "Eric told me that a VA major he met at a party when he was a freshman paid him 200 dollars to film him and a girl he didn't know having sex on a grave at a cemetery within earshot of a graveside service in progress . . . "

"Yeah," Bobby smiled, "that's an Eric story."

And the look on Bobby's face, well, for a minute the thought occurred to Pam that he never referred to her with such fondness.

"Do you think that was why he was messed up all the time?" Rachel shook her head disapprovingly. "Because he was scared by what was in his head?"

"I think he did drugs because he preferred it to being sober," Bobby said confidently.

"Or maybe it was simply because they were there, which has always been my theory," Pam said. "No self-control. Eric was the kind of guy who would always help himself if no one else minded.

"Which reminds me," Pam said, sensing this might be a chance to lighten the mood. "To us." She held up her glass.

When they clinked glasses, some of the wine spilled. Pam forced a laugh.

"To us," she said again.

"We're great," Rachel chimed in, following her cue.

"That we are," Bobby said. He was starting to come around.

When they had all downed their glasses, Rachel refilled hers again, and passed the bottle to Bobby.

He said, "This is really nice. It has been a long time."

"I wish we had some spare instruments lying around. We could make some music."

"I'll show you a spare instrument."

Rachel gave him an elbow. They both started giggling. The

whole thing between them annoyed Pam.

When Bobby thought of Eric, he didn't usually think about the last time he physically saw Eric. He usually had to remind himself that the band was in Weatherton when it happened, and that he had been standing in the snow, wearing only his boots and the blanket from the bed he had wrapped around himself when all the yelling had started, and that Eric was lying on a stretcher swinging between two park rangers who were wearing skis. Eric was covered by a blanket from the cabin that was identical in color and pattern to the one Bobby was wearing.

The last Bobby saw of him, Eric was disappearing over the edge of the incline, on his way down to the ambulance.

Bobby finished his glass, cracked open the night's last bottle of the red, even though he didn't really need it.

He was not feeling anything anymore.

"You know, I really respected Eric," Rachel said. "He had a weird way of thinking. He definitely had strange things going on in his head. But he was a good person. He wasn't violent; he didn't like to hurt people. He didn't like trouble, and he wasn't judgmental. He was cool. He just wanted to be left to go his own way, and he was willing to grant the same to everyone else."

"An ideal world where people are only allowed to hurt themselves?" Pam said. She was bugging Bobby a little now.

"He knew how to have fun," Bobby said. "He had a larger perspective on life. He was enjoying the big show. Besides, for me, he was one of those people it was easy to talk to. Probably the last good guy friend I've made since . . . "

He looked Pam's way, to see how close she was listening, half-wondering if he had said that out loud.

"Since you've moved in with me? Is that what you were going to say?"

They both stared at each other for a tense moment.

Bobby did not say a thing. Better not to go there. He smiled weakly, first at Pam, then Rachel.

"I encourage him to go out without me," Pam said. "Like we couldn't all use a little time alone."

"Save it for your own time," Rachel said. "I want to hear about the dark man."

Pam scowled at both of them, but didn't say anything more. Bobby decided to run with the ball Rachel had passed him.

"The dark man," he said, "is a messenger. A shadow moving back and forth across the face of the world, marking the people who are soon to die, so that Death will know the way to them . . . "

"Eric told you that?"

"Eric told me he'd seen him before. When he was a kid."

Pam, staring at the wine in her glass, said, "Does that mean Eric thought he could tell when someone was going to die?"

By her sarcastic tone, he could tell Pam had had enough of this Eric talk.

"You know what? I'm not saying anything other than what he told me. He thought he knew what it looked like, and he thought that he could tell when it was around. He believed he had seen it before. Maybe he was being paranoid. I wish I could describe it to you the way he described it to me, because it sounded really strange and it would only sound lame if I tried to put it into words for you . . . but he was so convincing at the time—maybe it was because we were totally stoned the day he was going on about it. But I believed that he believed it."

"Next thing you know, we're going to hear he was able to raise the dead," Pam said.

"I don't like to joke about things like that," Rachel said after a minute of pensiveness. "I mean, if a person believes he saw what he saw, who are we to question him?"

"I disagree," Pam said. "Because I'm not a fatalist. I don't believe anything is predetermined. And the fact that Eric was a complete drug addict would necessarily have to be factored in. Let's be serious—how reliable of a witness could he be?"

Rachel and Bobby exchanged looks. Pam wanted to

argue—she would say debate—but neither he nor Rachel was in the mood.

"Eric believed it," Bobby said, "and I believed him enough that I still get the chills thinking about him seeing death coming."

No one said anything for a minute.

"Bobby . . ."

"Yeah, Ray?"

"What do you think Eric was doing? What do you think he was trying to do up there?"

When he thought of Eric now, it was usually a night two summers ago that came to mind, when Pam and Bobby and a group of Bobby's high school friends who were in town visiting dropped mushrooms down at the park by the harbor. Pam and Bobby wandered off from the group, and ended up sitting by a pond, laughing at the ducks. They were tripping out, just beginning to get intimate with each other, and it was very warm and slow and tender sitting there touching each others' hands; not just holding, but actually feeling each others' fingers and palms, admiring and enjoying the texture of her skin and her fingernails, and they were talking and joking and laughing about the band and about Eric . . .

When who comes walking through the trees and right up to them, totally out of the blue, totally unexpectedly? Eric.

A chance meeting, even.

He wasn't looking for them, just kind of wandering around the oceanfront, looking kind of high, kind of out of it, vacant—not unusual for him. When he saw Bobby and Pam, and they saw him and waved him over, he sat down right there next to them by the pond. It blew Bobby and Pam away, no kidding. Pam and Bobby were near overload, and laughed like crazy for about ten minutes.

Then somehow, a while after that, they were all three kissing each other. And touching and taking off their clothes. Bobby remembered not being sure who was leading who into what because it was hard to say who was more fucked up.

It was not something Bobby wanted to get around.

Pam was watching him quietly.

What do I think he was trying to do?

"I think Eric thought maybe he was going to be able to fly. Just fly away from whatever it was that was bothering him."

Chapter 7

Office of the Dean
March 17

10:30 pm

As Evelyn readied herself to leave her office and head home, if only for a few hours reprieve from the problem growing seemingly exponentially in the Plaza, she scanned the room for anything she might be forgetting. And there, in the middle of her desk, in a place she couldn't have missed it, there was an unfamiliar black folder. She didn't typically leave her desktop with anything on it unless it was something she intended to bring home with her.

There was a business card attached to the cover: BRIGHTER DAY SERVICES.

And below that was a note from Mr. Harwood: "Following up on out-of-town leads. Attached is a rough preliminary report, a highly speculative attempt to build a narrative out of the information I've found so far. Edge."

She flipped through the pages inside. It looked like a report one of the students might have turned in. How much could he have found in a day?

She set down her bag, turned on the desk light, and sat down, bracing herself.

PRELIMINARY REPORT
Subject of investigation: **ERIC HARTIN**

The Press Gang broke four ways from Camp Idyllwood Rehab when the storms were their worst. Ronald Able went East. The North was yours. You lit the fire in the file cabinet in Yaegar Hall when the detention officers were switching their shifts. The winds can never be held long.

When you came home, when this all started, you pushed up the bedroom window with the new rake, and leaped through from the top of the fence, spinning over your knees like a penny, falling into the blankets that were waiting to rise and wrap around you. That night the bed was hard and musty, the sheets loose and wrong, missing the smell your mother's hands left behind while pressing them flat. And you could not sleep.

Her boyfriend Dennis came in and you stared at the wood-paneled wall because you knew he was going to tell you she was gone.

There are no chains, you thought.

Without turning on the light first to make sure it was really you, Dennis put his hand on your chest and said, "None of this is ever going to be easy for you, I guess." After he left and you closed your eyes, you squeezed them until the blackness gave way to streaks and stars and light breaking and finally with your eyes closed you saw again the grainy white lines in the wood panels. For a long time you stared at that wall.

That night, while your eyes were closed, something came. At first a curling whip of spice in your nose, then on your tongue in your mouth, making your eyes water. You saw the silver chain hanging, swinging in a thin line, back and forth, and the faint outline of his chin. The steaming air came into your face all at once—the sweat, the smell of old cigarettes, and you stretched out your arms around your father's neck and they closed on empty air, your fingers jamming into the wood.

Later, much later, still awake, at last you heard the rumbling, felt through your still sore fingertips the earth shaking far off. You heard the tall white tombstones shifting in their lines on the green hills, the earth cracking open, the stones breaking into rocks, the rocks into the pebbles, the ground giving way and giving forth.

You climbed the bedpost to reach the window in time, standing on your toes to push it open, to hang your head out in the night air. The whole wall was shaking by then, and coming closer you heard branches cracking off of trees, the roofs of houses breaking into pieces. The winds came, smashing through fences, rising up the wall in a rush into your face, blowing back your hair, chilling you, breathing around your neck, running cold over your scalp. Your ears were wet from the cold, but dripping even colder, whispering like ice, you heard your father saying, "You are master of the winds, caller of the storms, ruler of the air . . . "

It was only a moment.

The voice floated higher and higher away until you could not hear it at all and all you could see was a kite string hanging out in the street from a telephone wire swinging back and forth, back and forth.

You fell backward and the window slammed shut. The winds were hidden again. You slept with the covers wrapped tight around you.

———————

At a single-family home at 3267 Crystal Drive, in Sherman Oaks, California, Dennis Hale woke and showered, shaved, put gel in his hair, looked at himself through the stream on the mirror and wondered if he might be gaining weight. Then he looked at the top of the television, where he left the bong the night before, and where it should still be, but wasn't. He decided he needed a cigarette. But he only found his jacket where he put the pack the night before after five minutes of looking, and only then because the arm was sticking out from the coat rack behind the door. And the cigarettes weren't there anyway.

He stopped and thought about it a moment longer.

He thought he fell asleep with the television on.

Dennis sat down on the bed, and rubbed his hands up and

down his chilled legs. The desktop was clear, and the trashcan next to it stuffed full. All the bottles of alcohol were at the top, necks pointed down into the papers. The carpet around the trashcan was soaked wet in a circle.

The kid could be a pain in the ass, Dennis thought.

His guitar was hanging polished on the wall. He tried to make out the lines of his face in it, and reached for it to play, but he didn't have the time. Ashtrays were emptied and stacked, the drawers were all closed, keys, wallet, and change lying out in a neat row on the dresser. Not a piece of clothing in sight. Everything was probably folded and stacked somewhere in the house. In the garage, maybe.

Dennis held his breath and listened, as if he might be able to hear the kid's breathing through the thin walls. A chill ran from his legs to his back and he shivered. He pulled open the top drawer, half-hoping it would be empty, otherwise praying the picture of Karen would still be there. It was, of course, and lying face down until Dennis set it again on top of the dresser.

The whole room had been dusted. But Dennis could feel bits of potato chips sticking to the bottom of his feet when he walked into the hall. He tried to step around the creaking floorboards at first, but was too groggy for the effort. He was just getting started. It would be nice to hear his voice, Dennis thought to himself, and he let his heel rest hard on the board that would creak the loudest, a board the kid probably broke himself, as he pushed the door open far enough to peek inside.

In his head, Dennis heard Karen's exasperated voice saying, "The study, Den, the study. It's not anyone's room anymore." Eyebrows and lips turned angry and pouty. "Not anymore," she said. "Don't make this any harder." The memory of her voice melted his heart a little. "He isn't yours," she said. "He is not your son. He's mine and you can't understand how this hurts me, so listen to me please this once."

So he listened. And two days later he came home from

work and Karen didn't. Just like that, she was gone.

The creaking of the floorboard, done three times over, did not wake the kid.

It took Dennis ten minutes to find the coffee, the glasses, the silverware. He dressed in the garage by the dryer, where his clothes were piled in neatly folded stacks. When he pulled on his jeans, they were still warm.

There was no use in getting angry at him, Dennis thought. All it would mean would be not seeing him again for a longer while. He always pretended the kid was his. Dennis always left the window unlatched for him. No harm in it. Dennis knew he wouldn't be around forever to have the chance.

There were two pictures on the fridge, done on scraps of Idyllwood school letterhead with a pencil. The first was a picture of a street running over a beach straight into the ocean. In the second, five bums were dancing in a circle on the sand, their shadows forming a crown around them.

Dennis set out on the table an extra glass of milk and an extra glass of juice. He poured the cereal in the bowl for the kid, and left it dry, hoping the kid would think to add the milk to the cereal before he ate it. Dennis opened the drapes, and the sun came in, hot already. It was going to be another hot summer.

Dennis stood in the hallway outside the door, eating toast with jam, looking up every bite or two to watch the kid sleeping. He looked thin, Dennis thought. And too old and too beat up for what, 13, 14 years must be. Dennis would like to take him fishing sometime. He knew the kid would like it.

But the kid was at the age. Always been at the age. Always looking trapped, always running.

It took Dennis another ten minutes to find the bong in the chest in the living room. Karen used to keep it in there for special occasions only. He should have remembered that. But he was running late already. He needed to stop for some beer. Dennis snapped down two bowls. The blue smoke was still hanging in the room when he set the new *Fishing* magazine in front of the cereal bowl and grabbed his work vest. He decided also to put out two apples for the kid. And he started whistling when he grabbed his hat off the rack and closed the door behind him.

The air in the house after Dennis left was stale, hanging like a mist of dust over the kid while the sun burned through it. His lips were parched, his throat creaking dry. The sheets scratched away his skin. This wasn't the bed with pointy rocks in it, but he still felt them there under him. All night long he felt them scraping away the pieces and patches of his flesh. Each piece of loose skin balled sharply into another rock to scratch away more. When he started sweating the night before he could feel it all sticking to him, coating him as he rolled and turned and tried to find the cold spot.

He tried to lift his arm, to sly it between the mattresses for the cigarettes he stashed. But it was no use. He was too weak, his arms thin from losing so much skin. He swung his legs over the side of the bed and ended up on the floor, using both arms to snag a cig. When the smoke was in him, his legs and arms felt lighter already, and he climbed the bed again to drop the dead match out the window.

His hands shook when he finished the cigarette.

He tried to eat the cereal in the kitchen, but it was too dry and tasted like gravel in his mouth. So he put everything in the sink and added the Joy.

It was easy to clean.

While drying the back of the cereal bowl he saw his reflection in it. And a minute later beside his face in the reflection, he saw Jason's face. He said, "Shit," and jumped and turned. His foot missed the stool. His hand went into the water with the towel in it. The dish fell to the floor and broke as what breath was left rushed out of him.

But he was seeing things again that were not there. Jason was not there.

Shouldn't curse, the kid thought.

After everything was clean again, even the crumbs in the hall, his legs were shaking again. He leaned against the chair when he reached for the doorknob. When he set his hand on it he saw reflected in the glass above the doorknob another hand, which he thought was his own, pale and bony as it was, until the second hand came out of the glass, settling around his wrist.

Seeing things.

The kid held his hand against his chest a short while before trying the doorknob again. He needed juice.

He raised his hands when the door was open, closing his eyes and trying to imagine the voices in the winds, trying to call them. But they were no longer his to command. The night before they had tossed him here, tired of him, banging closed cabinets, sweeping clean tile and walls, then leaving him crumbled. They returned to Jason, to be sealed in the casket, away from him.

Already he felt his shoulders withering, bending into and toward each other, his skin, what was left of it, turning brown and hard, crumbling from him as he moved out into the street toward the bus stop.

"Father," the kid said to himself.

————————

The winds were too wild for you.

There was an empty lot on the other side of the hill at the end of the street, where the weeds grew in yellow stalks as tall as the trees, and in thick, reedy bunches, each one topped by a cotton crown of seeds. When the winds blew too hard into the lot, the white tufts lifted from the weeds and broke into a million white wisps thick in the air, weed seeds sweeping, swirling into every garden, through every open window, spreading, smothering the valley floor where you lived.

But the winds were too wild. They would not stop coming to you. They would bring voices and sounds in the night when you were holding your eyes closed to fool them, and the voices would not be singing and talking but instead you heard the sounds of people yelling and screaming and crying out in all the far off places. In the mornings when you woke up, you and your hollow bones were always in a new place. Your breath would always be dry, rasping and rattling in the wake of the winds, your skin crusting and cracked. You would always end up searching for water.

They came when you did not call, and when they did they stole your breath, and carried you with them wherever they would go. Until the day you knew it had gone too far, when you woke up in the sand with a piece of cotton, a weed seed, stuck to your tongue, and more blowing in the sky above you. They had pulled you too far, tossed you too hard, until you slipped out of their hands, away from their fingers, falling faster than they could follow. You went over a cliff, tumbling against the rocks down to the sand.

You waited there, not breathing, for a long time, knowing if you even whispered they might discover where you were. You waited there, not breathing, waiting for your fingers and toes to go stiff and begin to crumble into the sand, wanting only for the tide to pull you apart and away where the winds would never find you.

———————

At 112 Jubilee Way, in Venice Beach, California, the black coils were laid neatly now, curled and piled like garden hoses in the hall outside of her door. In the mornings, all the untangling always seemed to have taken care of itself, everything put back in order. Each step Adriel took forward was clumsy and wooden, the strings, which were attached invisibly to her arms and legs, lifting off their piles, dragging and scraping, ugly noise, on the hall floor behind her. Her leg lifted at the end of the hall and she turned with it, against her will crossing back down the hall, past her apartment door to the apartment door further down. Her hand was pulled to the doorknob by one thin, black line. She yanked it back, and, feeling the resistance, enjoying it, she crossed the hall again. She tried to wipe the strings away from her hands but succeeded only in smearing them, making them worse and tangling them in the wind chimes, which clattered chaotically and brought a strange blush to her face.

Adriel stopped herself. And turned and took three steps backward before stopping again, and turning again, and running for the gate. She held out her arms, catching the threads on the planters, the junipers, and the post. When she dashed through the empty, quiet yard, and when she pulled open the gate, she felt a burning in the back of her neck and heard the chimes ringing sharply. The hall behind her was a mess of black strands, the web thickest outside her front door. She pulled her head forward, and when she felt the line connected to her neck snap, she smiled, and the wind chimes crashed to the ground and were dragged into the black knotted pile at the end of the hall before they were silent.

She'd been feeling ill again. She'd been tired and emotional. She thought when she woke up in the morning that she was gong to start feeling really sick again.

Feeling is as good as being, she thought.

She was having nightmares again. It was all that time spent inside with Paul, in the quiet, where nothing happened and all the excitement, all the dreams passed by. People had to change themselves. At some point, they had to grow up and change. And then they would know better.

She wished to herself as she stepped off the curb and the gate slammed closed that somehow the back of the building would simply not be there when she returned, with Paul's apartment fallen into some hole, cleansed and removed.

The bus brakes shrieked out from across the street, and there was a final puff as it stopped. The squeaking wheels of a shopping cart being pushed along the boardwalk by an old man made her toes curl pleasantly in her pumps. And she sighed. The old man pushing the cart looked at her first, then whistled at the rag lady sleeping against the fence. Two skateboards passed by the old man, the waves thundered further back, and she could hear from around the corner the sound of the Hare Krishnas drumming and singing. She straightened her skirt, tossed her head back. It was so unnaturally quiet in the yard inside the gate, and so noisy outside. And Paul always wanted to stay in. A door opened across the street, and for a moment or two heavy metal music spilled out to the street. She felt her heart beat faster. The sun felt wonderful on her face and on her legs.

When she stepped up on the far curb and she saw the little blond boy coming off the bus, a cold wind rose off the beach, for a moment freezing her in her tracks. And, of course, she was wearing a skirt. The chill ran up her legs, and her chest tightened, the wind almost caressing her hair. The blond boy was staring at her and smiling. Paul would see him out the window and he would start talking about having kids with Adriel, as if that would solve everything.

The boy snickered and said, "Hey, sweet chili," and when she saw he was blushing, she had to laugh. She rubbed her hand in his hair when she passed him getting onto the bus.

Paul was always saying something stupid, trying to tell her what kind of person he was, what he was going to do, how far he was going to go. Always talking, talking, droning on, explaining, never listening to himself, never really leaving his apartment. At first she thought it was easy to see he wanted more. But she guessed that she had finally started listening to what he was really saying.

I guess I have high expectations. That's what my mother always said. I'm sure you remember telling me you didn't want anyone to count on you. That was your big message for the day. Just talking, though. Well, I don't want any part of anything like that. There are better things. It was just like you to find your voice at the end of the play, at the end of everything, after the most miserable hour of silence when I could not force myself to talk to you or look at you, an hour of keeping my eyes on the stage.

You waited until the audience was clapping and standing and the curtains were dropping for the second time and the cheering sound was flowing over us, distracting me, to finally say something, to ask what I was doing, to ask me what was happening. Far too little, I guess. It was easier to put on my coat and pretend I didn't hear you. I knew you wouldn't ask again.

Bye Love,

Adriel

———————

Fucking art majors, Paul Ivers thought.

He crumpled the note after Adriel got on the bus, after the bus pulled away, and tossed it over the edge of the balcony, where maybe she would find it when she came back from her adventures in the real world and she realized she had to sleep alone.

Paul only liked Adriel because she reminded him of Shelley. But some people had to fuck with everything. Nothing was good enough the way it was. Everyone wants something, he thought, and by the time you realize you're being parceled out and losing your ground, you're lucky if you have anything left.

A black BMW pulled into the bus stop, with five or six guys in it, all of them in coats and ties and dress shoes. Frat dicks on parade, from the look of it, he thought.

Paul shifted the deck chair. Jason and he got in late the night before, and Paul was going to go to Jason's room with him— both because Jason asked and because Paul felt like he owed Jason. Jason seemed totally distracted, so when Paul saw the deck chair out at the top of the stairs, and saw that there were towels out, too, he told Jason he wanted to sleep there and wake up with the sun on him.

Paul watched the blond kid cross the street. The wind had turned so cold he had to put his shirt back on.

He's the greatest little kid. Beautiful, too. Jason's little sidekick.

When the kid sat down on the curb and pulled an apple out of his jacket, Paul couldn't stop looking at him. He looked like a little king. He rubbed his apple, holding it in front of him, staring at it, licking his lips, maybe seeing his face in it, almost as if he was not sure whether or not to eat it. It was a relief, somehow, when he bit into it. Paul could even hear the crunch.

Shelley was John's girlfriend. Paul fell in love with her the first time he met her, after John had been dating her for five or six months. Shelley was too good for John. She was too smart, too funny, too sexy, and it was obvious John didn't treat her right, didn't tell her every day that she was beautiful, didn't hold her hand or touch her arm or whisper I love you in her ear every morning and every night.

They doubled on a date. And for some reason, John was scamming on Paul's date. That one was Kim. The one who always said I don't think so, who always wanted to know when she was going to be getting something out of their relationship.

They ended up all four of them skinny-dipping together in the ocean. When they came back to the house, John somehow pulled it so that Shelley and Paul had to rinse off in the shower together. Shelley didn't deserve that. Paul was going to keep his hands and his eyes to himself, but by the time they were in the shower they were so close together and he was hard against her stomach, their hands all soaped up and wet, sliding over each other until John's voice at the doorway surprised Paul and Paul fell back against the wall dizzy and shaking and flushed.

They all traded places then. And while Shelley and Paul were drying off, he watched her lift her leg onto a foot stool to run her towel along it. Paul leaned over her and ran his lips lightly up her spine, at the same time sliding two fingers into her from behind. Shelley moaned and pressed her hips back, lifting them, and Paul pulled out his fingers and fucked her that way for five minutes more, quickly, until the water in the shower turned off.

They didn't have time to finish, and promised each other to do so later, but Kim came out of the shower looking displeased and shortly thereafter Paul was alone on the couch jerking off while John and Shelley had make-up sex.

Paul rolled over on his stomach and tried not to think of the whole debacle. For a while, it was enough to watch the blond kid.

He's got to be cold, Paul thought. He needs someone who will take better care of him.

The kid ate the whole apple, spitting out the seeds when he got to them, then playing with the stem on the tip of his tongue. Once he finished with that, he walked over to the corner of the gate on the sidewalk, where the rag lady was lying.

Jason was tossing rocks at her this morning, when they came in, and laughing about it. Jason, Paul thought, can be a sick bastard.

The kid said to the rag lady, "you're going to have to do better than that if you want to convince anyone of anything."

The rag lady did not answer. She didn't this morning, either, even when the biggest rock hit her. Jason laughed at Paul when Paul said he thought he saw her fingers moving a little. Jason said that it was the weed confusing him.

The kid reached into her rags and pulled out a bottle, pouring what was left of it on the ground beside her, so that the dark liquor inside ran under her rags. He reached in again, pulled out another bottle, and was just beginning to unscrew the cap when she woke up and yelled for him to stop. The kid stepped back from her and tossed the bottle over her head, over the fence, into the back yard. The rag lady swung at him, but the kid jumped away easily.

He said to her, "I own the winds, old lady. I own the winds."

She swung again, and he jumped up on the boardwalk wall,

pulling another apple from his pocket, making as if he was going to throw it at her. Paul had to smile because the kid looked so fierce and proud.

The rag lady stood to her full height, and bits of sand, and rock, and pebbles rained down from her rags to the sidewalk under her feet.

She said, "I see your winds. No winds at all. That's what you have."

The kid's face screwed down real angry, and he threw the apple at her, whipping his hand hard. It landed in the folds of cloth covering her stomach, and it didn't look like she even felt it hitting her. She caught the apple when it fell out, bringing it up to her mouth quickly.

She said, "I have my teeth. I have my teeth. See if you can do any better," she said, and laughed.

The kid ran over to the gate, and Paul decided to go down to his room at the same time he heard the kid's foot on the first step. When they passed on the stairs and Paul said hello and smiled, the kid was too shy even to look up at him, and he ran the rest of the steps to the second story without a word.

Paul shrugged. It wasn't as if he didn't have other things to do. And now he had some money in his pocket. The scene at the play the night before was bad, but things came out all right afterward. Jason saved him from being left alone. He talked Paul into ripping off twenty empty kegs from the storage area at Teaser's and returning them for cash deposits all over town. And on top of that, the bud Jason had was choice.

A lot of little projects going, Paul thought as he passed Adriel's apartment door. The lease on his room was up in June, and not soon enough at that. The room was a pit. Toilet seat backup smelled like shit. That and the mildewed carpet. His mattress had three burns in it, pretty much useless. He didn't know why he always ended up in places like this.

When he reached door number four at the end of the hall

and he realized he was being watched, he looked over at the gate, toward the ocean, and standing there was the rag lady. With her hands wrapped around two of the black iron bars, the dark rags on her arms draped down like feathers.

"How did I know you would be there," Paul said.

The rag lady smiled and said, "Perhaps I summoned you."

———————

Jason came to you from the ocean, passing by where you were lying in the sand.

He said, "You look like you need a hand."

"Bigger than you," you said, and Jason went away over the sand. Every night after he came out of the water, Jason returned, sometimes walking close enough for a drop of water to slide off of his chest and into your dry mouth. Every night your answer was the same.

But you started following the trail of cigarette butts Jason left stubbed in the sand behind him. Every night you got a little farther from your place on the beach, always moving in the night so the winds would not notice your movement.

The cigarette butts on the sidewalk were the hardest for you to follow, because they rolled into the cracks mostly, and it was hard to tell which way they originally pointed.

One night you reached the apartment building on Jubilee. One night you went up the stairs to the quiet yard, thinking that this one time only you were going to look in his windows. And when you reached the top step, when you were staring down the hall toward his door, you smelled in the air the same smell of cigarettes you had been following in the sand. You looked over, and Jason was seated there on his throne, watching you, smoke coming out of his nose.

He said, "Can't stay away, can you?" His chest was bare and broad and rising, and you could feel the power of his breathing, the strength and control behind his upper lip. His eyes flashed and the cigarette smoke curled very precisely under his lifted finger and he smiled. And you bent down on your knee.

"I'll be your friend," Jason said then.

Later, he told you he thought it was wrong for one boy and one boy alone to have to hold all the winds. He said, "Every boy needs to be free." He said, "I will show you how to hold the winds."

He said, "Close your eyes now, and summon the winds." You felt his large hands moving on your arm, and felt even with your eyes closed the moonlight pouring over you through the bay window as you whispered for the winds.

There was no breeze, no warning for the storm that came down on you. You would have run but the belts held you down and then the table was too high above the floor, lifted by the winds, and you knew nothing would catch you if you fell. So you listened to the winds screaming until there was a pop and a pinch in your arm. And you felt in all those winds one single breeze being stripped away. And the winds left and you felt better. Jason sealed that one breeze in the casket.

This was the way Jason peeled the winds from you. Night after night you would summon the winds at his command and night after night he would remove only one wind. Each night he would take that wind and shut it in the casket.

"They're easier to hold in your hand," Jason said, "but first we have to peel them all away."

He told you that you were not ready to be master of the winds on the last day, when finally there were no more winds to be called. You were shaking and weak and tired when he closed the casket for the last time, locking it with a silver key you had never seen before. And he set the casket up high, out of your reach. He told you that was how you held the winds.

Then he told you that you were beautiful.

On Jubilee Way, Jason Sloane thought that things had been touch and go, touch and go lately. Too little touch, too much go, and he wasn't even going to try to figure out why or who was behind it until later. But somebody was fucking around. His connection, Sashia, wasn't taking his calls, and wasn't calling him back.

Twice this month, Jason thought, my line has been lighter, definitely lighter.

The knock on his door scared him back to reality. He didn't hear anyone coming up the stairs, only that fuck-up Paul going down. And the fear Jason felt clinched it. That, he decided before opening the door, was the instinct to trust. It was time to clear out.

When he opened the door, he got angry, because he suddenly realized who it was.

"I thought I told you to get lost, Jarhead," Jason said.

The wind was kicking up outside, and really cold. He would need to bring a jacket.

The kid tried to push his way in the door, but Jason shoved him back against the railing. When the kid straightened himself up, Jason could still see the attitude. He closed the door and went to the kitchen. Made himself a cup of hot chocolate and packed all the stuff into his stash box, which he set on the table after twice making sure it was locked.

Coming down to it, the stash box was really all he needed.

When he came back and opened the door again, the kid was, of course, still standing there. In a couple of years, Jason thought, when I'm finished with him, he'll be a young stud. Already was. And that was an E ticket if anything was. Solid property.

The kid said, "I don't have anywhere to go."

Jason said, "Who told you that already?"

The kid looked down at his feet.

Jason said, "Who helps you out, man?"

Jason knelt on one knee in front of the kid, put his hand on his shoulder, and squeezed. The kid tried to pull away, but Jason shook him up a little and squeezed tighter until the kid stopped resisting and took it.

Jason said, "Who do you always try to hurt? And who always takes you back?"

———————

The rag lady said, "It's better to choose while you still can, to commit to something you want. It's better than having to choose later from only those things you have left. It's better to let someone choose for you at those times when you can't choose yourself."

Paul nodded his head, yeah, yeah, because he knew she couldn't see him around the junipers. He picked up the bottle from the weeds in the corner. The rag lady's voice made him uncomfortable. All he wanted was to toss the bottle over the fence, so she had to run off to chase it. All he wanted was to be in his room above the first floor, and for her to be gone. The chilly breeze had turned into a strong, cold wind, shaking the palm leaves above the building, kicking up sand on the beach behind the rag lady.

She said, "I can show you a place. I can offer you a reward you will never have to share. I'm on my way to join the others," she said, "before the wars begin."

Paul slowed down as he walked toward her.

She said, "Let me make this choice for you and you will never have any regret."

She reached one of her rag-covered hands between the bars.

She said, "I know the way and need only someone to guide."

———————

Jason pulled the kid inside. His eyes were hungry. Obviously needing juice. When he started looking around the room like a hungry little animal, Jason slapped his head, knocking him into the hall table.

Jason said, "I made it clear, didn't I? You will get what you deserve when I decide you've earned it."

"Yes," the kid said.

Jason said, "Either I can count on you and you can count on me, or we don't count on each other at all."

"Yes," the kid said. And Jason's finger fumbled at his belt buckle before he could unlatch it.

"Can I still count on you?"

The kid said, "Yes," but his eyes shifted away a little and Jason knocked him again, this time using the belt.

When the kid answered, "yes" again, Jason believed he meant it.

Jason heard creaking far off in the back of his head, creaking like he should have heard before when the kid came to the door. Lots of creaking on the stairs. Jason opened the hall closet, and pulled his gun from the top shelf. He picked the kid up off the floor, wrapping the belt around his neck.

"We're in this together," Jason said in the kid's ear. "You and me," Jason whispered all the way to the door, with the gun at the kid's head. Jason couldn't tell if he heard something or if it was just the wild winds outside.

Jason's eyes settled on the stash box, and he knew that was what the kid was thinking about too. But for a second, Jason was distracted because he thought he saw shadows at the west windows and he snapped the belt loop tight a half a beat late. The kid butted his head hard into Jason's chin. He pulled the belt from Jason's hand, but Jason snagged his elbow, and swung it back until he felt and heard the crack.

"Stupid kid," Jason said, even as he saw there were five definite shadows at the window. The next thing he knew, the kid was all over him, his little fingers coming at Jason's face, his teeth flashing.

He pushed Jason back into the wall. Jason's head slammed,

and he felt burning where the kid, using his teeth, broke the skin of his shoulder through the shirt. The kid kicked him in the stomach, just missing his balls, and his little hand pulled at his lip, yanking it up past his nose before two fingers sank into Jason's right eye.

Jason knocked the kid off him, and when the kid fell backward, Jason felt something snap hard against the back of his neck.

The kid didn't even seem to touch the floor, but instead kept moving toward the back window. Jason lifted his gun at the same time he heard glass breaking across the whole living room.

Fireworks exploded around him and suddenly he was twitching, twisting, shaking, moving retardedly with a hundred stinging pains. The kid swept across the room toward the window and Jason saw how hard the winds were blowing and now he understood it wasn't fireworks he heard but thunder, the storm being called like the kid said. And the kid was the eye, sweeping with the stash box in his hands into and through the window, the books flying off their shelves in his wake, the plants falling over, turning sideways sucked out in his tailwind, the door banging open, magazines pulled off the shelves, the furniture, the glass. The lightning struck Jason again and again and again and even his drops of blood were drawn behind the kid into the blue white void as Jason's face slapped against the cold, hard floor.

Someone, he thought, someone at the door . . .

The bottle was just at her fingertips when the rag lady screamed at the sound of what could only be gunfire coming from the apartment building, deafeningly loud. Paul dropped the bottle, at the same time getting a full blast of wet sandy air in his face, before he looked up at the second floor and saw those five guys, who were too old, he could see now, to be frat boys. And they all had guns, pointed into and firing through Jason's windows. Fucking yuppie mobsters, Paul thought.

He ran for the back of the house, for the back gate, at the same time the back window of Jason's place exploded outward. A clump of wet rags rolled past Paul's feet as the kid came tumbling out in the middle of a shower of glass. And the guns were still going.

The kid rolled on the lawn, and Paul could see he had Jason's stash box in his arms, held tightly against his chest. A bloody key on the end of a bloody chain flashed in the sun before the kid stuck it into the box. The lid lifted off at the same time the gunfire ended and Paul heard sirens rising a couple of streets over.

Baggies and vials emptied out of the box, mixing with the rags and glass, rolling, dragging in the grass. Paul heard feet pounding across the hallway above, feet pounding down the stairs.

The kid grabbed a vial, sticking it between his knees, fumbling at the same time with his left hand and his teeth to open a syringe packet, which caught in the wind and was pulled away from him. The kid's right arm looked pretty sketchy. He reached across the grass with his left hand for another packet.

Paul grabbed the kid under his shoulders, knocking everything out of his hands. The yard was a whirlwind of glass and plastic, flashing and reflecting the sun, rags tumbling over and over each other.

Paul heard gunfire out in the street in front as he ran the rest of the way to the gate. Once they were out of the yard and away, running over the boardwalk to the beach, Paul whispered in the kid's ear, "I'm going to take care of you."

The kid turned in his arms, and without looking at Paul, with his little eyes closed tight, he wrapped his left arm, and his right arm as best he could, around Paul, and hugged him, his whole body trembling.

Paul tried to run a little faster in the sand.

END PRELIMINARY REPORT

Chapter 8

White Harbor University
March 18

Eric was awake and already restless by the time the kid finally started moving around. He was ready and waiting with a cup of water when he woke up.

And Eric was looking forward to trying some more of his Spanish.

But when the kid opened his eyes, it wasn't a peaceful awakening. More like a cat being startled out of sleep by the slamming of a door. He was up on the cot on hands and knees in an instant, alert, and backing himself slowly off the cot and toward the corner of the room while he searched out the exits.

Ready to bolt.

Eric stood still.

He did not seem at all the same kid Eric met the night before. He didn't even look the same. Last night he was bubbling. Now in his face there was nothing less than fear, and in the curve of his upper lip there was also something like anger.

Maybe that was just a dream I had last night, Eric thought, with the Spanish and everything. He waited a little longer, and then held the cup out to the boy.

The kid took it carefully, then gulped it down.

It isn't going to be so bad, Eric told himself. It's just a little kid. I can help him out of this. I can figure this out.

The kid set down the glass, and asked Eric, this time in English, without any kind of accent, if Eric had a cigarette.

———

Letter dated March 15, with March 18 Mexico City postmark

My Dearest Evelyn,

Sweet Serendipity has cast her glance my way, though I did neither recognize nor appreciate her attentions until long after our bus had arrived in Villacuerda. My only thought at the time was that I had to keep myself from screaming until I stood again on solid ground. My body, my mind, my very senses were so addled by the road here that only now, almost a week later, have I regained my equilibrium; I literally felt as if I had been shaken to pieces—physically, emotionally, spiritually. Imagine me wedged for two days between chickens and crying children on my way to what I am expecting to be a mildly pleasurable spiritual retreat and you'll understand that I very nearly suffered a nervous breakdown . . .

Certainly, Villacuerda is not in any form a pleasure resort. The terrain is high desert, the town isolated, the days dry and warm, and the accommodations primitive. It has the air of a town abandoned, much like the ghost towns left behind up north after the gold mines petered out. There are also many indications to be found of earlier inhabitants—carvings and tunnels and long-empty living spaces cut into the rocky mountainsides. There is an enchantment and a sense of timelessness to the terrain, a character unaffected, I suspect, by any who might settle here. So I think I have convinced myself the conditions are not so bad as they could be. We're in the hills, so there is an occasional breeze, and the nights can even be rather brisk. As opposed to the stark plains below, there is some brush here lending color to the locale; there are even occasional clusters of trees to catch some shade under if you really need it; and really, there is nothing like sleeping on a stone slab for a back like mine.

Evelyn, the stars are so beautiful at night.

For the most part, the town appears to function as a rest stop at the convergence of a handful of mountain trails. There is an air of impermanence to the downtown area, where properties and businesses (there are only nine such enterprises currently operating in the area) apparently have a high turnover rate. It is a very poor region; most of the population avoids this area I am in because there is very little offered here which they can afford, and there are not enough tourists from whom they can hope to make a dollar. There are hints the place may be undergoing the beginnings of an entrepreneurial new-age renovation—mostly billboards marking sites of future construction—but my happy impression is that things don't change too fast here, whether or not a person sets out with that purpose in mind. Everybody blames it on the warm weather and that soul-breaking road.

Today there are a number of curious new faces in town, from the look of them locals all, strolling along the Navajo-colored trail just off the porch on which I am seated. Although I've been told on several occasions that Villacuerda has a population of several thousand, I have been finding such numbers hard to corroborate, being that I've not seen more than fifty or sixty people in my short time here, and I've seen no other place where several thousand people might be living other than among the brush and bramble in the gullies between the hills.

Evidently, there are more people out today because the word is out. We're all waiting for a woman named Maya to arrive.

Evelyn, therein lies the story I could not wait to tell you. For here in Villacuerda, I am witnessing and taking part (albeit vicariously) and sharing with all those around me an occurrence that will one day be passed along and written down and eventually written off as urban myth, as lore of the southwest, or worse, as more new-age hoopla. Quite simply, I expect the day to end in a miracle, if it is not a miracle already that has happened here.

With that flourish, I will explain.

This story begins the day prior to our arrival, with a party of 15 people making the three-hour trek to Puerta de la Reina, which is also called the Burnt Spot. I've heard it is a most arduous journey, which is why I have not yet made the trip myself. I wanted to regain my strength.

On this tour of the Burnt Spot were three young girls. They are now seated at a table not ten feet from where I sit. Their names are Kaitlin, Divinia, and Sarah. Kaitlin is the only child of an Australian archaeologist at work on a dig at a site east of town, a woman I have not yet met. Divinia lives with her grandmother in Villacuerda while her parents are working in the States; she hasn't seen them in over two years. Divinia and Kaitlin are close friends who can usually be found playing somewhere around town, and Kaitlin frequently spends the night with Divinia and her grandmother. Sarah is the child of an Indian couple with whom I have had the pleasure of sharing several conversations in the last few days. They are both teachers, and are planning on backpacking north from here as far as Oregon before the summer.

Kaitlin and Divinia, having visited Puerta de la Reina a number of times before, separated from the group at the site, and headed south along the shore to pick among the rocks for shells and crabs and anything else they might find there, a sort of ritual with the two. Along the way, they stopped at one of the remnants of the wall that marked the southern edge of the town.

Kaitlin found there, lodged in a shallow nook, a small, square, rough-edged stone with carvings on it.

A short time later, the two were seated at the water's edge, admiring Kaitlin's find, with Divinia apparently feeling quite unhappy not to have found something special of her own. At a moment when she was feeling especially envious of Kaitlin, she looked up the shore at the same time the sun caught and flashed on something lying there in the sand, something newly revealed by the outgoing tide. As Divinia tells it, in her breathless manner (she is a very expressive child, very precocious), she looked up, and the mother ocean winked at her in answer to her prayers. Kaitlin witnessed none of this because she was busy studying her stone. Regardless, when Divinia went to see what was there on the shore, she found a piece almost identical to Kaitlin's, also with writing on it.

After their excitement at the coincidence had died down, they thought little more of their pieces than how nice it was that they both had found one, continuing on with their day until they heard the whistles blowing and returned to the former center of the town to meet the group for the trek back. They were showing their finds to the tour guide, a lovely local woman named Julia, when Sarah and her family returned from the northern side of town, where they had spent much of their day.

When they arrived, Sarah was cradling in her hand a strange little rock with markings on it. It matched almost exactly the stones found on nearly the opposite side of the settlement by Kaitlin and Divinia.

The girls quickly compared their finds. This all occurred with an air of novelty, as it was no great event to come across an artifact or two of the town that had once been there. The three stood in a circle, their hands a tangle in between them as they passed the pieces one to the other and around to the next, turning them over and over in silence until finally one of them said, "There."

To the amazement of the entire group—twelve people who had slowly gathered around these 13-year-old girls—they revealed, held in between them, three-quarters of a stone tablet. The pieces they had found fit together perfectly.

Julia was able to translate the carvings for the group. It was a contract, a simple promise cut crudely into a stone tablet, one of the sort of documents of friendship little girls make with each other when they are young and afraid of being separated; short and to the point, promising eternal friendship and devotion.

At the bottom, there were four signatures. Their first names remained only; the missing quarter held the last names.

After Julia read the names aloud, the girls reformed their circle, and went around one by one saying the names out loud and giggling, until Kaitlin stopped and said she was claiming the third name on the list as her own. Divinia and Sarah chose from the remaining three. And then around in a circle they went again, calling each other by these chosen names, laughing and laughing and laughing until all of the sudden they were crying, and then hugging and then, just as suddenly, they were falling against each other and sobbing uncontrollably in each other's arms. I've spoken to the entire party in the last five days—I've been quite a nuisance—and they've all said the same thing: it made their collective hair stand on end.

When things had settled down, Kaitlin asked out loud about the remaining, unclaimed name on the list.

"So then," she said, "where is Maya? Who will be Maya?"

When they got back to town later that evening, and the story was told and retold across Villacuerda, they found a possible answer. This is the very woman who is supposed to arrive today. Messages were already going in and out between Villacuerda and the town where she now lives by the time we had arrived.

As you can imagine, this chain of events has sparked near continuous debate and discussion; the matter weaves itself in and out of every conversation, staying alive until the last ember in the last campfire is put out at night. Much has been made of the fact that all three girls share the same birth date, exactly one year and one month after the floods that overtook Puerta de la Reina; the conclusion has been drawn that all but one of the girls named on the tablet died in that storm, Maya being the only survivor. The most agreed upon interpretation is that these three living girls obviously had some bond with the spirits of three others who were now dead. Some believe Kaitlin, Divinia, and Sarah are those three reincarnated; I am not inclined to accept such a tidy conclusion, but I haven't bothered to engage anyone in a debate on the specifics of the matter.

For the most part, these events have lent the town a rather jubilant spirit. Just about the only ones unaffected, of course, are the three principals, who fairly convincingly carry on as if they are oblivious to the attention, even somewhat resentful at the intrusion of being the center of our interest. You know how it is at that age—they'd rather be left to their own devices.

As you can no doubt imagine, it has been a most exhilarating week for an old woman who was starting to think she had seen it all. There is no telling when (or even if) Maya will arrive, but you can be sure we will be waiting.

I promise you will be hearing from me again soon. I hope you are well; I wish you could be here with me . . .

All My Love
Regina

White Harbor University

Eric and the kid were standing in the snow looking out across the Plaza. There was a guy somewhere out there with a microphone promising that everyone who wished to be heard would be heard, for the simple price of a one-dollar donation to be made at the Pan-Hellenic booth at the northeastern corner of the shantytown.

The speaker was right. It was a shantytown. The Plaza, the fountain, the lawn, all of it had disappeared under a vast structure of interconnected pieces of cardboard and wood. It was impossible even to see what it might be like inside, because the whole thing was covered by a loose patchwork of tarps, plastic drop cloths, and trash bags, all intended, Eric supposed, to keep out the snow and the rain.

There were several entrances and exits into the structure, and there were crowds of people streaming in and out of those, past trinket vendors who were still arranging their wares and club organizers who were handing out leaflets. People were crowding into the shantytown, and, while there was still some breathing space outdoors, that, too appeared to be dwindling fast. Some of the people were townies, but most of them were students. It looked like his mother's little ant farm was getting a bit out of control.

"Let's go," Eric said.

Then they were on their way.

Eric made a point of noting the location of Brother Matthew's kiosk before they headed into the mess. After yesterday's weird-out, he thought it best to steer clear of the god guy.

"You be the scout," he said to the kid, who was watching the crowd in open-mouthed silence, "so I don't get lost. We're going to be heading straight to and through the parking lot over there, and right into town."

The kid didn't say anything.

The windows on Eric's mom's floor of the administration building were all still closed, the shutters drawn.

She wasn't even here yet.

Eric picked the kid up, set him on his shoulders. Rested— for the first time in a long time—he was strong enough to carry him. Not that there was that much to the kid—he was all skin and bones.

"I guess I need to bring you someplace." Eric tried to look up at him, but he couldn't tilt his head back far enough to see him. While he was trying, flecks of dirt were falling on his face. He looked down at his shoulders, at his shirt, and saw it was already all over him, the copper-colored dust even streaking his pants.

The thing was, the kid was the one doing it, brushing himself off. All over Eric. There was probably a trail of it they had left behind them, too.

"You couldn't do that while you were still on the ground?"

"It wasn't bothering me then."

"Did you hear what I said?"

"What?" Eric recognized the tone right off. It was that difficult kid thing he was doing. Not listening.

"Is there someone who I can bring you to? Someone you feel safe with? Or somewhere? Like your . . . "

(*Mother*, the boys thinks, seeing in a faint and fast dying
flash in his mind's eye that her hair had bounced shining all around
her back when she said she had already warned him twice she
would stay only if he would go to the rehab center.)

Right before Eric was about to repeat himself again, the
boy started whispering in his ear.

Eric jumped.

"You scared the fucking shit out of me." He found he was
whispering, too.

"My mother knew a bad man," the boy said, and the feel
of his breath gave Eric goose bumps on his neck. "She knew one
day he would come to kill me after I was born. So she hid me from
him. And because she was afraid he would find her and force her to
tell him where I was, she hid herself from both of us. We're never
supposed to know where the other one is . . . "

"So your dad did this to you?"

He covered Eric's mouth with his small hand.

(The sky trembled overhead. The winds were here because
they too were afraid, the boy thought. He let go of the strange
man's head and held his hands up waving to get their attention. But
they didn't answer to him anymore. His father gave him the winds
one night, opened his mouth blew them right in. He thought at
the time his father loved him but maybe his father knew the winds
would tear him apart from the inside the way they did.)

"He is everywhere." Again with the whispers.

"Your dad is."

Maybe it was too soon to start pushing too hard.

"Okay, then, what about this Paul guy you mentioned last
night?"

(Paul saved him.)

"My friend." Finally, he wasn't whispering.

"Who is he?"

"He takes care of me."

"Doing a great fucking job of it."

He didn't say anything.

"He's not the guy who did this to you?"

"No."

"And he's not your dad?"

(The boy remembered there were angels there.)

"No."

The boy leaned up and away from Eric, which meant, Eric guessed, that he thought the conversation was over. There was some kind of commotion coming up on their right, and the second Eric saw that Brother Matt was at the center of it, he veered to the left. Some frat people were circling around Brother Matt, booing him as he made his way through the crowd, his eyes darting around, his face without expression. The yellow security jackets were already on the scene, keeping themselves alongside him as he continued forward, doing a little crowd control, making sure no one got hurt and in the process giving Brother Matt a sort of official air, as if they were escorting him wherever he wanted to go.

The sign he was carrying was what was upsetting everyone. Some of the more daring guys were even trying to snatch it from Brother Matt's hands. It was the last thing any frat boy or girl at WHU wanted brought up: the beating some of their alumni administered years ago to someone who had basically gotten lost and stumbled into their midst. The sign said her name. It read: REMEMBER CARLIE LONG.

Which Eric had to admit was pretty cool, especially since it was obvious that it still pissed them off to hear about it.

Stupid fucks, Eric thought.

"Well," Eric said as they walked on and away from the Plaza, "where is this Paul guy now?"

"That's what we're going to find out," the kid said.

Once they were in the parking lot, Eric lifted the kid up and off his shoulders and set him on the ground.

Then Eric took a good long look at him.

The sight made Eric think that however it was that he had ended up with his mother, he was lucky to have landed there.

This one looked like a little dirt boy. There were places he'd tried to wipe off that were still smeared, like his face and his hands, but mostly it was caked on heavy all over him. Eric still had no idea what the boy really looked like under all that junk.

When the kid was finished smearing the dirt around on his right arm, he held the arm out for Eric to see.

It took Eric a minute to notice what he wanted Eric to see.

It took Eric a moment to see the marks there.

He's got tracks on his arm, too, Eric thought.

Eric looked down at his own arm, thinking he would show it to the boy to let him know they had more in common than the kid might think, forgetting the fix he'd gotten yesterday until he saw the red mark.

Eric covered it with his other hand before the kid saw it, pulled his arm away, hid it at his side.

The kid didn't see a thing. He was staring at his own arm.

"This is how I lost the winds," he said.

If Eric closed his eyes right then, he thought he would be able to recall exactly the sensation of anticipation, the tingle that he got in his chest and the lump in his stomach right before the needle sank in.

———

Villacuerda, Mexico
March 18

5:15 pm

On the trail down from Villacuerda to Puerta de la Reina, Regina's tour group had been on a harmonious chord—they had moved in a close pack, the conversation had been engaging, and the pace had been brisk. It seemed they all shared something in common now, having all played the role of witness to the days and nights Maya and the three girls had spent together amongst them. They had all experienced the same electric thrill when Maya sat down at the table on the porch of the dry goods store with Divinia, Kaitlin, and Sarah, and set her piece of the tablet in its place at the center of the table where the other three pieces were already seated, assembled. When she slid her stone into place, the contract was made whole.

Now, it seemed, while the story remained to be told and retold, the intensity of that moment was dissipating, and slowly, slowly, the currents of everyday life again taking hold. Maya would in fact be gone by the time their party returned to town. She had promised to return in a month for services to be held commemorating the 14th anniversary of the tragedy. Sarah's family had been hinting that they'd fallen behind in their travel schedule, and Regina was sure they would be leaving in the next day or two. Kaitlin and Divinia were intent on attending the memorial alongside Maya, and indeed, it seemed many in their tour group, including Regina, were considering altering their travel plans that they might attend as well.

The day had also started with the promise of a sky clear and blue to the horizon.

Now, although the rain had not yet begun, there were only clouds to be seen.

Their group was now spread across the miles of the route back. There were some who had already begun the uphill portion of the trail that was the last link to Villacuerda. It had been a somber journey home, with hardly a word said between any of them.

Puerta de la Reina weighed heavily on their minds.

It was as utterly devastated a landscape as Regina had ever seen—barren but for the black stumps of dead trees dotting the prairies of cracked silt, and the remnants of the perimeter walls. It was a place where still not even a weed of green appeared to grow. Regina's first thought upon seeing the city had been to wonder why, in all the stories she'd heard in this last week, none of them had mentioned the oppressive weight that hung over that place, the terrible sadness in the air.

Julia, their tour guide, had walked them about and told them stories of a childhood in Puerta de la Reina, of farmers and soldiers and orphanages and garment factories and colored boats down on the sun-speckled water. Regina had only been able to stare at this young woman in disbelief, unable to attach her picturesque remembrances to the harsh physical reality around them.

"The government offered to set the land aside as a reserve and a memorial for the people of the area, many of them relatives of those who died," Julia was explaining to what remained of their group. "Of course, the port was unusable because of the storm, and there were many bodies still to be unearthed and identified and properly buried. In addition, there had been extensive salt-mining up the coast during the seventies . . . and years after the rain had ended we realized that both salt and much of the attendant excavation waste, which had simply been dumped in pockets in between the hills, leaked into the soil and had been spread by the waters across this entire valley. The salt was at such high concentrations that it killed most every plant before it could start to re-grow. As it had always been, the people here were left to face these problems alone.

"And while the Mexican government would unofficially acknowledge the gift of the land as an apology, the apology was not to be made public, and the conditions of the agreement were that neither side would specify exactly what the apology was for."

When Julia said the word apology, Regina thought perhaps she understood the girl's motivation in committing herself to this exercise of forced remembering, an effort that could only promise to harden her.

She does this as penance for the guilt she feels in having

survived, Regina surmised.

"Hello," Julia said, and it was in a tone that abruptly drew Regina from her thoughts. But Julia wasn't speaking to her.

Her words were directed instead at a man on the trail behind them, a man Regina was sure hadn't been with their party when they left town this morning, a man she had not seen before, although she did feel instantly there was something about him that was familiar. He was indeed not the type of man who would be easily overlooked. He was large, broad-shouldered, unshaven, beer-bellied, and dressed in a stained brown suit that must have been 20 years old. He looked and smelled as if he had not bathed in days.

Regina was immediately uncomfortable with the way he examined Julia as he approached their group.

He didn't respond to her as if she had just spoken to him, although obviously, by the smirk on his face, he was aware she had.

He simply walked on by them.

Julia caught up with him, matching his stride, as did Regina, walking somewhat behind them.

Julia asked, "Where did you come from?"

"I joined the party late," Regina heard him say. "I was half an hour behind the group on the way down. I hitched up with everybody for the trip back, but I guess I've got a problem with taking my own pretty time doing things. Sorry about that, Sweetheart. My name is Edge."

When he offered his hand, Regina was sure Julia would not take it.

She didn't seem the type of girl who would answer to "Sweetheart" from a stranger.

But indeed, she did take his hand and shake it.

"Julia."

There was something about the way she said it— something about the way her hand lingered in his hand and her eyes lingered on the man's face . . .

"The pleasure is all mine," Edge said with a lecherous grin.

Regina rolled her eyes. There was simply no accounting for taste.

———————

Eric could see it as his muddy companion's confidence started to waver as they got closer to the harbor; it was pretty clear soon after that the kid really had no clue where he was leading them. He made lots of stops, he looked confused, he said to himself over and over again, "Oh, I know where we are . . . " when Eric knew he didn't.

Eric let him go through the whole routine of realizing he really was lost. After a while, Eric actually started to feel sorry for him.

They stopped at Sid's place when they got down to the apartments near the pier. Sid had a studio one block from the water, and Eric hadn't dropped by for a bit because he'd been so short on cash. Like he never seemed to have any. Like, he couldn't remember the last time he'd gotten his "support" check from his mother.

Eric was hoping he could talk Sid into smoking him out, at the least. Dealers tended to understand. A guy needed to get by.

It turned out Sid was so glad to see Eric—almost inexplicably so—that he gave Eric a couple joints from his cigar box, without Eric even really having to ask. It was strange when he smiled at Eric and handed him the joints—Eric got the impression Sid thought he was dead or something. Sid also gave the kid a cigarette to smoke on the porch while Sid and Eric partied inside and shot the breeze.

Fifteen minutes later there was another knock on the door, and Eric and the kid were on their way out to make room for the next person in line.

Sid's has always been a busy place, Eric thought. Good prices, always a warm atmosphere. In and out.

Eric was on the sidewalk two minutes later looking at the

joints in his hand, thinking he should make himself scarce more often, if this was the reward. A few minutes after that, they were standing on the beach, staring out into the Atlantic.

The kid was quiet while he was looking at the ocean. When he turned and examined the pier, his shoulders drooped, and he bowed down his head.

"This isn't where I should be."

Eric swallowed and waited a minute before agreeing.

"But this is where you are. Did you hold onto those matches Sid gave you?"

He handed them to Eric.

Perfect. Another beat or two and a joint was burning in between Eric's fingers. He felt better already. He studied the boy. He wasn't dumb, Eric thought. He really didn't think the kid was playing him.

This isn't going to be so easy, Eric thought.

The kid looked at the ocean, at the sky above it, at the houses behind them.

" . . . this isn't where I remember," the kid said at last with a shrug. "Everything is in the wrong place. I don't know where to go now."

"Maybe we should just sit down on the sand here and talk about it." Eric was channeling his mother. "Maybe we can figure out what happened. Do you want to try?"

He looked doubtful. But he said okay.

He was actually kind of starting to grow on Eric.

"You have to do me right, okay? I don't want to hear the fairy tale crap anymore, or whatever stories you've made up for yourself. I won't give you a hard time for things that aren't your fault—there is no reason you should be like this. Do you understand that? You deserve better than this. This is a serious situation. You could have died last night if I hadn't found you when I did. So now we're going to do things my way. And we are going to start with you giving me some answers."

Chapter 9

Fourteen Years Ago

Paul had tried to help him from the very start, and not because he wanted something from him. He knew after a while that Paul was not like everybody else. Paul taught him to be like a man, to toughen up, because you never know what the world's got planned for you next, other than there's a good chance anything notable is going to hurt somehow. This was one of the first things Paul had ever said to him, after they had spent most of a day moving south.

The advice had come right before Paul had explained to him that because the two of them had seen the bad-ass gangsters who killed Jason they would have to make themselves scarce if they didn't want to be dead too.

Jason, with all his needles and belts—he was always sticking something into him whether he begged and cried for it or not. Jason had stolen from his veins the very winds that were the only gift given to him by his father the sky king.

Jason had deserved to die for that alone.

He was lucky someone else got to him before his dad did.

Because he wanted to be tough like a man, and they had already lost so much time taking care of his broken arm, he did not tell Paul he was sick until they were far down into the roads of Mexico. After the sweats and the chills and the aches and the pains, after the scabs started itching on his arm until they felt like the tips of matches, on a long road, not a car in sight, he had started shaking, and throwing up, and found he could not walk any further.

Paul had him lie down off the road in the dirt on his back while he went to find help. Paul said before he left that he didn't know where they were going to find help because they hadn't seen anyone in a long time.

He did not remember how long Paul was gone, or if Paul had ever really left; he thought he remembered sometimes Paul was there—he remembered seeing Paul's face looking down over him—and sometimes Paul was not. This was all happening because the bad spirits Jason had put into him did not want to leave his body, and they were messing with his brain to get him to let them stay. All that was clear were the bugs crawling over him and out of him there in the dirt, the roaches on his legs and neck, the ants and the spiders with their long wispy legs that crawled out of his ears and ran races down his arms, the fleas underneath his toenails and the flies, the beetles, and bees, and terrible things he'd never seen before stinging him and biting him and sometimes just scratching him with their feet as they walked.

Until the bad spirits had been driven out, he had to keep screaming to keep them from crawling down his throat.

When he woke up later, he was someplace new, and he didn't know where.

Paul had found them jobs on a small boat moving people and their stuff around, picking the stuff up and taking it up and down the coast to different towns and piers and houses to drop it off. Sometimes they would take tourists or pals of the boss out into the gulf to fish or dive. Every week they would stop at the dock and pick up their instructions—twice a month there would be money for them, too. When they had their days off, they would take a dinghy out to fish, and then later in the afternoon if they'd caught something good they would go along the docks beneath the mansions that lined the cliffs and sell their catch to the cooks and servants who would meet them there.

His hair turned blond and white like Paul's, and they were both very tan.

He liked it when Paul told people they were brothers.

Those were the best days of his life.

Once in a while, when they had a break and they were in the area, Paul would stop in the place he called La Reina. They

never went there for work, because it was not in their territory.
When they got ashore, Paul would give him some change to buy
fruit for lunch, and the two of them would separate for the day.

There were so many children everywhere in La Reina that
he was never afraid the soldiers would notice he did not belong
there among them. On one of their visits to La Reina, when he'd
just left the dinghy and begun walking through town, he came
around a back-street corner, and saw behind an empty building
other kids standing waiting in a line that led to a hole in the wall
that went around the town. Through that hole as he peeked around
the corner, he could hear the sounds of other children laughing
and playing.

In front of the hole were two large boys—the biggest of
all the children there, bigger than he was for sure—standing with
their arms crossed, blocking the entrance. As he watched and
listened, though he could not understand their language, he could
easily tell this was a game they were playing. A game they played
all the time.

A short, heavy boy would approach the person at the
front of the line and ask a question. The whole group in the
line would be listening in, and usually would giggle at both
the question and at what the person standing in front had to
say. Then the short, heavy boy would tell that person to do
something—one boy had to cross himself and say ten hail Marys;
another girl had to sing a short song—in front of the whole line.
With that done, the boys guarding the hole would step aside and
let that person through the wall.

He had watched until the line was gone. Two boys were
turned away, one for having a bad mouth, and the other for
talking back to his teacher, and both of them had run off crying.
Which had made him think maybe they would try to stop him
from getting through if he got in line. Which is why he didn't. As
he was watching, the guards and the questioner went through the
hole, so no one was left on the street.

When he was sure no one else was around to see him, he crept up to the hole. He tried to peek in at the very same time someone on the other side slid down the panel that blocked his view.

At the end of those days, Paul would meet him back at the boat. He was always in a good mood after La Reina, and he usually came back to the dock whistling, with food and cigarettes for them to share, and for the rest of the day they would do nothing else but lie around on the boat smoking cigarettes talking about what they wanted to do, where they wanted to go next . . .

One day Paul said it was time to cut themselves free. He said he never meant to get in this kind of business. Not after what happened in Los Angeles. They had just picked up two small boxes to deliver to one of the mansions up north. They brought along the raft they'd bought from a tourist who'd been heading home; Paul inflated it, and set one of the boxes they were supposed to deliver in it with only some of the food and only some of the water and only some of their stuff. Paul said he'd rather have brought the dinghy, but he was sure they would notice it was gone and get suspicious.

In just a few minutes after the time when Paul said he'd had enough, the two of them were in the raft, rowing themselves away from the boat. Paul said he had kept the one box only because they were going to need to have some kind of nest egg when their cash ran out. Otherwise they would have nothing.

Their boat, which was moving the other way very slowly, and was maybe five hundred yards away, exploded. And exploded again.

"Keep rowing," Paul said to him when he stopped to watch the fiery debris flying up and then falling down into the water.

What was left of the boat sank very fast.

"We're dead people now," Paul said "Just keep rowing."

"We want to put all of this badness behind us."

It was late at night, their second night in La Reina, their new home, when the noises on the other side of the wall began.

The shack they had moved into was attached to the back of the sewing building. There was a tall chain-link fence around the sewing building that ended and began on either side of their shack in the back but did not enclose them or the stables or the gardens. There was a second gate that went around the whole compound, the sewing building, their shack, the gardens, the stables, and the houses and bunkers where the managers lived and the owner sometimes slept.

Their job there was to care for and guard the animals (two cows, four goats, and all the chickens), to tend the gardens that grew the fresh fruits and vegetables for the managers' meals, and to keep the grounds clean.

Paul had laughed a lot the first night the noises started. He had laughed and laughed and when he was done laughing his cheeks turned red as he explained that the women in the sewing building were criminals, and that they were locked inside sewing as punishment for all the bad things they had done. Paul told him the sounds they were hearing at night were the sounds of the seamstresses agonizing after endless hours of work as they prepared themselves for bed in time that they would be rested enough for another day of agonizing work.

Mostly they would hear the noises on the weekends; but after a while there they realized it could start up any night, or not at all. The sewers would pound their hands against the floorboards, and slap each other while laughing wickedly, and scream and pound and scratch and bump the walls. Paul told him they were hitting their hands that way against the wallboards just so that the feeling would return to their cramped fingers and hands. The women would bounce on their beds to exercise their legs because they were chained to chairs all day and forced to sit without moving them while they worked. They would cry and grunt and moan and sometimes cry out or scream as they tried to straighten their bodies and fall asleep. They shook in their beds long into the night. There would be the voices of men, too, sometimes growling and shouting, or saying bad words. Once, for hours, a man slapped a woman and told her to keep it down over and over again when she cried.

The first few nights, Paul thought it was funny. But after the first few weeks of not going out anywhere where someone might see them, Paul would get mad at him on the noisy nights; they would be lying in their cots trying to fall asleep with all that racket going on next to them, and if he said even a word to Paul, Paul would tell him to shut up, to go to sleep, to close his eyes, to close his ears, to go away. He would lie there in the dark silently listening to Paul turning and moving restlessly in his cot, listening to Paul's hard breathing, unable to tell if Paul was crying or else praying under his breath or just wiggling his toes real fast under the sheets until finally after a while Paul would catch and hold his breath, and then there would be a sigh that followed as he let that breath out, and only then would Paul finally be falling asleep.

Everything would be okay again in the morning.

Finally, Paul said it should be okay for them to go out and be seen. His beard had grown in and he had dyed both their hair black so no one would recognize them. When the noises started that night, Paul got right out of the shack and told him he was going to look around, to see if there was anything he could do to make them be a little quieter.

He tried to go along, but Paul told him he would go alone.

Paul did not return until morning.

The women were just as noisy as usual.

He had gotten very worried waiting for Paul. He had been up early and was watching the sewing building thinking Paul was never going to come out of there when he saw on the shadier side of the building four little girls walking around inside the sewers' gate. He had never seen children near the compound yet, and so he watched them while he was feeding the hens. They didn't see him at all. They slipped out through a break in the chain-link fence, ran across the dirt to the outside gate, and there slipped through another break before scurrying off to town.

Paul came back hours later, whistling and looking very pleased. Paul rubbed his head without a word, handed him a new carton of cigarettes and went to work beside him in the garden.

―――――――――

White Harbor University
March 18

Finally, Eric needed a break from listening to the kid talk, and kind of started tuning him out. What he really had to do was figure out where to go for the night. He could scrape by, sure, but with the kid along that somehow didn't seem right—the idea of him seeing the things Eric would describe as getting by seemed kind of embarrassing.

On the other hand, if worse came to worse, wherever they managed to spend the night, it wasn't as if it was going to be a step down for the kid.

The problem was really that it sounded like just about the whole world had done its dirty business with the kid. His dad was some violent bastard who filled his head with nonsense, and his mom stuck him in a home and bailed, leaving him to wander the world. Then this guy Paul came along and stole him from some pusher who got himself whacked, and this Paul ran off with him to Mexico as his own sort of unofficial witness protection program.

He's gotta be shitting me, Eric thought. But then, just look at him. And it wasn't helping Eric at all, anything he was saying. They were nowhere closer to figuring out where to put him.

Eric's other problem was figuring out how best to ration the one joint and the one roach they had left.

It was snowing harder, it was cold, it was windy, and night was close.

The kid had grown on him enough that he wanted to put him into more capable hands. Because all they were going to be getting outside was cold. At least Eric was. The weather didn't seem to bother him at all.

They could head back home, he thought, get comfortable in that big warm house, kick back, and relax. Eric could smoke half of the remaining doobie, and still have enough left over to help him fall asleep later.

Eric used a couple of twigs off the ground to hold the last nub of the roach as he tried to suck a last hit off of it.

It might just be time to hand this one over to mom, he thought.

Then they were on the move again, heading home.

———————

Office of the Dean

As the day progressed, confusion reigned over the Plaza. Students and local citizenry vied for space on the snow while protesters argued amongst themselves and with other groups of complainants. Speaker after speaker strode to the platform representing one group after the next, mostly sororities and fraternities, and the crowd became increasingly belligerent.

Toward the late afternoon, when there looked to be less than an hour of light left in the day, Evelyn began to hope for a respite. She and Victrine had earlier decided on the language of a memo that would effectively close the school in the event of a downturn in the weather, a possibility considered more and more likely by the hour, according to the reports Victrine had been monitoring on her radio.

So now Evelyn looked out her window at the crowd below, wishing it were later in the day, wishing that it would begin to snow.

She was watching when Brother Matthew strode dramatically to a position on the walkway leading from the parking lot to the Plaza, and threw off his robe, leaving him standing there in a loincloth. He reached over the wall next to the walkway, and lifted up what appeared to be a makeshift yoke.

The crowd around him parted as he walked slowly, dragging his yoke, toward the steps of the administration building, where the podium with the microphone had been placed today—yesterday's open speech zone having been enveloped by the growing shantytown structure. Matthew was shouting as he walked, but his voice was only a faint noise, indiscernible against the noise of the overall crowd.

When he reached the steps, he shrugged the yoke from his back. He then sprinted up the steps toward the podium, before which the current speaker now stood dumbstruck. Matthew reached the podium and then, surprisingly, passed it by, and without breaking his stride, yanked from their stands the four flags planted there beside the podium—the United States flag, the flag of Maine, the flag of White Harbor, and the official Pan-Hellenic standard—and charged back into the crowd.

He disappeared beneath the cover of the shantytown, and then came rushing out the other side moments later in a commotion, with those four flags and now several others in his hands—fraternity and sorority standards, the unofficial shantytown flag that had been planted on the inaugural day of the extended camp-out, as well as the standards belonging to any number of the other special interest groups represented on the Plaza floor.

The yellow jackets of campus security were clearly visible to Evelyn as she watched from above, and they pursued Matthew during much of the course of his sprint. He raced wildly at the end, veering right and left to grab at every flag he could see, even wrestling with the people holding them, until at last, apparently sensing he was soon to be apprehended, he lurched away from the Plaza holding above his head the cluster of banners he had collected.

When he seemed to be headed in a straight line toward the parking lot, his pursuers converged on that line. Some of the people in the crowd reacted by joining in the chase. Others, of course, were making more of an effort to impede the security detail.

Matthew was nearly at the spot where his exhibition had begun when someone grabbed him by his loincloth and pulled it down, pulling Matthew down to the ground at the same time, and knocking the flags from his grasp. Within seconds, a man stood up with the loincloth in his hand, waving it in the air triumphantly to cheers from the crowd. Matthew rolled in the snow for a second, disoriented, before his pursuers piled on top of him. The flags came down all around and on top of the struggling group, draping over them all, effectively obscuring for a minute or two Evelyn's view of the melee continuing underneath.

In the ensuing commotion, as she watched the flags being trampled and torn up in that pile, one thing soon became clear: Brother Matthew had escaped.

———————

Fourteen Years Ago

Puerta de la Reina

One night Paul left without him, all washed and cleaned up, saying he wouldn't be back until morning. He had waited only a few minutes, until Paul was out of sight, before he went out behind him.

In the dark of the moonless night he was not worried about being seen slipping through the break in the fence around the sewing building; and once he was hidden in the blackest shadows cast by the eaves, he moved boldly down the side of the building to the place where he thought he'd seen the girls coming out; he searched so long in the dark with his hands for a point of entry, a door, a window, anything, that he began to despair of ever finding it.

Finally, his searching hands came for the fourth time across a knot in the wall, level with his chest.

More out of frustration than anything else he poked his finger in.

And there was a click.

A panel popped forward from the wall, hitting him in the knees.

He knelt down and crawled forward breathlessly into the damp darkness of the building, feeling with his hands, listening closely for the sound of anyone who might be inside waiting to catch him. He could hear the same sorts of sounds he listened to at night, only here they were closer and clearer. There was a small space inside where he could stand, with a ladder going up. At the top, he stepped off into a narrow passageway with a high roof that disappeared to the right and to the left into darkness. It was crowded with pipes and boards and foam and wood supports. The only light there came from further inside the house, through pinpoint holes in the boards on the inside wall of the passageway.

He followed the sounds of a woman murmuring and squeaking metal springs to the second such hole he came across, through which he could see the wavering light of a candle, in a small, square room.

There were blankets on the bed, moving all around.

That was it. That was all.

He could not even see the woman who was murmuring, or understand exactly what she was saying. He slowly followed the passageway around a corner, and coming across another crack in the wall, looked and saw it was another view into the same room, this time from above the bed. The blankets were no longer moving and the woman underneath was now making a cooing noise.

The passageway ahead was longer than the first, and there was a line of pinpoints along the wall, and he went from one to the next, looking in each one. In one, he saw a soldier who was sitting on a wooden chair with his pants and underpants around his ankles on the floor. He was still wearing his uniform shirt and hat and boots. There was a woman on her stomach across his lap. The back of her dress was lifted up and her underpants too hung from her ankles. The soldier was spanking her. Ten slaps he counted and then the man reached between her legs and pinched her there until she squeaked and then said "Ow!" He laughed and put her skirt back down and rocked her body on his lap while he swayed his head around and his eyelids fluttered.

Then he lifted up her skirt again and spanked her some more.

In the room after that was a man sitting on a bed who was crying onto a woman's shoulder. She rocked him back and forth, patting his back with one hand while she pulled at something in his lap with the other.

There were many empty rooms after that.

When he got to the last room on the row, he looked in and saw another soldier, there with another woman. She was watching the soldier unzip his pants. He took them off, and then his underwear, then standing there naked in front of her he folded them both and set them on the uniform shirt which was already folded flat on the chair. The soldier looked like he didn't feel well at all standing there naked in front of her. When he was done undressing, he sat down on the edge of the bed. The woman took off her robe and also was naked, and sat down on the bed next to the soldier. She pushed him on his back and started playing with his thing while she rubbed her hand across his chest. The soldier closed his eyes. She squeezed and rubbed it for a while until she had made it hard and straight, and then for a while her head was over it and her hair made it impossible to see what was happening.

Then the man got up from the bed, and stood there beside it, looking very different than he had a few minutes before, staring at the woman while he squeezed and rubbed himself.

That was when he realized what was going on in the room below him. He recognized it because of the way the soldier was acting now and the way he looked standing there reminded him of Jason. He felt very bad for the woman, because he knew any minute now the soldier would turn her over onto her stomach, tell her not to make a lot of noise, and put it someplace it would hurt.

But the man did not turn the woman over. Instead, she spread her legs wide apart and pulled him on top of her. The two of them spent a little bit trying to get his thing into her, and while they were trying, the soldier stood back and, from above, it was clear that she had someplace else to put it.

Finally, the man did just that, and the look on the face of the woman after he pushed it in said it was causing her anything but pain. She made all sorts of noise that sounded like it felt good. She grabbed and squeezed his hairy, white cheeks as he pushed himself in and out of her. The bed squeaked faster and faster, and after a very little bit the woman started moaning in his ear, and dragging her fingernails up and down and around his back.

A few minutes later, the man was grunting, pushing himself into her like crazy.

He reached into his own shorts and there found he was as hard as the soldier down below. So hard it ached. With just the touch of his fingers against the head he felt it throb and then burst in a warm rush that spread as it jerked and spurt and filled his shorts with juice.

The woman was starting to make all sorts of little cries and squeaks herself when something happened that stopped her, and the soldier slowed down and stopped moving. The soldier rolled off her and onto his back beside her. It was still sticking up, hard and straight and glistening.

The woman leaned over it and started licking it.

He was shocked for a moment by the fact that she did this.

He felt stunned as he pushed away from the wall.

He had never felt anything like that before.

He all but ran back to their shack, where he rolled his sticky shorts up in a ball and stuffed them under his cot, He climbed into bed, where he stayed, breathing hard, his mind racing with wild thoughts, until he drifted off to sleep.

It was all he did or thought about for the next few weeks.

He would wait through each long day to see if Paul would be going out that night. Paul sometimes went to drink and play cards with people he'd met in town, and sometimes he would say he was just going out to wander. Other times Paul would wash himself off, take what he said was a little something extra from the package they'd brought with them from the boat, and leave without saying where he was going, only that he would be back the next morning. Paul would always tell him to hold down the fort as he was going out the door.

In those few weeks, he saw every kind of thing he could have possibly imagined a man and a woman could do to and with each other. Most of what he saw was just like the first couple he had seen, only with different people each time, and usually lasting much longer, and usually with the woman looking more bored than pleased. Sometimes he would have to hold his breath in the dark to keep from laughing, because it could all look so funny.

Sometimes what he saw frightened him. Yelling men hurting women, punching them, pulling their hair, throwing them around, doing whatever they wanted to them, putting it into them anyplace they wished. After a short time he knew the faces and bodies of the worst men, and he would not watch anything else when he saw one of them in a room, because all he would be able to focus on were the tears and the fear on the faces of the women with them. One of the house managers scared him most of all. Whenever he was done he would leave a woman lying there crying and bruised on the floor or on the bed, bleeding between her legs, and choking for air because he'd squeezed her neck too hard, or else just rubbing the forming bruises that showed where he socked her or slammed her against the wall.

At the beginning of those few weeks he would always go

home right after he had done it for himself once. That was enough. At the end of those weeks, he left only when the flesh between his legs was too sore to be touched or handled anymore.

On what would be his last night in that dark place, he was nearly numb, and standing there regardless with his shorts dropped to the floor and both hands on himself, looking in on a room where two soldiers were sharing one woman, when he heard a sound that did not seem to come from inside the room.

It sounded like a giggle.

He looked around the passageway, breath held, his heart jumping about wildly in his chest, one hand still on himself as he bent to reach for his shorts . . .

But there was nothing there. No one there.

Maybe it had come from another one of the rooms?

He believed that probably because he was only partway done.

When he turned back to the wall for a last peek, one man was on top of the woman, and the other man was hovering over the two of them, touching them both in different places . . .

A voice standing very close to him in the passageway made him jump.

"Disgusting animal! Smell it in here! What have you been doing here, spraying it all over the place like a tomcat? You're going to clean up all your dirty little seed!" It was a deep, commanding, woman's voice. He recognized it immediately as the same voice he'd heard through closed doors at the owner's house on the occasions he had been there to drop off vegetables from the garden.

He backed away from her, but tripped on his shorts.

She grabbed him by the nape of his neck as he fell and then dragged him along behind her. She was so rough with him that had he not been wearing his shoes and socks, he would have left his shorts at the spot where she'd found him.

They walked out of the passageway after much bumping

and cursing into a room filled with large wood sewing machines that were covered with dust and cobwebs. They went through a door and up a staircase, down another hall and toward an arched open doorway decorated with colored sheets through which, as they approached, he could hear the sound of women laughing.

The owner's woman started speaking out loud in Spanish even before they got into the room. As a result, every person inside had stopped talking to turn and look as she walked in, pulled him to the center of the room, and dropped him down on the floor. When the owner's woman told them what he had been doing, the room was filled with clucking and booing while they all waved their fingers at him and his privates.

He stood to pull up his pants, disoriented, near tears from his shame, when he heard one voice in that room which sounded familiar as it laughed away at him.

He turned to see that it was Paul, standing in a doorway leading to another sitting room, next to a pretty girl. He was nearly doubled over, red faced, and nearly crying from laughing so hard.

The sound proved infectious, and the rest of the room soon joined in, until all of them were laughing at him.

Chapter 10

White Harbor
March 18

Mom's not home yet, Eric thought. The house is kind of spooky in the dark.

Eric felt weird being there at first. Like he didn't belong. Or worse, that he shouldn't be there. But the kid was pretty wiped out, so there was no room for second-guessing.

He gave the boy a quick tour of the place, so he knew where everything was, and by the time the tour was done—when some of the lights were on and he was telling the kid a little bit about what to expect from his mother when she did get back—Eric started to settle into the familiarity of the place. A little.

At the end of the tour, the only problem was that the kid wouldn't take a bath or a shower. Eric told him it was safe, that he could lock the door, that he was not some kind of pervert who was going to hassle him or anything. He needed to be clean. Didn't he want to be clean? Eric tried explaining to him that it would give Eric a chance to wash and dry his clothes so he didn't leave more of a trail through the place than he already had.

Eric tried everything he could think of, but nothing worked.

Talking to kids is apparently not my forte, he thought. I guess I'm not that connected to that part of myself. I don't remember what it's like to be a kid.

What Eric ended up doing was getting out Kennedy's old bedding—the designer label sheets and blankets his mom washed after Kennedy died and then stuffed in a cupboard in the laundry room and never touched again—and spreading them all over the floor in front of the fireplace in the den, right where Kennedy used to fall asleep.

He gave the kid a few minutes alone in the room with the lights on to get comfortable with it. While he was doing that, Eric took a quick jog up to mom's bathroom to browse through the medicine cabinet.

He dipped into a few things there. Painkillers and muscle relaxants, mostly. And his Mom always had tranquilizers.

Just one or two to tide him over, nothing she would miss.

By the time Eric got back downstairs, the kid was already in dreamland.

Seeing him curled up there reminded Eric of Kennedy.

What a great fuckin' dog he was, Eric thought.

He turned off the light, stepped out onto the back porch, sat down on the step there, and listened to the night wind and watched the snow.

He finally let himself smoke that last joint.

While Eric was sitting there, just zoning out, an image popped into his mind, a picture of himself, and all the rest of the band—Ray, Bob and Pam, and Nate and Marty.

The others were laughing at him, and he was sitting there in front of them, with a joint in one hand, a beer in the other, and what was really just a stub of a cigarette hanging from his mouth, and he was looking for a third hand to grab the shot of tequila Bob was passing his way. In his mind's eye, he saw himself in a mirror on the room's faux-wood paneled wall.

When was that, though? They were in a cabin, maybe, in the mountains? Was there someone else there, too? Why did he remember hearing other voices there?

In the end, it didn't ring any bells, and Eric let it go for later

----

Office of the Dean

By early evening, there was still no word on "Brother" Matthew's whereabouts.

Evelyn leaned back in her chair, facing toward the window. The cigarette she occasionally dragged on smoldered in an ashtray on the windowsill. Before she left on her errand, Victrine brought her transistor radio into Evelyn's office, allowing Evelyn to listen in as the weatherman talked about the unusually turbulent weather patterns—low-pressure systems colliding with high-pressure systems, continuing darkened skies over New England, projected snow hazards, preparations being made across the region if this turned out to be as big as it looked on the satellite shots, crowds clearing the shelves at local supermarkets up and down the seaboard.

Victrine was already on her way with the campus closure memo, and to make arrangements to have transportation on standby to carry the shantytown inhabitants home.

If the storm would move in now and begin in earnest, Evelyn might actually manage to see all of her concerns resolved at one time. A blizzard would drive all but the most dedicated away, and if she could find a way to send those buses and their occupants back where they came from, the spell of the moment would be broken, and they surely would not be returning another day. They were young. They would be quick to move on to another of their philanthropic entertainments.

The foul weather would distract the local media from the campus happenings. If not, friend and foe alike among her peers, among the board members, and even in certain local groups, would take immense delight in her dose of bad publicity. Her critics would have something new to crow about, and she was certain most of her supposed supporters would be only too quick to offer their own opinions as to what she had done wrong in dealing with the situation—beginning with the fact that she had not consulted with each and every one of them at the outset.

With the phone resting on her shoulder, she leaned to pick up the cigarette. She dialed the number for campus security. She would have to ensure that in the event the weather turned as bad as projected, those camped out below would be adequately supplied and looked after. They would have to open up some of the buildings to house anyone who they couldn't bus away. They would have to requisition certain supplies, and there would have to be a staff member on at the food commons in the morning, and after that, she had to place a call to the campus hospital . . .

The sound of an unfamiliar voice in her office . . .

"Tell me, Dean Hartin,"

. . . made her jump in her chair.

"What kind of game are you playing?"

Matthew was in her office. Standing twelve feet from her desk, with only three tattered, torn, wet flags for clothing—the White Harbor University banner, a banner from a beer company, and a Delta Delta Gamma sorority flag. They were all tied around his waist. His dark hair was disheveled, his thin, pale, shivering body wet from head to toe, and he was breathing so heavily that shots of spittle were coming out between his chattering teeth. His eyes were wide, and he was clearly agitated. By all indications, judging by previous heated "debates" with him, he was well on his way to some mad diatribe.

"I thought we agreed," Evelyn said as she rose from her chair, her composure for the most part restored, "that you would be allowed to remain here only so long as you did not make more of a nuisance of yourself than your calling required."

She heard the voice on the other end of the phone say, "Campus Security."

Matthew heard it, too. He jumped at the desk, grabbed the phone cord, and yanked it from the wall with some small struggle.

Although this surprised Evelyn, and even alarmed her somewhat, she sighed loudly.

"You have a handful of minutes before they respond to that call."

"Why are you allowing this to happen?"

"I will not have a debate with you, in this manner."

"There is no debate to be had. Tell me where he is, Dean Hartin. Where have you put him? Where have you had him filed away?"

"Who, Matthew? Who are you looking for? What are you looking for? Please, you've disrupted the campus, you've invaded my office, interrupted my work, all to be heard, and now I'm listening, and you are not making any sense," she said, thinking perhaps that was too magisterial an approach. However, her tone seemed to give him some pause, so she continued. "You have my undivided attention. I want to resolve this with you before the police arrive to arrest you. That way we can both sleep better tonight." His eyes moved quickly to the door and back.

If only I could be sure they were coming, she thought.

"He is wandering this place, planting in each footprint seeds that have already grown into the weeds on your doorstep. Someone needs to trim the weeds. He doesn't belong here."

She was confused. Was he referring to the shantytown and the protests?

"At the least, I need to baptize him. Because it won't stop with this. This is only the beginning of what he can do, what he will do." Matthew looked at her, and saw something in the look on her face that made him stop.

"I saw him yesterday." He nodded at her knowingly. "You should have hidden him better. I saw him out there in the middle of that crowd outside. You shouldn't have let him taunt me. "

Still she wasn't following him.

"I saw your son yesterday."

It took her a moment longer to realize that by her son he might mean Eric, and then to connect it to the idea that Eric was the one Matthew was looking for, and to realize that Eric was the one to whom this conversation until now had applied. In those few moments, the room and all its various shadows seemed to spin and bend around him as they reached for her.

"What are you talking about? What do you mean you saw him?

He nodded his head at her.

"I understand you better now. I know your secret. I know you had a son and then you lost him, and then suddenly a few years later you had found a replacement. I know it now. Your son died and so you stole another. But that's what you get—the one you stole was a monster."

The mention of Eric had shaken her, as he had known it would.

"I don't . . ."

"You do!" He said, stepping forward. She knew he was coming for her a moment before he moved. He charged around one side of the desk, and she ran around the other side toward the door. He caught her before she had crossed half the room to the door.

It was all weirdly familiar as he pulled her around by her hand and she tried twisting away from him; he held on and pulled her to him, and when he had both hands on her shoulders he shook her violently.

With a call, Evelyn thought, feeling weak and small in his hands, she could confirm Eric was in his hospital bed where she had left him. This was all a mistake.

"Tell me where he is. Before he tears this place apart, we need . . . we need to help him. We need to stop him."

She had been here before. Only the face of the man had changed.

"Stop," she said. "Matthew. You can't have seen him . . ."

As she spoke, it did not at first register that it was Victrine charging across the room toward them, because the speed at which she moved was so incongruous with her size. "You couldn't have seen him yesterday," she repeated.

Victrine was in fact behind Matthew before he knew she was in the room.

She grabbed him by the back of his neck. Matthew's face was nearly as shocked and disbelieving as Evelyn's when Victrine yanked him away from her. His eyes clouded over with a look for Evelyn that was all accusation. He tried to turn, to struggle out of Victrine's grip, but with hardly any more effort than a grunt, Victrine swung him around into the wall. She held him pressed against the wall, banged him against it once, then, while he was stunned, spun his body around, and grasped him again by the neck, this time from the front, and held him pinned.

Her palm alone was as wide as Matthew's neck.

"Hold still, you," Victrine said, and when it seemed he was not going to do that, she knocked him against the wall again and again, with such force that at first Evelyn did not even think to move, she was so stunned at seeing Victrine's ferocity. Each bump stunned Matthew enough that his movements lost some of their urgency.

Evelyn ran to Victrine's desk and dialed the police, while scanning for something in the room they could use to restrain him. Through the doorway, she could see he was still moving, trying to pull Victrine's fingers away from his neck. He managed to stick out his knee, right into her stomach.

Victrine cried out, "Glory!" But instead of buckling, she squeezed her hand harder, shifted her grip slightly, and lifted him higher off the ground. He instantly started choking for air, and he could hardly flail his arms against her. Victrine held him aloft until the choking noise tapered off, and his eyes rolled and his eyelids flickered and he seemed like he might be dying.

Only then, did she open her hand and allow him to drop to the floor. Although he gasped when she released him, his eyes did not open when he hit the ground, and he did not stir.

"Is he dead?"

"I don't think so. If he's not, he won't be out for long,

though he shouldn't feel much like moving regardless. We should tie him up." She picked up the telephone cord that had been ripped from the wall, and, after unhooking it from the desk phone, had him hog-tied in no time. "Watch him file a lawsuit for my treating him like a farm animal." Afterward she checked to make sure he was, indeed, breathing, and nodded toward Evelyn to let her know that was so.

"What do you think happened to him?"

"God knows," Evelyn said. Her gaze went to the windowsill, to the balcony, and beyond into the night.

If only she could fly away. Was that what Eric had been thinking?

"911," a voice on the other end of the phone finally answered.

Evelyn set down the receiver, and walked to her window.

There were colored, flashing lights outside and below. Looking closer, through the veil of falling snow, she saw there were police cars underneath those lights.

Evelyn wondered how they could already be here. She looked more carefully outside. She turned back to Victrine and thought guiltily that making sure Victrine was all right should have been her first concern.

But Victrine recognized instantly the troubled look on her face.

"Lord, Evelyn, what now?"

"There are White Harbor patrol cars in the parking lot," she said. She put on her glasses, hoping to see better. When she turned to reach for her binoculars, Victrine was beside her, handing them to her.

"Armed police on our campus, and no one called to let us know?" Victrine said softly, "The world's gone near mad."

They both turned and looked at Matthew when Victrine's desk phone rang.

"Well, let's be getting away from the man," Victrine said.

"We'll go out and wait by my desk. Leave the door open so we can keep an eye on the bugger. Half expecting him to start lifting himself up and come after us like a horror out of a movie."

"He's just a man," Evelyn said. They looked at each other for a few seconds before either moved. When Evelyn quietly said, "Thank you," Victrine nodded only slightly. The look in Victrine's eyes before she turned away was impenetrable.

———————

Villacuerda, Mexico
March 19

Her body aching from the hike, Regina gratefully inhaled the fragrance of frying eggs mingled with the musty smell of rain, carried past on a cool gust of wind, and watched silently as Julia sweated over the coals. Of their hiking party, only they two had as yet appeared for the breakfast Julia had promised all takers, although Regina was certain that man Edge was probably skulking about the town somewhere, if not watching and listening to them at this very moment.

Much to Julia's embarrassment, Regina had commented the evening before, as their party arrived back in Villacuerda, on Julia's apparent attraction to Edge Harwood.

He had simply brought to mind, Julia had assured Regina in confidence, memories of a boy she had a crush on as a child. Edge was older, fatter, uglier, and smellier, Julia had giggled, but something about him had taken her back for a moment, she had said, blushing a bright red.

So this morning Regina had steered clear of the subject.

"Julia, why were there so many children living in Puerta de la Reina?"

"Orphanages. There were many of them, filled with children who had been moved there from all around the country.

Most were simply parentless, homeless children picked up on the streets of the bigger cities, where they lived and survived as beggars and were considered detrimental to the tourist industry. There were several military installations outside of the town, and, in town, the attendant brothels that served them. Between those two over the years many children resulted, and these also fed into the system, either when their fathers finished their tours of duty or their mothers died; there were also the displaced children from the local communities, who supposedly the orphanages had originally been built to serve, as well as the children who were not at all displaced, who lived and played on the streets around their families' homes."

She had a slight, enigmatic smile on her face while she spoke.

To Regina, it sounded sad.

"It's hard for me to think back on it now, to view it from this older, objective perspective, wherein it must be classified as the result of political and economic oppression by a government toward the country's indigenous peoples, and an unrelenting violation of human rights.

"I knew and played and grew up with many children who slept on the streets every night, and never realized I was in the midst of a tragedy. There were so many who were there for so many terrible reasons, and we had so very little, yet almost all of my memories of La Reina are fond.

"I spent part of a happy childhood there. That is what I always remember when I am there. For a child, it was almost always just another day on the playground."

———————

In Eric's last dream before he woke up, he found himself in a hospital bed.

The doctors, the nurses, everyone who passed in and out of his room, they were all scared of him.

He could see it in their eyes—they didn't want to get near him. Some had crosses cupped in their hands that they flashed his way discreetly. Others had Stars of David hanging from chains around their necks or hanging from their ears, or other talismans—a rabbit's foot, an Eye of God, an ankh, or a chain of beads, or simple pieces of string tied around the fingers.

Some of them prayed under their breath as they stood over him checking his vital signs . . . as if that would protect them.

There was one nurse less afraid than the others. She didn't cross herself, she didn't stare at him; she just went about her work. That was what he liked to see. Someone actually doing their job.

When she finally turned to leave the room the light flashed for a second on the long, silver blade of the knife she'd been hiding behind her back.

We all have our crutches, Eric thought in his dream.

He woke up on the couch in the den. When he opened his eyes, standing in the doorway staring at him was a little blond boy.

Eric had to think about how familiar he looked for a minute before he figured out the kid had gone and washed himself up. Something Eric said must have done the trick.

Only, Eric realized, the kid didn't really look the way he'd imagined he would look. Much heavier, for starters. And shorter.

He looked down at the bedding on the floor, and saw there, asleep, the kid. Eric's kid. His dirty little kid.

When he glanced back at the doorway a second later, the blond kid was gone.

It took a minute more for Eric to place the face.

That was the kid he'd seen in his mother's photo albums in the attic. Eric thought he might have caught glimpses of him before in the house. The first kid. Curt. The one Eric replaced.

That was him, Eric thought.

———————

Fourteen Years Ago

From the morning after the night he had been caught in the sewing building, when he showed up at the side door leading to the kitchen and was met there by the woman who had caught him, La Reina started to feel like it could be a home for him.

Her name was Lydia, and for the next three days she met him at that door holding a bucket of water, a scrub brush, and soap, all of which she would hand to him to carry to the back of the building. Under her supervision he scrubbed clean the walls and the floors of the passageway that ran behind the back rooms, beginning on one end and working all the way to the other, giving those floorboards and those walls the only cleaning they had probably ever gotten.

Lydia spent most of those three days hovering over him, watching him work, and making him listen to her. She told him on the first day that when she had been younger she had been a movie star, that she had had hoards of fans who had followed the adventures of a character she played in over fifty films. She was famous for portraying a woman whose trademark was that she would kill her lovers after sex. The twist that kept them coming back was that each time she killed a different way.

She told him many stories about the sewing building, and as the week progressed, she introduced him to some of the women there, and explained to him the order of their house. The oldest women had been there the longest, and were shown the most respect simply for having survived so long. They were retired from the work in the rooms at the back of the building. Instead, they sewed by hand morning, noon, and night to convince the managers they were still useful to keep around, and they would tend to the children of the house during the mothers' working hours, using that time to pass along their needlework skills.

Next were the women who did the real work, the women he had seen so much of already. In the light of day, most of these women looked older and tougher than they had when he had seen them in those dimly lit rooms. A few of them might have once been pretty, but years at the mercy of men had left marks on each of them, some easier to see than others.

Lydia counted herself among this middle group, though she knew no one else felt the same. The rest of the women so resented and talked about her behind her back because although she had started out as one of them, now she was the owner's favorite. An exclusive position, Lydia had explained to him, sounding bitter. Regardless of what she did, the other women would say that Lydia lorded her position over them, that she thought she was better than they were.

As a result, she kept mostly to herself those weeks when the owner was out of town, when she would be restricted in her movements to the sewing building premises.

The children of the house were its greatest treasure. They were rarely to be seen about, and never on those nights when the soldiers and the men from town would drop by. That was a house rule. There were no boys living in the sewing building, only girls, and their mothers intended that they would not suffer under their sentences. The children enjoyed some freedom, and were allowed to sneak out of the house and past the fences regularly to play in La Reina.

Alma was the oldest girl, and she was the one Paul had set his eyes on.

Once he was in on the secret of the sewing building, Paul had confided to him that he had had a thing for Alma since even before they moved to town, since the day during one of their earlier expeditions to La Reina when he had seen her walking along the shore. Even though the back rooms of the sewing building were the main reason Paul had visited La Reina in the first place, he hadn't known Alma lived there until a later trip, when he'd caught a glimpse of Alma being hurried up a staircase. He'd been back many times since, but never again for the sex. He returned time after time only to court Alma.

She was too young, he had told Paul, worried that what Paul wanted with this beautiful girl was what all the men who came to the sewing building seemed to want.

But Paul, embarrassed, had said he didn't want Alma just for that, not for that at all right now, he had said. That would be too fast to really enjoy himself as much as he could. I like her, Paul had said. I think she's sweet. And so very beautiful. And so shy. And she smells so good. No, anything even seeming like that and she would never see him again, and her mother would put a pitchfork up his ass besides.

You see, Paul had said, that's why I didn't tell you the truth about the sewing women. What you see in there is not what sex and love are about. That's for people who don't have the real thing. That's where I went before, before I knew Alma. Real love begins with the challenge of getting a pretty flower like her to trust enough to open up and smile at you as if you're the sun . . .

Julia was Alma's younger sister. Julia only tolerated Paul's "little brother" because Alma and Paul insisted. If, on any given night, Alma and Paul were going out someplace, Julia would not be included unless they went as a group of four. Alma wanted to have the option of telling Julia to run off with Paul's little brother when Alma wanted to be alone with Paul.

But Julia learned to play along, because it turned out to be the next best thing to being with the object of her adoration, which also was Paul. She thought everything he said was funny, and every idea he had a good one. Some days Julia would stop by their shack as if she came to play, and she would stay all day waiting for the chance just to see Paul, to say hi to him, and to get a smile back from him.

Julia was the one who finally took him to the hole in the wall, and explained to him the game the children played to get through to the shady, grassy meadow on the other side. She helped him make up the stories he would tell the boy who played St. Peter when he was finally questioned about his parents, his home life, and his sins.

Days and nights they spent as a group, Paul, Alma, Julia, and he, occasionally along with other girls from the house, and more times than not a kid or two from the town who joined them along the way.

They would wander around town, walk the nights away at the beach, watch the fishermen bringing in their nets, climb in the hills around the town, picnic in the meadow, or else sit on a corner sucking on ice drinks Paul would buy.

In the afternoons after tending to the animals, he would inevitably end up in the loft in the sewing building, sitting with the women and Paul as they talked and laughed. The older women and the younger girls would be joined by the working women, and as a group they would work on clothes for the members of the house or else for the orphanage. They were a hard-working, sometimes scary group who had been so long together they got along like family.

As the spring wore on, the package Paul had brought with them from the boat was soon more than half gone, and Paul started keeping him up at night talking about what they were going to do for money when their supply ran out. Paul would wonder aloud in the dark if they should start planning on moving on, or if they should try to figure out another way to extend their stay through the summer.

At the end of those three days of scrubbing the passageway clean, as they were preparing to head back to the front of the house, Lydia had turned to him with a most serious look on her face.

"I told you I know 50 ways to kill a person," she said. "I'm not even going to try to think of something new to do to you if I or anyone else in this house catches you sneaking around back here again.

"This is not a place for you to be. Do you understand?"
He nodded his head, petrified. Yes.
It was really the only family he had ever known.

Chapter 11

March 19

It was hard to tell what time it was when they finally got breakfast going. The electricity had been out since early morning. The clocks were all stopped at 4 am.

The kid had cereal. Eric was so out of it from the muscle relaxants that he didn't notice until after the first bowl that he hadn't given the kid any milk. The kid didn't seem to mind it either way.

The lights in the kitchen flickered back on. The hum came back into the house. The telephone rang a few seconds later.

The answering machine picked it up.

"Hi, this is Rachel calling. Eric, are you there? Are you going to pick up the phone? Or are you just going to stand there listening . . . "

The kid looked at Eric. Eric shrugged at him.

"I'll call her back later."

" . . . Okay, well, anyway . . . I'm planning on stopping by today to see you. And I'm going to be leaving campus soon. So make sure you're around. I have some stuff I want to talk to you about . . . "

"We're going to have to clear out when you're done," Eric told the kid when the message ended. "I don't want to have to explain you to Ray."

A few minutes after the message machine clicked off, the power blinked off again.

Eric wondered where his mother was. It wasn't like her not to come home, even if she only had time for a snack or a catnap.

Knowing her, he thought, it's not because she's out on a hot date. She's probably pulling an all-nighter at the school.

That's where we'll find her.

White Harbor University

After one set of police officers had taken Matthew into custody and Evelyn and Victrine had answered an hour's worth of questions, Evelyn had gone down to the Plaza to deal with the combined forces of the campus police and the balance of White Harbor's police squad, which amounted to three more squad cars on top of the two already on campus.

She was incredulous, horrified, and outraged at the sight of armed officers on her campus, and as she approached them, she momentarily envisioned herself taking refuge in the shantytown alongside the protesters and resisting such an unnecessary show of force. But it was only a few steps later, after seeing a few stray flakes of snow dropping around her, that she changed course.

Following a short conversation with the lead officer, and with her full blessing, the assembled security forces began rousting people from the camps and clusters of smaller structures that surrounded the main shantytown structure. Victrine worked her phones and her computer to make sure everyone had a place to go and a way to get there. The early hour, the carryings-on of the two previous days, and the presence of armed officers made the process go surprisingly smoothly. At 3 am, they weren't ready to battle and it wasn't long before the campus custodial personnel were able to begin clearing the debris left behind.

It was 5 am when that task was complete and they turned to the shantytown structure itself. It was decided that she would enter first, before the police, to appeal to the shantytown inhabitants to leave.

So it was that Evelyn, megaphone in hand, was wandering through their temporary shelter, admiring the students' handwork, feeling no less than impressed at their industriousness. What a few days before had been a cluster of cardboard boxes had grown into a maze, a neighborhood of cubicles and huts and tents and boxes stacked on top of each other or set up side by side, connected by tubes or joined by scaffolds and ladders, each living space personalized in some way or the other by its inhabitants, whether it was drawings or bumper stickers, or brightly painted Greek symbols, or pyramids of beer bottles by the doorway.

There were also, in a few dark corners she passed, places where students were simply sleeping on the ground, some in sleeping bags, some under blankets or sheets or towels, some apparently relying on the shared body heat of a neighbor or three.

There was another sound she heard as she walked about that did not seem quite right . . .

When she was closer to the source, she was sure it was the sound of children laughing, and it worried her more than anything she had seen or heard in here so far. Why, Evelyn thought, would there be any children here at all?

———————

Harbor View Hospital

The hospital parking lot was still as Rachel crossed it; but for the breath of the wind through the trees and the sounds she herself made trudging through the steadily falling snow, the walk from the bus stop passed in silence. The cars she walked by were capped with enough white powder to have been parked there most of the morning. There was no one else to be seen, no deliverymen, no doctors, no ambulances, no visiting family members, no patients being wheeled around in chairs, none of the human traffic Rachel had encountered on her earlier visits.

Hers were the only fresh footprints leading up the steps to the lobby.

Coming through the front doors, she felt nothing less than

heroic for having made the effort to get here. How sad was it the only loved one getting a visitor this morning wouldn't remember it?

What could a person possibly do in here all day all week all month all year but get sicker?

It was dark inside, and also quiet. The power was out?

The lobby appeared to be vacant.

They're probably on a skeleton crew because of the weather, she told herself. The staff probably had their hands full. Or else this was what qualified as customer service in the healthcare sector, circa the new century.

She had come this far. Her feet were numb from the cold.

It would be ridiculous not to at least look in on Eric just because it was a little spooky in here, she convinced herself.

Villacuerda, Mexico

"My mother was arrested," Julia said, "and jailed for killing her husband. I couldn't tell you whether or not he deserved it, though she always assured me he did, and I've never had reason to doubt her. She was young and attractive, and eventually she was transferred from the prison by people unknown to her—it could have been the police, it could have been military officials, prison guards, judges, a very wealthy citizen. At one time or another she's told me any and all of those were involved . . .

" . . . regardless . . . she was moved to what amounted to being a brothel near what was at the time a military outpost in Puerta de la Reina, which is why I've always assumed the military was ultimately responsible for her being there. This was to be her prison for 20 years, the place where she would have three children who would never meet their fathers."

Harbor View Hospital

Rachel wound her way back through the corridors from Eric's old room—where he had been last time she visited—and then began to look for his new room. Why were hospitals always so labyrinthine?

Where was everybody?

Where was the staff?

Who was looking after these people?

Minutes later, she stopped midway down what she thought was the right hallway.

She looked back the way she had just come.

Was someone else in the hall back there?

Or were her eyes playing tricks with the shadows?

It was darker here than in the lobby. There were fewer windows looking out on the grey snowy day outside. Her eyes were still adjusting to the light. Shouldn't a place like this have a backup generator?

"Hello?"

No answer.

There was no one there.

She took a few more steps, and immediately there was that feeling again that she was not alone, a feeling that someone was following behind her.

She hurried on.

Whether or not she was being paranoid thinking the patients might have rioted and killed all the staff (and were now stalking her), Rachel was greatly relieved to find herself at the new room.

She stepped inside and there was Eric, looking very much the same, asleep on the bed. She let go the breath she hadn't even realized she was holding.

Get a grip, Rachel.

"Hi, Eric."

It was even darker in his room than in the hallway outside.

"Boy, am I glad to see you."

What little grey light there was came through two small windows at the top of the wall, on either side of the bed.

"I was getting the willies big time walking around this freaky hospital."

She could hear through the window something in the sky above that sounded like thunder. Rachel shivered. She would have brought a flashlight. Or some candles.

Bobby and his stupid dark man, Rachel thought.

———————

Villacuerda

"At the end of April that year, my sisters and I were awakened in the middle of the night by one of the women of the house. She was yelling, calling out to all the rest of us to join her in the sitting room.

"Her name was Lydia. This was a woman I was afraid of all of the time I lived in that house. The years we lived with her, I was sure she was a murderess; I found out later she was there for making dirty pictures. Which better explains to me her position as the owner's girlfriend. I never did think she was very pretty."

"Her gloves and her new dress—gifts from the owner which hours before I had thought were so very beautiful, much too beautiful for her—were covered with blood."

"Lydia had been with the brothel's owner that evening. All the older women knew this already; they had been speaking badly about her the whole day. She was resented for the privileges of freedom she enjoyed; for the fact she was a whore to only one man, rather than to many.

"Lydia told us the owner had received a phone call earlier in the night from some person unknown. In front of her, he had taken on a very panicked air. He had begun packing his clothes. He had made several phone calls, after which he had woken his driver, and later, after he had packed his last silk socks he had looked at Lydia as if he had suddenly just remembered her, and paused, and stared, and pondered, and then told her she should prepare to leave with him.

"Lydia told us she asked him what would happen to her if she didn't want to go. The owner took her concern as coyness. He told her he would not feel right sending her back into the whorehouse to die. He said it would be dishonorable.

"As you can imagine," Julia said, her eyes wide at the remembering, "At hearing this, a great amount of murmuring went through all of the grown-ups there. It was already night and we were alone. Were we in any danger?

"Lydia agreed to go with the owner. He had been pleased to have his way with so little argument. She told us he kissed her, and told her he would fuck her there in their clothes if the situation were not so urgent.

"And when he had turned from her again, and bent to zip up his bag, she told us she picked up his pencil off of the nightstand next to the phone, and brought it down into his back, right where she had thought his heart would be, if he had one.

"She told us she stabbed him many times because it was not a big heart he had in him, and she had to make sure she got it. The way she smiled," Julia shivered, "we were all a little frightened of her, I think. Her eyes were somewhere close to mad, or else the blood on her made it seem that way. She told us that after the pencil broke, she had beaten him with the telephone receiver until he stopped moving.

"All I remember after her talking to us is the confusion. I remember Lydia ordering everyone around, telling us all what to do, where to go, what to pack. She handed out knives from the owner's kitchen and sent some of the women to the managers' houses, others down to the front of the house where the guards were. Bodies were moving, racing, running around in the dark of the house, some whispering, others cackling out loud, and my mother was telling my sisters and me to get this and that and this and that . . . and in what seemed like very little time at all we were all together, outside, slipping out through the holes in the gate with as many of our personal belongings as we could carry. It felt like a strange miracle that no one was coming to stop us.

"My sister Alma and I stopped by the shack where this boy I was talking about earlier lived with his younger brother. The two of them tended the gardens and the animals. I do not know where they came from before they started working there, other than that they were Americans."

Julia smiled a smile she had saved for him all of these years. Her first crush.

"We had only a few minutes to warn them. Only the younger brother was home. We told him to come with us, and we told him he would probably die if he did not. But he refused to leave without his brother, and we understood, because we didn't want to leave without his brother, either." She chuckled a little at that, shaking her head side to side. "He ran off to town to try to find him. All we could do was tell him to hurry back."

"That," Julia said, "was the last I saw of them . . . the last I saw of Puerta de la Reina, of the house I grew up in." Her eyes were brimming with tears, but none fell. She stared at the empty air for a silent moment, long enough for Regina to consider making some excuse to leave the room, if only to give Julia a moment to gather herself.

Instead, Regina began looking for a handkerchief. Eventually, she pulled her pocketbook out of her jacket. She opened it on the table in front of Julia. Inside the plastic pocket protector, alongside the aspirin and the band-aids and a folding toothbrush were several pieces of tissue, flat as paper. It was one of the few places that seemed to keep dry even in a downpour.

Beside her, Julia made an unintelligible noise. It sounded like a gasp.

"What was that, dear?"

Regina held out a piece of tissue.

"That's him." Julia said, her voice incredulous. "That's him."

"Who?" Regina looked around the room, to see if someone had joined them without her noticing.

"That That That. Him." Julia jabbed her finger at the photograph in the window on the inside cover of Regina's pocketbook, "That's him! I can't believe it!"

The photo was a Christmas card Regina had received more than a decade before. Evelyn's first formal photograph with her newly adopted son, Eric.

It was Eric that Julia was pointing at.

"That's the boy I was just talking about! I remember him, I remember him. Do you know him? She said, "Oh! I think I remember his name!" She snapped her fingers twice. "Jared. This is him. Jared. All the morning long I've been trying to remember his name and just like that now . . . "

It took a moment for Regina to understand what Julia was saying. It was longer before she spoke. That name, Jared, or the echoes of the sound of that name spoken aloud, the weight and truth of it echoed through the chambers of her mind, filling her thoughts with a discordant jumble. In her imagination, she thought she could hear gunfire, she thought she could hear faceless, nameless mothers praying for their wayward children, she thought she could hear a deep-voiced man advising someone to paint his door with the fresh blood of any animal they had available and to hide inside, and she pictured poor Eric lost and searching for his friend while everything burned around him.

Regina heard in the sound of the thunder footsteps approaching.

But she was torn from her thoughts by the sound of someone yelling outside. It sounded like a man screaming out in the rain.

Julia tilted her head at the sound, but was not ready to move onto the next thing yet. "Apparently," Julia said, "you now have some things to explain to me."

The front door burst open. Kaitlin came charging in, soaked by the rain, a look of fear on her face. She was wearing what looked like the stone from La Reina as a pendant on a silver necklace.

"That man! That man from the Villacuerda hike!"

Julia asked which man, but Regina knew instantly who the younger girl was talking about.

"Mr. Harwood," Regina said.

"Yes. Him. I saw him just now, two minutes ago, just now he was outside the window, that window," she said, "looking in on you. I saw him there and I was watching him . . . "

Julia was already moving for the door. "What the hell . . . "

"And then he just disappeared! I saw it! He was standing there one minute, standing around in the rain, listening through the window, and then something happened to him, as if he had been hurt. He yelled like that! You heard, right? And then he just disappeared. Like the rain just washed him away . . . "

Harbor View Hospital

Rachel was stunned when she saw how thoroughly Eric was bound. His ankles were tied with cord to the metal stirrups as well as to each other, as if to keep him from running, while wide bed belts were fastened around his knees, his waist, and his chest, no doubt there to hold him down during a seizure. There were straps and smaller belts and more cord around his arms and his wrists, and his neck was in a bracket that fit him like a loosely fastened collar.

It looked to Rachel that underneath all of it, he was in something resembling a straitjacket . . . like some serial killer.

"Talk about overkill," she said. It actually did make her feel better, talking to him. She figured it could only be good for him to hear another person's voice in the room, something besides the sound of the wind whistling through the windows, something to fill the quiet of the hospital around him.

But it was difficult for her to look at him tied up like a prisoner.

It wasn't as if he was fighting.

His fingers on his right hand were nearly blue.

Picking and choosing carefully, she began loosening some of the restraints.

What were they thinking? What kind of place does this? Do they just tie him up to the bed and check on him later?

As she was pulling at a cord knotted tightly around his left wrist, she felt a slight tremor run through him. It started at his neck and then ran uninterrupted down the left side of his body, down his leg to his foot, which twitched twice.

"Eric?"

Was she being too hasty? However inhumane it may seem, there could be a rhyme and a reason for this.

There was that sound again. It was thunder. For a moment the winds outside were really gusting.

Does it usually thunder when it snows?

Simultaneously, both of the windows above her slammed shut, pulled closed by the vacuum created by the wind.

Rachel jumped up from the bed, startled.

"Oh my gosh!"

The room was instantly quieter. The window frames creaked ominously.

Oh my gosh, she thought.

With a sharp crack, both panes snapped outward from their casings, and shattered on the iron grates outside; Rachel screamed out in surprise as the broken pieces crashed and chattered against the metal bars and were snatched away, pulled out into the storm and snow outside.

Forces of nature at work, she thought to herself as she stood frozen in her place . . .

Eric was starting to twitch around again.

Get a grip, Rachel. Get a grip.

It was a moment more before she was ready to acknowledge the feeling . . .

. . . that something was not right in the room.

Everything loose on the countertops was suddenly rattling around her—vials and tubes and antiseptic-looking metal canisters and jars filled with syringes all took to shaking as the wind rushed into the room; everything loose on the bed stand next to her was swept off onto the floor. The intravenous apparatus rolled away from the bed until the tubing that connected to his arm was taut. The doors on the cabinets banged opened and closed while the sheets on the bed waved and flailed about wildly. The circular clock on the wall above the bed swung back and forth on its nail like a pendulum.

It was almost too much, that nearly irresistible feeling she experienced of panic rising, coming over her as she started to turn to the door.

I'm out of here now, Rachel thought, and she noticed as she turned to the door and the room turned around her how much darker it seemed to be. It felt like she was moving against water as she reached for the door handle. Her arms were heavy. The terrible cold coming into the room had washed through all her layers of clothing. She pulled on the door, cracking it open, and then thought for some reason that something was standing behind it, something was waiting on the other side; something worse than all of this, she thought with a panicked certainty—whatever it was she had felt in the hallway behind her, this was where it had been headed. As the door opened wider she thought she could hear and feel the quietest whisper of something coming through that door into that noisy room . . .

. . . something she could not see, but someone, some

presence she could feel . . .

. . . something moving, passing so close by that she could feel its cold breath . . .

(*Are you my*)

Rachel screamed and backed from the door, away from it, whatever it was.

Eric fought wildly against his restraints.

The thunder roared outside.

Rachel thought, Sweet Jesus, God, Mother, Father . . . are not around to do a thing to help you, Rachel . . .

It was just her and Eric and whatever it was in that room with them.

"Stop it! STOP IT! GO AWAY LEAVE US ALONE!"

Which was useless. Who was she talking to?

Things were falling, clanging, and crashing to the tiled floor around her.

She reached with more determination for the door.

When it was open, she paused outside the doorway long enough to wonder which way to go down the dark corridor outside.

Rachel turned slowly, readying herself to run.

Fearful, heart racing, she stood to the side of the doorway, took a deep breath, and peered around the door frame, looking back into the room one last time at her friend before she fled . . .

Eric was sitting up in the bed facing her.

Rachel shrieked.

He was still in the hospital jacket, but he was free of the rest of his restraints.

From the blank look on Eric's face, she could not even be sure he saw her, or knew she was there.

"My name . . . ," he said in a dry, creaking voice.

"You're Eric," Rachel said quietly.

"My name . . . ," he said, his face without expression, his open eyes more vacant than she remembered them being, and somehow angry. And frightening.

"My name," he said as he stared back at her, "is Jared."

With a sharp crack and a terrible tearing noise, a section of the roof disappeared into the sky, taking the iron grates with it. It was as if a tornado were hitting.

Rachel wondered, Do they even get tornadoes in Maine?

In only a matter of seconds, and right before her eyes, Eric and most of the contents of the room—whatever wasn't anchored down—were sucked up by the wind and swept from the room through that gaping hole in the ceiling.

Rachel screamed his name.

But Eric was gone.

Except for the sound of the wind outside, everything in the room was still and silent.

Gone.

Rachel waited without moving, stunned, for a few moments.

She looked around the room desperately.

What do I do?

She wanted to scream again.

Instead, she ran.

Chapter 12

March 19

Eric and the kid were crossing through a park on a short cut route to campus when Eric felt something twisting inside of his stomach. Something similar, he thought, to what he was feeling after that nice nurse lady shot him up. Like prey exposed.

Eric's heart started pounding real fast in his chest. He started feeling light in the head. My dad is out there, somewhere, Eric thought. He is everywhere around us—watching us as we leave, trailing behind us, and then waiting for us wherever we go—ahead at the school, behind us back at home, scouring the streets in between . . .

Near the middle of the park, Eric stopped and waited, hoping, praying for the feeling to pass. Because he couldn't think of any place safe enough to hide.

He couldn't think of any place they wouldn't be found.

The only place to go was the school.

He had to find his mother.

Are you my son?

The kid tugged on his arm to keep going. Eric said, "Hold on a sec, hold on a sec."

When he didn't stop tugging, Eric lost his temper a little.

"Shut the fuck up for a second," Eric said.

Then Eric saw that something had shaken up the kid, too, more than anything Eric could have said to him. Eric felt bad right away for raising his voice. For cussing.

The kid's wide-open eyes were filled with fear.

Eric asked him, "You felt whatever that was too?"

Eric felt a chill when the kid nodded yes.

Then they were off and running.

It should have been that when they left the park, they would have crossed a street in front of a small neighborhood church. Down half a block from the church, they would have crossed another street, and walked right onto the campus.

But the truth, Eric thought, was that he had not been paying much attention to where they were running, and all of a sudden, it seemed they had turned down into some low-rent part of White Harbor he didn't recognize. By this time, the air was a shifting veil of snowflakes, making everything harder to assess.

When he looked back the way they had just walked, Eric saw cops out across one street. They had passed by them without even noticing them there. It seemed like a fine place to get lost in, or else to find a corner to crawl into.

It was deadly quiet, first of all. No one milling around, even though it had to be near midday by now. Must be that everybody had holed up for the storm, he thought.

Eric wanted to go slowly, to look around, but the kid was not waiting for that. He was just pulling Eric along by the arm, whispering, "Come on, come on, come on."

All the doors and windows they passed were closed. There were people sleeping here and there in the gutter, or on the sidewalk, or just sitting up against a wall.

We've got to find a hiding place, Eric thought.

When they came out at the mouth of the alley, that was when Eric got that feeling again, that tightening in his chest. The hair on his arms stood up. A chill traveled through him, and a shiver, and a sense that whatever it was they were running away from was waiting down the path whichever way they chose to go.

"It's my father," the kid whispered urgently, "it's my dad. We have to hide."

His fear was infectious.

We have to hide.

They both stared at each other for a few seconds, listening for something out there beside the storm.

It was out there. They both knew it.

Eric turned himself in a circle, looking at everything all around him, wondering where they should go, what they should do. As he turned in place he stared at the structures around him, and there was something familiar about them, something he remembered about the look of them that he had seen someplace else—small buildings packed close enough together to resemble tenement halls or the projects . . .

The kid was off to his right. He yelled out, "Paul? Paul, is that you? Paul? Where are you?"

His voice sounded so loud to Eric.

The earnest way he said it, almost as if he'd caught sight of his old friend, left Eric almost expecting someone to answer back.

But there was no answer. They only waited a little bit longer.

————————

Evelyn slipped her walkie-talkie into its holster after confirming to the head of campus security that she, too, believed the structure had been completely cleared. Still feeling uneasy about allowing them to bring down the construct, she hadn't given them permission to start—and they wouldn't do anything until she stepped outside and gave the approval in person.

She only wished she'd had the presence of mind to bring along a cigarette.

She was certain earlier that she had heard the sound of children at play inside the shantytown, but there had been none among the hundreds of people evacuated. As she had continued forward through the structure, shaking her head at the number of personal items and the amount of trash the "protesters" had left behind, she'd started to feel like she'd gone too far through the structure for her not to have reached the end of it. She could not see the end of it.

So before she exited the building, she sought out a perch from which she might get a better view of the encampment. She found a section where the students seemed to have managed to build a second-story level. Cardboard boxes stacked on top of plywood crates. There was even a perch outside the cardboard second story—clearly intended for viewing. She didn't want to climb the exterior, and wondered if she might find a ladder inside, so she walked into the plywood framed first-level doorway, crossed through a room the size of a large telephone booth, and stepped into another cardboard-walled room. Instead of a ladder, she found a staircase made of wood. It looked almost professionally done.

It felt sturdy enough, as she took the first steps. It even had a railing. When she reached the eighth and top step, she stepped onto a solid floor made of wood, and found herself in a small, simple hallway, also made of wood. She walked in the direction she believed would bring her to that balcony perch.

And in a way, it did.

But it wasn't a cardboard-walled room she walked through to reach that balcony. It was an actual room, simple, wood-paneled and with no furniture and a door on the opposite side of the room that opened to a balcony that looked out on a little street.

It was noticeably darker than when she had entered this structure, Evelyn thought as she stepped to the edge of the balcony and looked out. There were small buildings across the street that looked primitive, made out of a combination of boulders and wood. In the dark, the other structures on either side of her position looked like buildings out of a very poor, underdeveloped community.

She didn't know how to react to what she was seeing as she

stepped out onto the balcony. It was impossible, and yet, there it was. She felt as if she was hallucinating, and yet with every moment it seemed more real.

When she looked down, she noticed on the street that there were people all over the place, curled up in blankets (or not) on the sidewalk or on the curb—many, many of them, all sleeping away the night.

Evelyn reached for her walkie-talkie, and found that it was no longer there. She looked at her pants, and then at her own clothes, and realized they had changed too. This outfit had to be ten years old.

But before she could puzzle over that mystery, she heard the first muffled reports that came from some other far-off, dark corner of the tent.

She watched as a lone figure wrapped in a sheet appeared at the mouth of the second alley over from her perch. There was enough noise from the snowstorm outside that she could not hear the sound of his or her footsteps. The person's movements were so frantic as he or she looked about from side to side in the street, then raced under Evelyn's perch to another alley, that she wasn't sure what to think. He or she ran around the corner and disappeared into the night.

———————

Eric followed the kid through a jagged line of narrow spaces running between buildings and houses, with the two of them finally running into an opening between two yellowing concrete structures. It was not wide enough to be called a walkway. There were several doors on either side of them as they pushed to the end, but they stopped knocking on doors after wasting too much time outside one where they could hear the people inside trying to pretend they weren't there. At the end of this line between the buildings, they encountered a chain link fence. The eave of the building on the right extended out far enough that it prevented them from climbing the fence. There was no way for them to continue forward.

What was worse, the narrow space they settled for turned out to be no good for the kid. He was claustrophobic or something, Eric concluded. Turned out that nearly being buried alive was a handicap.

When Eric told the kid it would have to do because it was all they had, the kid only got more agitated. Eric told him to try taking slow deep breaths.

Instead, he darted past Eric, heading back out the way they came, not even trying to be quiet, banging the walls and the doors as he hurried on, with Eric chasing right behind.

"We have to stay down," Eric said over and over.

"He's going to find me. He's going to find me."

"He's not going to find us if we stay hidden."

But the kid was not listening to Eric.

He's freaking out.

Eric grabbed him by the back of his shirt.

The kid was ready. He was waiting for that. He came back at Eric swinging and kicking.

I don't want to have to pop him, Eric thought. Although he was tempted.

Instead, Eric did what he'd seen boxers do when they couldn't take another hit. He pulled the kid into a clinch, wrapping his arms around the kid's, almost hugging him. The kid kept struggling, but couldn't land any shots with his arms pinned. Finally, he kicked Eric's leg good and hard.

Eric hugged him even tighter.

Suddenly the kid stopped struggling. He stopped fighting, and instead he started squeezing Eric back with his little arms. It startled Eric a little bit, the fierceness of the hug. He could tell how scared the kid was by that hug. Eric was scared, too. Between the two of them, their fear was almost tangible.

The kid was the thing for the moment, Eric thought. Have to keep him safe.

The kid's thin arms were trembling with the effort of holding on. He held his breath, leaned into Eric, put the side of his face against Eric's chest, so that the top of his head was in the crook of Eric's neck.

No one's probably done this for him in a long time, Eric thought. Me neither, it feels like.

For a moment, it was almost as if they were safe.

But it was time for the moment to end. The boy had a grip on Eric, and he just squeezed harder and harder. Eric patted him on the back finally, and he tried to give him one last solid squeeze before he let go so they could get back into that hiding space. But Eric couldn't get a firm grip on the kid after that. Even though he was right against Eric, it felt like he was slipping away from Eric's hands. It was as if he was disappearing in between Eric's arms . . .

Eric looked down as the kid's head sank into his chest, as the kid's body and arms and legs disappeared into Eric's body.

He's going into me, Eric thought, horrified.

Eric tried to look over his own shoulder, as if the kid was going to be materializing out of the other side of him, thinking that maybe he would see those little arms coming out of his back.

But there was nothing there.

When he looked down, the kid was not there either.

Eric was holding air. In between his arms, air.

"What the hell?"

He's gone, Eric thought. The kid is gone.

Eric inspected his chest, his stomach, his neck, pressed on his skin, on his arms, even on the spot where the kid had kicked him earlier.

Where'd he go? Eric was stunned. How did he do that? Where did he go?

I have to get out of this tight space, Eric thought. Before I start to scream.

He wondered: Did I think that? Or was it the kid thinking that?

As Eric raced out from between the two buildings, he thought he could feel the kid inside his chest, breathing in his breath, making his heart race, listening, waiting, desperate, fearful, thinking

It's my father come looking for me, the kid whispered from somewhere inside.

As Eric stepped out onto the street, he nearly staggered as a cascade of memories washed over him. It hit him in a wave. Faintly familiar images flashed through his head in a wild rush.

He remembered running up and down the streets of La Reina in the dark of night, up and down empty, unpaved, sun-baked roads lined with spare, dilapidated buildings. He smelled the salt in the ocean air as he searched for Paul.

All the doors were locked, the lights out, the drunks passed out on porches or in the gutters where the smell of vomit was almost as bad as the smell of the dried piss.

At first, he didn't believe Julia when she came pounding at the door, telling him he had to leave. He thought she might have been playing a trick on him, perhaps to ditch him so she could follow Paul around for the night.

But when he looked out the door behind Julia, there were women waiting in the dark of night in a line, and he realized she might be telling the truth.

These women had an air to them, anxious and excited, waiting patiently, their eyes aglow at some undefined promise in the air. They were wearing or carrying or covered by robes and shawls and blankets and army overcoats; some were carrying rolls of cloth, others holding knapsacks and bags of fruits and vegetables.

They'd picked the garden clean.

Two of them were holding chickens in their arms.

Then he raced through La Reina street by street, looking

for Paul, worried about being left behind. He needed to find Paul
before he could leave. He must have looked down every alley,
and in each one children slept bundled together in boxes, or lying
alone under trash, faces etched with concern as they looked up at
whoever it might be racing into their midst.

Without finding Paul . . .

He stopped looking only when he heard the noises start.
Noises like he'd heard before, on the day when Paul first saved him.

Eric felt very exposed standing there alone in the alley.

That sound, he thought. I know that sound. Was it coming
from the north? Quiet, quiet, quiet, Eric told himself, like he was
talking out loud and not just in his head.

It's gunfire, Eric thought.

The noises were coming closer. Someone wrapped in a
sheet came running down the street toward Eric. It turned out to
be another boy, and he was wrapped in tattered white clothes that
looked almost like a shredded sheet from a bed. He approached
quickly, and nearly silently, then ran past Eric, his eyes fixed ahead
of him. Then he ran off.

Eric realized he should still be looking for a place to hide.

The noises from the north moved steadily toward Eric. The ground
and the air began to shiver, then to tremble. He smelled smoke in
the breeze.

He didn't know where to go, but he knew he had to, so
he began trying to retrace the path he'd taken to this spot. On
the way, he saw more kids, dirty kids, skinny kids, street kids,
scrambling through the streets, most of them running south, away
from the noises.

"Run!" They were shouting. "Run to the meadow! The
soldiers are coming!"

The street was instantly awash in children who eerily and
chaotically raced and scurried about with hardly a sound or another

word spoken. Bodies previously lying inert on the sidewalk or
on the road sprang up and sprinted away, and the street he was
on became a whirlwind of arms and legs and bodies, of worried
and strangely familiar faces. Bodies emerged from every shadow,
moving in every possible direction in response to the approaching
gunfire, driven by the sounds that filled every wide and suspicious
eye with fear. Most were wearing rags. He could see—as the breeze
picked up the leaves and dust and dirt and dried vomit and pee
kicked up by all the running feet, stirring it all together—some
were clutching their meager possessions against their chests. They
appeared at the mouths of the alleys they had just been sleeping
in, confused and terrified and alone, with urgent voices whispering
in the night, telling Eric to run with them, to fly from here even
as they wondered what it was that was happening, whether or not
it was the end of the world or only potentially the end of their
lives. They charged into that street and raced away. In the dark of
that moonless night, Eric could see clearly, beneath the fear of the
approaching gunfire, the despair on their hungry, cold, lonely faces.

For as long as he could remember, Eric had believed in
something that he, when he was younger, called the dark man. It
was not a person, exactly, as he understood it. More of a presence.
It had crossed his path more than once in his life, and when it
did, when he'd felt that cold feeling, then it meant that death
was coming to someone nearby. His mother's friend, his Aunt
Regina, once told him she thought he might have some gift for
premonition, and that the sensation that overcame him on odd
occasions, that feeling of panic when there was no visible cause for
worry other than that the shadows seemed to be moving on their
own, were a manifestation of his gift. However she wanted to put
it, Eric believed the presence of the dark man was a prelude to the
box. The dark man was there when death was coming.

In the kid's memories of the streets of La Reina, the dark
man was everywhere that night, frolicking among the dark spaces,
dancing between the fleeing children, his dark scythe gleaming in

their wake.

Eric didn't want to know what happened that night—but neither could he stop himself from remembering.

———————

They ran in every direction below Evelyn.

There was no order to their flight. They ran over each other, they pushed each other aside, they each one made his or her own route. It was nearly a stampede. The occasional inhabitant would open a door to look out on the commotion outside; if they stepped out too far for that peek, or did not close the door quickly enough once they'd had that peek, then they would be pulled out from under their roof, or else nearly crushed in the rush by those outside to get inside. Doors opened rarely closed.

Many residents simply ran from their houses, joining their peers in flight, with no questions asked. They were all there below her, in various states of dress, with sleeping bags and sheets and blankets wrapped around their bodies, all intent on escaping whatever it was approaching.

———————

The popping noises were down the block and a street or two over, and coming toward him. The sound of the hooves of horses was so loud, so close, and Eric remembered running, and looking back to see what really was pursuing them, at the same time some of the kids around him started falling down in the street.

Eric started crying.

There were sharp cracks and then the people around him were falling as they ran. They spun around in wobbly uneven circles, crying out as they fell forward or to the side, the breath catching in their throats as they twisted and dropped or appeared to trip, or tumbled, blood running everywhere while their shrieking screams spilled all over the place. Only kids could scream like that.

Mankind versus its innocents. The one thing inevitably consumed everything. Innocence died.

———————

The killers moved in a wave, quickly and methodically. From the moment they came into view, their guns were constantly firing into the clusters of running bodies ahead of them. Many had escaped. The ones who had moved the fastest, who had responded quickest, the ones who fought the hardest to get through and ahead of their peers. Those who fell behind were left screaming for help as those around them were cut down by bullets. They were left to climb over the bodies of others, to use the bodies of the fallen as shields to cower under and behind, to pound their fists in vain against the doors they passed as they fled, to watch their companions and friends and brothers and sisters dying, to call in vain for someone, anyone, to help them.

Evelyn cowered inside the building, inside the doorway, only daring to peek out once or twice while the worst of the mayhem was ongoing.

It seemed like it was only moments after they had first ridden into Evelyn's view when, having come down the alleys, having killed or injured so many, the murderers continued on their way and out of view. It would be a while before the sound of gunfire was far enough away for Evelyn to hear the storm again.

———————

When the other kids started falling down, Eric remembered following someone down into an alley as the horses were nearly ready to trample them.

Up a stack of boxes before climbing a drainpipe to the roof.

By the time he pulled himself to the top, the other person

was running away along the rooftops, already too far away from him to follow. Instead, Jared spread himself flat on the roof as the horses thundered by the mouth of the alley he had just been in. He heard guns spitting fire above all the other noise.

Here and there other kids scrambled across rooftops, also running away.

The men on the horses were not long about their work. They did not pause. They swept down the street outside and moved onto another, leaving dead bodies and crying children everywhere behind them. Just when he thought it might be okay to move or maybe to go down and see if he could help anyone, he heard more men coming along on foot, shooting their guns less wildly, stopping all the crying and the screaming they came across, finishing the job. He waited for them to be done, until the whole army of men had moved on to the south, until the street below was quiet again.

———————

The second wave of gunfire caught Evelyn by surprise, and sent her scurrying for cover again. When those men seemed to have moved on, Evelyn waited for excruciating minutes before she made her way, crouching, down the wood paneled hallway, down the well crafted staircase, to the telephone-booth sized room, where she paused. She wanted to get outside to help anyone who might be assisted, anyone who wasn't dead.

Evelyn held her breath, and then walked forward not more than 10 steps, to find herself once more standing inside the shantytown structure, with not a body in sight. The storm outside was the only sound filling the space.

Evelyn thought, What just happened? She steadied herself. What the hell was that? Some sort of hallucination? Am I so tired I'm dreaming while I'm awake?

Then, like déjà vu, she heard the sound of footsteps

approaching. The sound filled her instantly with dread, and she found herself looking for a place to hide other than the building she had just been in.

She looked up to find a skinny young woman approaching her. Familiar looking, obviously a student, the girl hesitated before taking the last few steps that brought her face to face with Evelyn. "Dean Hartin."

Evelyn recognized the voice immediately. It was Eric's friend, Rachel. Evelyn knew she visited Eric regularly at the hospital.

"It's so weird. I thought I was on the right bus line coming back from Eric's hospital," Rachel said. "I even thought I had a pretty good idea of where I was when the bus finally stopped because it couldn't go any farther on the snowy road. But once everyone else was gone, and I walked what I thought was a good part of the distance back to campus, I realized that I didn't recognize the part of town I was in. Like, it was the poorest neighborhood I'd ever seen in White Harbor. But I just kept going in the direction I thought was the right one, and I don't know, just a few minutes ago, things started seeming familiar, and I found the shantytown. I'm so glad I found you because I was coming here to look for you."

She paused. "Where are we?"

Evelyn said, "I'm not sure I know anymore."

"I was just at Eric's hospital," Rachel repeated, breathing hard, her cheeks flushed. She was trying to keep her eyes averted from Evelyn's.

Evelyn held her breath. Please, she thought, he can't be dead.

"Eric isn't at the hospital anymore," Rachel said after wrestling with how to say what she had to say. "I was just there, and he's gone." Her eyes drifted to Evelyn's, and again she averted them. "This is the only place I could think of where he would want to be. I don't know where he went. He just vanished."

Jared ran all the way back to the sewing building.

It was on fire when he got there. Not the outside, not yet. But he could see the smoke and the flames licking out the broken front windows.

The front gate had been left swinging wide open.

There were bodies of children, none of them anyone he knew from the sewing building, lying in the courtyard.

The attackers had already been here.

He watched the house burn, not knowing where to go nor what to do next. He wondered if he would ever see Paul again.

That was when Paul walked around the corner of the sewing building.

As Jared watched him, Paul ran to the front door of the building with a crazed look on his face and began pulling at the chains that had been locked across the front doors. When they wouldn't budge, he started kicking at the doors, trying to knock holes in the wood.

Jared yelled out his name, and Paul looked all around for him.

When he spotted Jared standing there outside the gate, he whooped and ran over and lifted Jared off the ground and hugged him hard and that was when Jared knew again that everything would be all right. Jared knew Paul would save him. Paul later said that as soon as he had realized there was trouble, he came back to the shack to find Jared, and had been searching for him since.

Jared whispered to Paul that the sewing women were safe, that they had gotten away. Jared could see the relief in Paul's face at knowing his Alma was okay.

Together, Paul and he tried for a while to follow after the women, to find their trail, where they had gone off to, which crack in the walls around Puerta de la Reina they had slipped through.

But the sewing women had long since vanished into the night.

Finally, he and Paul settled on the road to the East, to Villacuerda. Paul said it didn't matter where as long as it was away from La Reina.

And, "as long as we're together, champ, we'll get by. We're all survivors in this life, Jared. Because that's what we have to be."

Eric felt a great welling in his heart at remembering Paul's words. He could almost say he remembered the face, the blond hair . . . but he wasn't quite there. He could hear in the howling of the winds outside the sounds of townspeople people yelling as the fire spread. He could smell what could only be the smell of flesh burning.

He and Paul ran through the back streets, and almost instantly the rest of what was happening in town seemed like it was happening someplace else, someplace farther away. He and Paul were both safe and all of that was happening to someone else. The soldiers were gone, and it seemed okay for them to be out, and they were both happy to have found each other after all that had happened.

As they were nearing the eastern edge of town, they heard voices behind them beginning to wail. They could see down through the rows between the houses the shadows of people running the opposite way, back toward the town, some carrying buckets of water.

The fire spread behind them. By the time they neared the wall, flames had swallowed the sewing building and the manager's house and the owner's building. Other parts of town burned from other fires set by the attackers. And all of the fires were spreading to nearby rooftops.

Chapter 13

Jared and Paul came upon two men standing, talking, out in front of a bar in the middle of the last block of businesses before the east wall. Jared was nervous because he thought they were soldiers. He thought everyone they saw was a soldier. The bar was closed.

Paul had whispered to be cool, because the soldiers were long gone. The two men had been talking to each other as they approached, but then the men stopped talking and looked at Paul.

Eric, nearly lost in the memory, became dimly aware that he was not alone on the street anymore. He'd wandered in a stupor somewhere he didn't recognize, and now he realized he was approaching a man who was just standing there, watching him.

It turned out to be the gardener standing there.

The Edge man.

Edge didn't look that great. He was holding his right side with his left hand.

"What happened to customer is king?" Eric yelled out to him. "I've been looking for you so long I'm nearly sober."

"Sure you are," Edge said. "You don't know sober."

"Is this any way to run a successful business?"

Edge snarled at Eric, "This is all you think of me? This is all I am to you, just some lousy dealer? Someone who came along just in time to replace your last lousy dealer? After all the fucking things I did for you?"

Whatever the hell that's all about, Eric thought. "You're still a lousy dealer."

"I was meant for more than this," Edge said cryptically. He sounded pissed off, Eric thought. "I became this for you. I wasn't meant to be immortalized as this fat, pathetic, lecherous loser, carried around in your head that way. Something I would have never had to be if I hadn't been looking out for you."

"You were my source, big guy. That was our relationship. And then you left."

There was a noise they both heard. Boom, boom, boom. Almost like thunder. Edge tilted his head to listen.

One of the men outside the closed bar, Eric remembered, wanted to ask Paul a question.

———————

Edge walked toward Eric, down the alley, and Eric was trying to judge by his posture if he was coming over in a fighting mood, or if he just wanted to not have to shout to be heard. Eric asked himself: Was he ready to get his ass kicked by some big loser dealer?

When he was about five feet away from Eric, there was that noise again, but slower, boom, boom, boom, and Edge paused. He looked at the sky, and he looked at Eric, and he stood there a minute. He looked at his own side.

Boom. Boom. Boom.

Edge sighed.

"C'mon," he said to Eric. "We need to move."

Eric stared back at Edge for only a few beats before he nodded his head once. Edge turned and started walking in the direction of the booming noise.

"This is all your fucking fault," he heard Edge say.

As Eric fell in behind Edge, Eric remembered Paul smiling in the dark at the men in front of the closed bar, and one of them lifted his hat.

Jared smiled, too.

The one guy stepped in front of Jared, really close to Paul, and then Paul made a noise that did not sound right.

The man who had lifted his hat said, "This is in exchange for the boat. The rest is because you pissed someone off you shouldn't have."

Jared saw a portion of the blade in the other guy's hands before it went into Paul again and again and again and again and again and again.

Eric thought, Paul was stabbed?

Jared's friend Paul was dead.

"He's dead," Eric said out loud as he went around a corner a few steps behind Edge. There Edge stopped and pointed at the cellar doors behind the weather-beaten two-story building they were standing outside.

Something inside was trying to get out, and beating powerfully against the doors to get out. Boom. Boom. Boom. Someone had bent a metal bar between the door handles to keep them closed.

Edge gestured to the doors, and then slowly collapsed, crumpling down on the sidewalk. The hand that he'd been holding against his side was covered with blood. Nearly as soon as he was on the sidewalk, blood started to pool around him.

Eric said, "What the fuck happened?"

Edge looked at him as if he couldn't believe Eric was asking.

Then Edge said, "You happened."

Boom. Boom. Boom.

"Is that my dad in there?"

"Kid, listen. I don't know what the hell you are. I don't know how you're doing all this. I don't know what your father is, but from everything I've heard and seen, and the fact of you being whatever the hell you are, I'm guessing he's some scary, scary bastard, and I understand why you wouldn't want him to find you."

Something happened to Edge's face as Eric listened to him. It changed. Or maybe Eric just was able to see, underneath the puffy cheeks, the sagging neck, the black mustache, that there was someone familiar. Edge's hair was lighter and shorter—the sideburns were gone, and the years fell away from his eyes and his face.

"But this isn't your dad you're running from here, Jared. He might be looking for you, but this is something else. All this stuff is in your head. This is all about you, Jared."

That was the last thing Edge said as the life went out of him. Only he wasn't Edge anymore, he was Paul. Just the way he looked the last time Jared saw him, after the guy who had lifted his hat grabbed Jared. He wouldn't let Jared touch Paul. He wouldn't let Jared say goodbye.

When Jared fought back, the other guy jumped in to help.

They tried to carry him away with them, but Jared was fighting too much, making too much noise. The other guy let go for a second, and while Jared fought with the man in the hat, he heard something metal being moved behind him.

Then he was being pulled off the man with the hat, and then he was being thrown like a pebble, bouncing down stone stairs, falling into a pitch black hole in the ground. Jared looked up the stairs in time to see the glimmer of a background of stars before the heavy cellar doors slammed shut.

He heard the sounds of the doors being blocked. He realized they were going to leave him there. Trapped.

———————

Eric stared at the cellar doors. He grabbed at one end of the piece of rebar that had been bent around the handles, and pulled at it, but he was too weak to move it. All the while, the pounding continued to rattle the doors.

Eric looked around the street for something he might use for a lever. He wouldn't wish such confinement on anyone. He remembered the terrible cold and dark of that cellar, not knowing who or what might be in there with him, sure there wasn't anyone left out there in world who would care enough to try to find him. There wasn't anyone left to save him.

He remembered crying, sitting on the bottom stone step in

that cellar. He cried at first because he was hurt from falling down the stairs, bumped and scraped, cut and bruising all over. He cried because he hated the man with the hat and the man with the knife and he was frightened by them. He cried because they were the only ones who knew where he was; he was scared they might come back for him. He was afraid they would leave him there. He cried because he was afraid, alone, in the dark, and because the soldiers had killed and hurt and chased away anyone here who might have called him friend, anyone who might have come to look for him.

He cried so long for his friend Paul, wishing he were here and not lying dead on the street above, wishing he would save him again, wishing he could have gone with him. It never felt like it was going to get better, it never felt like his tears would stop, it never made the hurt feel better. It only made him feel worse.

He cried until the cellar floor started to puddle with the water from his tears. He cried until he was almost screaming. He raged and he yelled until high up and above his sadness gathered into a storm over La Reina. Even underground as he was, he heard it answer back. He heard the winds roaring in conflict above him and when he did, he was thinking they would all pay for this. For Paul, for the women, for all the children who had died here in La Reina.

He called the winds, knowing and praying deep in his heart they would never truly abandon him; they would not give up their search for him. He called them to him from every direction— north, south, west, and east. When they could not find him they grew frustrated; the more he sobbed and screamed, the more they felt his pain, the angrier they grew. The more desperate they were to find him, the more frenzied they became, until the thunder was a steady, beating rhythm, until the lightning was nearly a constant fire across the night sky.

He cried until the water on the floor of the cellar was lapping at his ankles, and then at his knees. He had to move up the steps to keep dry. He cried so loud, so angry, so full of rage that finally his father the sky king heard him.

That night in the ground beneath La Reina he understood why his mother had run away.

For in that black cellar, with the water from his tears nearly at his knees, he heard the most terrible sounds coming from the murky darkness below him. From the bottom of that pool formed by his tears, he heard that terrible voice.

Are you my son?

Something in that black cellar was opening up, trying to drag him in.

His voice filled with fear and dread, he said, "Father?"

He felt a terrible fear in his heart when that voice responded.

It's time to come home.

Eric closed his eyes and he could smell that cellar, he could feel that agonizing fear, knowing it was all Jared could do to hold his sobbing breath, because even that noise would have been an invitation for whatever it was to consume him.

Eric remembered, too, the stories he had told himself when he was young, the things he believed when he was a kid, the lies he told himself about the father he never knew, the mother who did not want him, who never treated him well. The life he lived because he was so alone.

He remembered that sitting in that cellar, even though he knew there was no one and nothing in the world left for him, even though he was alone in the dark with something so terrible, all he wanted was to live, to have a family, to have friends, to be normal in a way he knew he would never be.

When Jared could not be silent any longer, when he started crying again, he cried out once more for the winds to save him.

Eric found a pile of rebar at the side of the building, the same place those other guys had found it, no doubt. He grabbed a bar and returned to the banging cellar doors, and he worked the bar in his hand between the sections of the bar that had been bent around the door handles.

Eric knew now how this had ended the first time. The cellar doors glowed and grew hotter as Jared cowered there, as his father's spirit sought him out in the dark. The lightning outside raked desperately against the doors trying to get to him, as the fury of the storm reached its peak and the ground all around him shook from the thunder, as water flooded the world above him.

He was Master of the Winds.

He would be free at any cost. No cage would hold him long.

The cellar doors exploded, screeching metal twisting apart above him, giving in to the onslaught of the storm, and the winds were on him in a moment, plucking Jared in a spinning spout from the rushing waters, sweeping him madly away into the sky, promising to carry him to a place where he would be safe, where his father would not be able to find him.

The winds saved Jared. They threw him across the world to the streets of Maine.

Eric knew where that story led.

But this, today . . .

He pulled back on his piece of rebar, and slowly the bent piece started to move. Eric leaned his weight into it, and at the same time the bar bent another fraction of an inch, whatever it was that had been pounding from the inside hammered it again, and the doors flew open, accompanied by a push of pressure that threw Eric ten or more feet backward, where he landed on his butt in the snow.

Seeming to rise out of the middle of the great wash of water that poured forth from the open cellar doors, a body was propelled out, and into the air above that hole in the ground. It was dripping wet, and covered in mud, and Eric thought it looked like something raised from the grave. It floated there, just floated there, several feet above the ground, and it stared at Paul's body, and it looked around the street slowly.

For a moment, Eric saw its face straight on, twisted by fear and rage into madness. He saw the face of the kid he'd spent the last few days with, and the face of Jared in his memories. He saw his own face. It turned its head again.

It looked back at Paul.

To itself, it said, "Die." Eric heard it. It turned to Eric, raised its arms, and screamed, "Die!"

Rachel, with Evelyn close behind her, could see the plastic-covered entrance to the shantytown ahead when she heard an odd cracking noise behind her. What she saw when she looked back was that the far side of the shantytown was now open to the air—it was, in fact, gone. All there was in its place was a driving wall of snow, a blast of frozen white pressure that was plowing through the shantytown, kicking up debris before it, and crashing through the rows of structures like they were cards. It was headed for them.

As she and Evelyn turned to sprint for any kind of cover, they were lifted off their feet, thrown backward, and then Rachel felt as if she was being choked and tossed by the pressing gusts of freezing air. Rachel thought that in the air, in the flurries all about her, she could see faces that seemed to be calling out to her . . . were they angels come to take her home?

The wave of white air swept Eric off his feet, pulling him and his filthy doppelganger in a swirling flurry into the sky.

"You don't know it all yet," it said as it grabbed at Eric's arm, and pulled him close, as all the while they moved further and further from the ground. Eric pushed him away, afraid of a repeat of what happened to the first kid he'd found. He didn't think there was room for anyone else in his head.

"You don't know about the two soldiers who stood out in the field on the other side of the wall that surrounded La Reina on the night of the attack. There was a hole in the wall they had noticed, and on the night of the fire, they took turns firing at the hole every few seconds, every time another child would crawl through."

Eric grabbed its hands as the buffering winds threw them together high into the sky, through to the heart of the blizzard and then above it, into and through the bitter cold, and ice and snow.

"You don't know about the father who raped your mother, the one she couldn't get away from and then wanted back, who she said changed his shape so many times to subdue her, who then left her in a field to die, who haunted her whenever she looked at your face."

Eric didn't know what to say. Hearing such things cut at his heart. As it continued to rant, Eric stopped listening, concentrating instead on the struggle to keep its hands away from him.

No wonder I'm so fucked up.

This, Eric thought, was not his father.

That was what Edge meant, Eric thought. *This is all you.*

Master of the winds, Eric thought. Caller of the storms.

Am I finally ready to die? . . .

Eric saw as he looked around that they had been carried above the clouds. For the first time in longer than he could remember, he could see the lights of stars scattered endlessly across the dark sky overhead, and the moon that swung so majestically underneath them. The clouds, the rain, the snow, the storm, the earth, they were all at his feet, beneath him. It was a moment of overpowering calm, of stillness, filling him with a sense of peace, of serenity, that he had never known or felt before in this life, an utter calm that was so very much like sleep . . .

Eric looked into his own angry face and understood this was his own death he was facing. Somehow, way back when, by luck or fate, he somehow cheated death, and now it was time to pay things even.

Ruler of the air. What will it be like to sleep forever?

Eric remembered standing near a cliff in the snow. Not at all feeling the cold of the night. He'd awakened from a dream that night in that cabin near Weatherton, not long after falling asleep.

He had dreamed he had been walking down a street toward a house. His home. It was the house he grew up in, although he hadn't remembered it for what it was that night above the Hayward Cabins. There had been a lady on the sidewalk outside this house, pulling letters out of the mailbox.

There had been a white fence. There had been a barking dog in the yard. Brothers, maybe sisters, laughing somewhere inside.

The lady had looked up at Eric as if she knew him.

He had realized that he knew her too.

They had stared at each other for one trembling moment.

This was his mother, he had dreamed. Karen.

She had said to him, her upper lip trembling, "Jared?"

Then they were hugging there on the sidewalk, both of them sobbing

In this dream, he had called her mother.

Eric had woken up seconds later.

Crying.

Wondering what this dream had meant.

Why had he had it? Why had it hurt so badly?

He knew that night it was because it would never be that way.

He'd headed outside for a smoke. Climbed up the hill beside the cabin, hoping to put some space between him and the others before he broke down completely.

A night like they had just had, a great show, a great night with friends, for some reason it had only made him feel worse. He had been tired of this pain he could not explain . . . he had been so tired of the noise in his head.

When he reached the top of the hill, he had felt he could no longer fight them.

He had listened to the voices in the air as he stood on that hillside, listened as they called to him, as they promised to take him away and to make him better.

He had decided to jump, to quiet them once and for all, to silence them . . .

. . . to join them . . .

And now here he was. A lot of good all of this had done him.

He thought to himself, Wasn't there a time in every person's life when he gets to wake up and the nightmare finally ends? Or does the nightmare never end for some people?

And then he thought, This is a nightmare.

I must be dreaming. Am I dreaming?

. . . and with that thought, Eric was awake. His body was cold and wet and covered in mud and filth. He opened his eyes at last. He was back in his own body. His arms were extended, his hands clutching at empty air. He was alone.

I am whole again, he thought. He felt whole again. He thought, there is only one of us. One fucked up self.

Alone above the storm.

Eric patted his chest with his hands.

He wondered, How many of us are in here?

He wondered why the wind was whistling in his ears.

And realized what was happening was that he was falling through mist . . .

. . . through clouds . . .

He was falling from the sky.

Instinctively, he opened his hands.

And called for the winds to save him.

March 20

Rachel opened her eyes in darkness, and didn't know where she was. The air was musty and cold, the floor she was lying on was wet, and she was shivering cold. When she tried to move her hands, to lift herself, she realized she was still grasping the Dean's hand.

She sat up, and said, "Dean Hartin?" She gently lifted the Dean's arm, and was relieved when the Dean began to stir immediately. Rachel looked around the dark space, and saw to her side what appeared to be a short stairwell. Above the stairs was a long white line of light that ran down a section of what appeared to be the ceiling. She realized she was looking at a space between two doors.

She thought, We're in a cellar?

She set down the Dean's arm and climbed the steps to the door, pressing her ear to the crack. Evelyn's eyes followed her.

"It's quiet out there," Rachel said. "I think that's the sun."

She put her hands on the right door and pushed. It moved a little, and a little snow got in. She did this two more times, letting a small pile of snow form at her feet. Rachel turned around, climbed up one more step, rested her back against the door, and then pushed again. This time, with some sustained effort, the door moved, and then pushed open.

The early morning sunlight was a blessing for her. Rachel climbed one more step, and flipped open the other side door.

She went back down to help Evelyn up the stairs, and when they stepped out into the light, they realized that the cellar they were climbing out of opened right in the middle of the White Harbor Plaza, where there had never been cellar doors, or a cellar, before. The whole Plaza area was covered with snow and debris, but, due perhaps to the early morning hour, the scene was still. Evelyn would even have described it as serene after the chaos of the previous night. Evelyn noted in her quick inventory of the scene that the University buildings were intact, the protesters evacuated, the buses and police cars gone from the parking lot . . .

"Look," Rachel said, and she pointed.

Evelyn saw there was a small depression in a snow-covered area off the main walk. In another month, it would be a grassy lawn area. In the center of that depression, lying in the snow, ringed by mud, there was a body. There was something unnatural about the way the body was positioned—one of the legs looked askew. Because he was wearing his hospital togs, they both knew it was Eric.

Evelyn's Journal
Entry date: May 6

Another cardboard box, this one file-sized and not suitable for habitation, is packed up and stored away in the attic. We will keep this one as a reminder of this dark time period, because we will want to remember, but we will store it away so we can move away from it. Inside this new box are journal pages, newspaper clippings, letters from Regina, Edge Harwood's unusual investigative report, cassette tapes donated by Eric's friend, Rachel, and other bits and pieces that will remind us—when we are truly ready to remember—what Eric went through, and what we all experienced.

Tonight, we will celebrate our continued recuperation with a few songs being performed at the campus recording studio by the band Eric says that Rachel has reconstituted for their senior year. Regina has agreed to accompany me, and I'm told we might even expect Victrine to make an appearance.

Eric is recovering still. He will be recovering for the rest of his life. His broken leg is healing nicely, and he has started seeing a therapist so he can work on processing his feelings about all that has happened to him, and all that he has learned, and he is also in a rehabilitation program. These comprise his new curriculum.

Clearly, there are forces at work in Eric's life that are currently beyond his or my ability to control. Taken separately, the accounts I've heard about my adopted son are impossible and nearly absurd; that Regina might have met someone on the other side of the continent who knew Eric as a child or that Rachel did indeed have the encounter she described at the hospital on the night Eric disappeared, those stories would have been taken as lunatic by any mother. Together, the coincidences, such as Regina encountering the private investigator I hired—and haven't heard a word from since—are enough to make me believe we may finally have a name which I can believe is really his.

To me he will always be Eric.

How was it possible that such a magnificent creation as a child could slip through the cracks of a modern society time and time again, until there was no clear sign pointing to the place he first came from? How was it possible there could be no one to care enough to watch over him along the way, to come after him when he was lost, to protect him from whatever or whoever it was that brought him to my doorstep?

Eric has been reserved in sharing some parts of the story. He, too, has seen Mr. Harwood's report, and since then, his answer to many of my questions is to reference "the winds." How did he get out of the hospital? The winds took him. How did he break his leg? It would have been worse, because he fell a long way, if the winds hadn't softened his landing.

Since Regina has returned, she and Eric have spent quite a lot of time together, talking. I admit to being a little envious, now that she is so interesting to him. She has met people from his past and knows things about him he had forgotten. There is no competing with that. Foreseeing an eventual family trip to California, and then Mexico, some time in the immediate future, I told him that I probably have enough information to track down, at the least, his parents' names. I asked him, Was that something he would want to do? The idea clearly made him uncomfortable. He said he was more worried about them finding him than he was interested in finding them. "The winds brought me here, Mom, to Maine, to you, because my parents didn't deserve me, and you did. Who are we to question their wisdom?"

Also by James T. Riley

HILL PEOPLE

www.ingramcontent.com/pod-product-compliance
Lightning Source LLC
Chambersburg PA
CBHW020828260626
47169CB00003B/884